CROOK O' LUNE

CROOK O' LUNE

A LANCASHIRE MYSTERY

E. C. R. LORAC

With an introduction by Martin Edwards

Introduction © 2022, 2023 by Martin Edwards
Crook o' Lune © 1953 by The Estate of E. C. R. Lorac
Cover and internal design © 2023 by Sourcebooks
Front cover image © NRM/Pictorial Collection/Science & Society Picture Library

Sourcebooks, Poisoned Pen Press, and the colophon
are registered trademarks of Sourcebooks.

Published by Poisoned Pen Press, an imprint of Sourcebooks,
in association with the British Library
P.O. Box 4410, Naperville, Illinois 60567-4410
(630) 961-3900
sourcebooks.com

Crook o' Lune was first published in 1953 by Collins, London.

Library of Congress Cataloging-in-Publication Data

Names: Lorac, E. C. R., author.
Title: Crook o' lune / E. C. R. LORAC ; with an introduction by Martin
  Edwards.
Description: Naperville, Illinois : Poisoned Pen Press, [2023] | Series:
  British Library Crime Classics
Identifiers: LCCN 2022061916 (print) | LCCN 2022061917
  (ebook) | (trade paperback) | (epub)
Subjects: LCGFT: Detective and mystery fiction. | Novels.
Classification: LCC PR6035.I9 C75 2023 (print) | LCC PR6035.I9 (ebook) |
  DDC 823/.912--dc23/eng/20230105
LC record available at https://lccn.loc.gov/2022061916
LC ebook record available at https://lccn.loc.gov/2022061917

Printed and bound in the United States of America.
SB 10 9 8 7 6 5 4 3 2 1

INTRODUCTION

In *Crook o' Lune*, first published in 1953, E. C. R. Lorac weaves a mystery puzzle into a novel of rural Britain. The story is unusual and the characters well-drawn, but the strength of the book is undoubtedly its setting. The events take place in Lunesdale, a lovely but (at least in comparison to its northern neighbour, the Lake District) unfrequented part of north-west England.

Lorac's series detective, Robert Macdonald, arrives in Lunesdale in the fourth chapter. He hasn't been summoned to investigate a crime; rather, he is taking advantage of a fortnight's leave to accept an invitation to stay with his friends Giles and Kate Hoggett at Wenningby Farm. He had fallen in love with the area during his first visit (recorded in *Fell Murder*, also published as a British Library Crime Classic) and returned in *The Theft of the Iron Dogs* and *Still Waters*. Now he has inherited a sizeable legacy "from a thrifty Scots uncle" and is looking ahead to his retirement and buying a farm in Lunesdale.

Macdonald isn't the only person to succumb to the charms of the area. The first three chapters are seen from the point of view of Gilbert Woolfall, a Yorkshire businessman, who has also benefited from an inheritance from an uncle. He is now the owner of a remote farmhouse called Aikengill, in High Gimmerdale, and is currently trying to sort out his late uncle's papers and history of the family. In the opening pages he finds himself exhilarated by his return to the area. A "sense of enchantment… always possessed him when he looked down at the huddle of ancient stone steadings hidden away in this vast solitude of hill country."

Gilbert finds himself increasingly tempted to make Aikengill his permanent home, rather than selling the property. While walking, he encounters young Betty Fell, who wants to marry Jock Shearling and offers to look after the house for Gilbert while he is away at work. The present housekeeper, Mrs. Ramsden, is planning to go and live with her sister in the village of Dent, but she too finds it a wrench to desert the charms of Lunesdale. Gilbert is soon disturbed by a couple of visitors. The first is Tupper, the disagreeable Rector, who has persuaded himself that Gilbert's Uncle Thomas should have made a bequest to supplement his stipend. The second is Daniel Herdwick, a veteran local farmer, who has the grazing rights at Aikengill and is interested in buying the property.

It is fair to say that the mystery element of this story is a slow burn. Lorac seldom indulged in melodramatics, and the ratcheting-up of suspense was not her highest priority. Yet there is something quite subtle about the way she lays the groundwork for a case that will eventually intrigue

Macdonald. At first, the only crime that seems to disturb the tranquillity of the neighbourhood is sheep-stealing, but a fire—which proves to be a case of arson—results in a tragedy that is all the more shocking because we care about Lorac's people. From that point, the plot thickens nicely, while the characters remain more substantial than those sometimes found in Golden Age whodunits. Among the unexpected touches are a couple of references to T. S. Eliot.

Even as the mood darkens, we never lose sight of the appeal of Lunesdale. A sketch map of High Gimmerdale (drawn by the author, a talented artist) is included, and at times the descriptions of the countryside are quite lyrical. And as Gilbert Woolfall says: "When people in the south say that the county of Lancaster is dense with industrialism, and smoke-grimed cities, I should like to drop them on to Bowland Forest and let them sense those square miles of high moorland devoid of any habitation at all." We are certainly not presented with a "chocolate box" or "picture postcard" view of the area. Farming in the hill country is tough, and Lorac makes no bones about the harsh realities of the lives led by the locals or the nature of a small community in which gossip "is blazoned abroad with the velocity of the infernal combustion engine."

Period touches include the faded war-time posters concerning "Anti-gas…decontaminating measures," while the local dialect is handled more crisply and less obtrusively than in many vintage mystery novels. In a foreword, Lorac says that she wrote the story "to give pleasure to kind friends from far and wide who have written to me and asked for another book about our valley, not forgetting Giles and Kate Hoggett…

Incidentally, the house I have called Aikengill is not for sale, nor is it to let. I live in it myself."

Crook o' Lune offers an excellent example of Lorac's method of blending fact with fiction, both in terms of characters (the Hoggetts were based on her sister Maud, and her husband John Howson) and places. There is a real Crook o' Lune (i.e., a bend in the River Lune, which turns back on itself just below Caton), and the title is highly appropriate; in the United States, however, the book was renamed *Shepherd's Crook*. High Gimmerdale is Lorac's version of Roeburndale (which, to complicate matters further, is itself mentioned in the book), while Kirkholm is Hornby in disguise. Gilbert Woolfall arrives at Kirkholm station at the start of the book and at the time of publication there was indeed a station at Hornby. Alas, it closed more than half a century ago.

Although many of the locations in the story are fictionalised, Slaidburn in the Forest of Bowland is not. There is an endowed school there, as well as in other villages in the area such as Wray, on the edge of Roeburndale; a school endowment also features in the novel. The historic inn in Slaidburn where Macdonald has an evening meal, the wonderfully named "Hark to Bounty," serves home-cooked food to appreciative customers to this day. The name, which appeals to Macdonald, is said to derive from a remark made by the local squire, whose favourite dog was called Bounty.

During the course of researching the topography of the novel to help me in writing this introduction, I visited Roeburndale and the surrounding countryside and dined and stayed at the Hark to Bounty. (It's a tough job, acting as Crime Classics series consultant, but someone has to do it!)

I am pleased to confirm that I share Macdonald's enthusiasm for the inn, which for many years housed an old manorial or "moot" court; the courtroom still exists on the upper floor. I learned from the staff that Lorac herself stayed there, and I'd guess that she name-checked the pub in appreciation of hospitality received.

My thanks go to Lena Whiteley (who knew Lorac personally) and her son David for their kindness while guiding me around "Lorac country" and telling me some of the stories behind her stories. Among other things, they explained that the crookedness that lies at the heart of the mystery was inspired by a real-life occurrence in the area where Lorac lived.

Lorac was the principal pen name of Edith Caroline Rivett (1894–1958), who moved to Aughton in Lunesdale during the Second World War, to be close to her sister, and became a much-loved figure in the village. Her home, the model for Aikengill, was Newbanks (now Newbank Cottage). Her strong personality shines through her fiction and is evident in *Crook o' Lune*, not least in her compassion for young Betty and the distaste shown for religious hypocrites and malicious gossips. Like Macdonald, she was not a native of Lunesdale, but once she had settled in the area, she never wanted to leave. Reading this novel, one can understand why.

—Martin Edwards
www.martinedwardsbooks.com

A NOTE FROM THE PUBLISHER

The original novels and short stories reprinted in the British Library Crime Classics series were written and published in a period ranging, for the most part, from the 1890s to the 1960s. There are many elements of these stories which continue to entertain modern readers; however, in some cases there are also uses of language, instances of stereotyping and some attitudes expressed by narrators or characters which may not be endorsed by the publishing standards of today. We acknowledge therefore that some elements in the works selected for reprinting may continue to make uncomfortable reading for some of our audience. With this series British Library Publishing aims to offer a new readership a chance to read some of the rare books of the British Library's collections in an affordable paperback format, to enjoy their merits and to look back into the world of the twentieth century as portrayed by its writers. It is not possible to separate these stories from the history of their writing, and as such the following novel is presented as it was originally published with the inclusion of minor edits made for consistency of style and sense, and with pejorative terms of an extremely offensive nature partly obscured. We welcome feedback from our readers.

FOREWORD

Here is another story about Lunesdale, written to give pleasure to kind friends from far and wide who have written to me and asked for another book about our valley, not forgetting Giles and Kate Hoggett. To all of you, in U.S.A. and Canada, in New Zealand and Australia, I can give an assurance that a place like High Gimmerdale really does exist, in the fells south of Lune. No inhabitant of "Wenningby" will have any doubt about that. But will all of you please remember that this is a story, no more? If I have used some real facts, such as the sheep-stealing on Whernside, and if I have taken liberties with ancient history and adapted Benefactions to the base uses of detective fiction, it is only to make a story whose very roots grow in the place. No character in this book is real—except perhaps the Hoggetts, and they bear me no ill-will for having turned even their cows into fiction. And to those of you overseas who think you might be descended from bygone Teggs and Fells and Shearlings and Lambs, well, the folk in this valley are a fine race, so good luck to all of you.

Incidentally, the house I have called Aikengill is not for sale, nor is it to let. I live in it myself.

—E. C. R. Lorac

1953

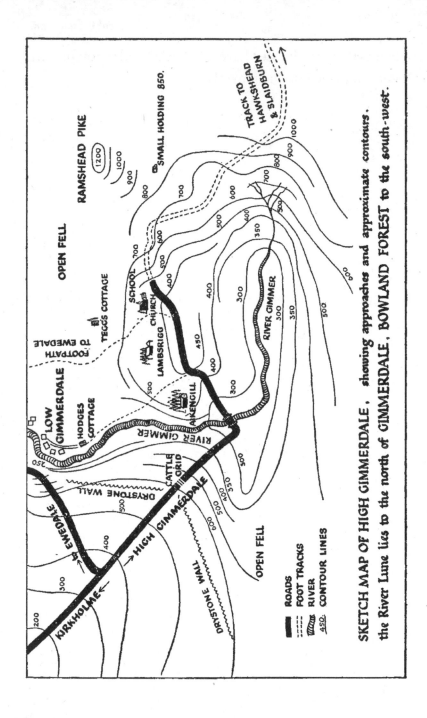

SKETCH MAP OF HIGH GIMMERDALE, showing approaches and approximate contours. the River Lune lies to the north of GIMMERDALE, BOWLAND FOREST to the south-west.

CHAPTER I

I

GILBERT WOOLFALL WAS ALWAYS CONSCIOUS OF A SENSE of exhilaration when he got out of the train at Kirkholm. A quickened pulse and a feeling of well-being seemed to wipe out all the tedious problems involved with the complex economics of industrialism which were his normal preoccupations as a business man.

Kirkholm is a very small, quiet station in the Lune Valley, on the railway line which connects the industrial towns of the West Riding of Yorkshire with the ancient city of Lancaster, hard by the west coast. For part of its route the line meanders in the shadows of the great limestone fells of the Pennine Range and above the green dales and rich woodland of the Lune Valley. It is an important section of line to the farmers and country folk who fetch their gear from its small remote stations, but it seems vague and slow to those urban folk who occasionally chance to travel by it. The places and territory it serves are little known to civilisation—if that quality be the monopoly of cities, as the word implies. How many townsfolk are acquainted with Lunesdale and Ribblesdale, Swaledale and Dentdale, Giggleswick and Bucka Brow, Trough of Bowland and Langstrothdale?

But to Gilbert Woolfall these were now real places—not merely place names—and the knowledge of them exhilarated his mind as the keen air from the fells exhilarated his body, making him feel not only more alive, but very glad to be alive.

Gilbert was the only passenger who alighted from the train at Kirkholm, and after a friendly greeting with the station master, he went out into the peaceful station yard and found his car, parked ready for him by the garage lad. With a sigh of satisfaction at the peace and solitude of the place, he drove out of the yard, turned sharp right over the railway bridge and down to the Halt sign where the main road ran east into Yorkshire. Having crossed the main road, he began to climb immediately, up into the hills.

It was a glorious spring evening, the sun still gilding the crests of the high fells, though the valley was already in shadows. At first, the steep narrow road ran between hedgerows in which the first blackthorn was spreading a mist of white, and the willow catkins were blobs of gold, but after a couple of miles the hedgerows gave way to dry-stone walls, the arable land dropped behind and the road rose even more steeply to the open fellside. There was a cattle grid across the road at the top of the hill, in addition to the gate which used to bar the road: stone walls ran to right and left as far as the eye could see, dividing the cultivated land from the rough sheep pasture. Once his car had bumped over the cattle grid, Woolfall delighted in the unfenced road, in the grand sweep of fell which stretched away unbroken, ridge beyond ridge of moorland, to the great dome of blue sky overhead. He drove on until he reached a level stretch and a firm piece of turf where he could pull the car off the narrow road, and then he got out and strolled over the rough ground to an outcrop of rock from whose topmost ridge he could see the stone-flagged roofs and the wind-clipped trees of High Gimmerdale, tucked away below, all unsuspected, in a fold of the high fells.

Gilbert Woolfall stood there for a long time, trying to analyse the sense of enchantment which always possessed him when he looked down at the huddle of ancient stone steadings hidden away in this vast solitude of hill country.

His forebears had lived in High Gimmerdale; generations of them. For five centuries at least—and who knew how many more, back to the dawn of history—Woolfalls had tended their sheep on these fellsides, had lived on the site of the sturdy stone house whose ancient flagged roof showed long and grey against the wind-swept beeches behind it. They had lived and worked, married and begotten families, died and been buried, in that small place hidden among the hills.

It was sheep country. The name of the hamlet, the name of Gilbert's family, the names of nearby steadings and nearby neighbours, nearly all were connected with sheep and the wool trade. Gimmers, tups, tegs, rams, wethers, hoggetts, ewes—all the terms so familiar to sheep farmers and so bewildering to the uninitiated—were woven into place names and patronymics. Woolfall, Herdwick, Fuller, Shepherd, Shearling—every name was derived from sheep.

The sheep were around him now—rough fell sheep, their fleeces long and unkempt, their dark noses nuzzling busily among the undergrowth for the fresh grass which was just beginning to grow under the dry bents. Their fleeces were not white or creamy, like the wool of the tall Shires' sheep, nor the fat beasts of the South Downs: here they were dark grey, as though they had developed a protective colouring which made their shaggy backs indistinguishable from the rocky outcrops among which they pastured. Their lambs were lighter in colour, but they were still so small that it was difficult to pick them out in the undergrowth: the lambs kept close to their mothers, sometimes trying to pasture in imitation of the diligent ewes.

Gilbert Woolfall stood very still, watching the flight of lapwing and curlew, listening to their call, while the ewes, gaining confidence from his immobility, disregarded him and pastured around him without fear; the wind swept by steadily, cold and exhilarating, and the sun sank behind the ridge of Claughton Moor.

Gilbert Woolfall was fifty-five years of age. He had been born in Bradford, son of a prosperous wool merchant; he had had a good grammar school education and taken a science degree at Cambridge. Then he had become a chartered accountant. He had worked hard, made money, married, and had two sons. His wife was dead, his sons set on their own careers, one in London, one in the Merchant Navy. He was prosperous, respected, very busy (head of his firm now)— and a bit lonely. But he was essentially an urban product: in mind, as in speech and habit, he belonged to town. And yet he stood here, on the windy fellside, looking down at the stone house which his Uncle Thomas had restored and made comfortable, and his one desire was to live in that house himself. Miles away from any town, he reflected, high up in the fells, remote from any neighbour who shared his interests or habit of mind—it was a crazy idea. With one half of his practical, businesslike mind he laughed at himself. What could he do here? He couldn't start farming—least of all sheep farming—at his age, and sheep farming was the very essence of High Gimmerdale: the only reason those stone houses had been built here was sheep. But with the other half of his mind he was aware that something deep down inside him responded to the remoteness and serenity of the place, something tugged at him, told him he belonged here, as his forefathers had done and that if he sold that ancient house which Uncle Thomas had left him in his will, he'd know for the rest of his life he'd made a mistake, as well as lost an opportunity.

I I

Conscious that the wind was growing keener, the fellside greying to twilight, Gilbert Woolfall walked back to the road, while the ewes leapt nimbly away from him, bleating loudly to their offspring, who panicked from mother to mother, butted mercilessly until they found their own dams. As he reached the summit of the road, he saw a girl pushing a bicycle up the hill and he called a greeting to her.

"'Evening, Betty. It's been a lovely day again. Lambing finished?"

"Good day, Mr. Woolfall. We've finished lambing down at

Ramsthwaite, but Jock's still got some ewes in the paddock at Lambsrigg. It's always a bit later up here."

Betty Fell, daughter of Christopher Fell, a farmer of Low Gimmerdale, was a fine strapping lass, tall, deep-breasted, rosy-cheeked, with crisp curly dark hair and bright dark eyes. Woolfall knew that Betty Fell and Jock Shearling were courting, and Gilbert hoped to see them married while he was still at High Gimmerdale. Suddenly she spoke again, abruptly, more quickly than was customary to northern folk, as though something urged her to get her words out.

"Mr. Woolfall, may I ask you something?"

"Of course you may. Would you like to come and sit in the car? It's cold up here."

"No. I'd rather say it here. If I don't ask now maybe I'll never dare. Are you going to sell Aikengill, Mr. Woolfall?"

Aikengill was the house Uncle Thomas had left Gilbert, the long, low house with the ancient, undulating flagged roof which Gilbert had been gazing at just now.

He tilted back his hat and rubbed his head, not knowing how to answer, for he sensed that a lot depended on his answer, for himself, for Betty Fell and for Jock Shearling.

"I don't know, Betty. Honestly, I don't know. I haven't decided yet."

She looked at him keenly, her eyes bright, her face flushed, her breath coming quickly.

"You like it here, don't you?" she said. "You feel it's home-like."

"Yes. I do like it here and it does feel like home, strangely enough," he said. "Why? Are you and Jock thinking you'd like Aikengill?"

"We couldn't buy it," she said quickly. "We haven't the money, and if we had, it's too big a house for us, and too good a house, but would you let us live there, just in the old kitchen and the room up above? We'd look after it for you, Mr. Woolfall, so it'd always be ready for you. And if we'd only got somewhere to live we'd get married, come Easter. We don't want to have to share with Jock's folks." She broke off and then added in a rush: "I've got it out. I've asked you—you can only say no. Jock'd be that mad at me for daring to ask you."

"No reason for him to be mad. You'd a perfect right to ask," replied Woolfall. "I believe your folks and mine were connected by marriage a few generations ago. We're by way of being kinsfolk, Betty."

"I know," she said. "A hundred years ago it was, Dad says, an Elizabeth Fell married a Martin Woolfall and came to live in Aikengill."

"So that if your children were born in Aikengill, it'd be their home in more senses than one, and I should be their cousin about a dozen times removed." He spoke without ulterior thought, just as the idea came into his mind, but even in the greying light he saw the scarlet flush race over her face and cursed himself for a clumsy fool.

"Don't be sorry you asked me about the house, Betty," he said quickly. "I can't promise anything, but I'll think about it, and I'll let you know."

"Thank you ever so. We would look after it for you, Mr. Woolfall, and it'd always be ready for you whenever you fancied coming, with fires lighted and all cleaned and comfortable. And I'm a good cook and Jock'd keep the garden nice."

He laughed at her eager voice. "Quite a lot to be said for it, on both sides, isn't there? Well—I've told you I can't promise. There's a lot to be considered—but I'll think it over."

"Thank you very much, for speaking so kindly like, even if you don't let us come," she said. "Good night, Mr. Woolfall."

"Good night, Betty. Bless you both, and good luck," he rejoined.

I I I

Woolfall got back into his car, switched on the spot-lights and drove carefully down the steep hill to the bridge over the little rushing river. He remembered the first time he had driven to see Uncle Thomas at Aikengill: there were no warning signs on the rough road and he had run down cheerfully in top gear, not sighting the bridge until he was almost on to the parapet—it was a sharp turn and a narrow bridge. He had just avoided piling his car up on the stone wall, but his bumpers had left a mark on it which made him ashamed every time he saw it. Now he took the hill sedately, in low gear, crossed the bridge at walking pace and turned sharp right up the hill on the farther side to the group of stone buildings which were so unexpected in that remote spot. There were two big barns, their walls and flagged roofs in good condition for all their ancientry. Between them was the remains of a little stone house—"one room up and one down." It was roofless, its beams rotting, exposed to the weather, but the tracery of the mullioned windows was still intact and beautiful, as was the flat Tudor arch above the great stone door posts. This little house, according to Uncle Thomas, had been the original "messuage" of the Woolfalls, before they had built Aikengill in the early sixteen hundreds. Aikengill stood on a levelled terrace to the left of the road and at right angles to it; higher up still, on the right, stood Lambsrigg Hall, a severe stone house built in the early nineteenth century on the site of a more ancient building. Above that again, on the open fell-side, was the gaunt little church, a tiny building with narrow gables and a steep flagged roof, angular and unbeautiful, but somehow moving in its stark plainness, with stunted pine trees seeming to crouch beside it.

Gilbert Woolfall ran his car into the stone building which now did service as a garage for Aikengill—it was a disused shippon—and let himself into the house. It felt warm and cared for, and there was a good smell of cooking which reminded him he was very hungry. The entrance hall was a big square room, with mullioned windows to east and west, and doors in its north and south walls. In Aikengill all the ground-floor rooms opened out of one another, so that when all the doors were opened you could see the full length of the house. He opened the sitting-room door and called: "Good evening, Mrs. Ramsden."

A woman's voice answered from the far end of the house: "Why, Mr. Woolfall, you're late. I thought you'd missed your train or summat. Your supper's ready—I was afraid it'd spoil if I put it in the oven."

"Thanks very much. Put it on the table straight away and I'll have it at once."

He threw his coat and hat on to a chair in the hall and went through the sitting-room to the dining-room, whose open door led into the kitchen, whence came a good savoury smell and sizzling.

"I strolled over the fell a bit to enjoy the view," he said, "and the time went faster than I thought. It's a grand evening."

Mrs. Ramsden laughed a little: she was a middle-aged woman and she had been housekeeper to Thomas Woolfall during the five years he had lived at Aikengill. "You're just like your uncle, Mr. Woolfall. He loved going up the fell to look down on these old roofs. You'll never make up your mind to sell this house, the way you're going. Now sit down and make a good supper. I've got you some kidneys and they're just grilled to a turn."

It was a very different meal from the more ceremonious dinner which Gilbert's housekeeper would have served in his town house, but no hungry man could have wished for a more satisfying supper. The kidneys (grilled over a clear fire) lay on top of thick slices of bacon, surrounded by fried potatoes, golden brown and sizzling. The bacon was farm bacon (Mrs. Ramsden's brother-in-law kept pigs, and Mrs. Ramsden had her own ideas about how much bacon a man could eat, ideas unconcerned with rationing). Gilbert fell to and enjoyed his supper; the grill, followed by apple tart, and the apple tart by home-made cheese.

Mrs. Ramsden came in and collected his plates, chatting cheerfully about local news and ending up by saying:

"Mr. Tupper called to see you after tea. He said he'd call back about eight o'clock. Reckon he's gone to supper with Mr. Herdwick. Maybe Maggie Herdwick wasn't any too pleased, but I didn't reckon it was my place to ask him to supper here."

Gilbert Woolfall laughed. "Quite right, Mrs. Ramsden. People oughtn't to ask themselves to supper these days."

"Oh, parsons are a law unto themselves. Leastways, this

one is. No sense he's got." Mrs. Ramsden was a Nonconformist and had no opinion of "priests and suchlike." In any case, the Rector of Ewedale-with-High Gimmerdale was not greatly loved by any of his flock, least of all among the hill farmers. Gilbert Woolfall had no liking for the Rev. Simon Tupper, but put the best face on it he could.

"Oh, well, he's been wanting to see me for some time, so perhaps it's a good thing he decided to wait. Put out the whisky and sherry, Mrs. Ramsden—or is he Teetotal?"

"Him! Not likely," she retorted. "Get what he can when he can, that's his motto. Now before you go and settle down by the fire, I'd best say what's in my mind. My folk over in Dent are on at me to settle what I'm going to do. My cousin Alice isn't too strong and she wants me to go and live with her if so be I leave Aikengill. Now if you wanted to come and live here, Mr. Woolfall, I'd stay and do for you as I did for your uncle. I like the house and I like Gimmerdale, but I don't want to go on by myself here as I've done this past month. It's no sort of life for a body."

"You're perfectly right, Mrs. Ramsden," Gilbert replied. "I've been very grateful to you for staying and looking after the house for me. As you know, I wanted to go through my uncle's papers carefully before I had everything packed up, but it's been a longer job than I thought."

"I know! I know," she said, half laughing, half protesting. "Your uncle, he spent goodness knows how many years writing his family history and that, and you've got so interested in it you just spend all your time here with those old deeds and records and that—but I don't see there's going to be any end to it the way you're going on. This time next year you'll still be tracing how John Woolfall bought his bits of land in Queen Elizabeth's time."

Gilbert Woolfall laughed. "Perhaps I shall," he replied, "but I've no right to expect you to go on staying here just to make me comfortable when I manage to come for a night or two."

"But what'll you do once I've gone?" she asked. "I can't see you cooking your own supper, and as for cleaning the house—well!" and she threw up her hands helplessly.

"Look here, Mrs. Ramsden. I'm going to tell you something in confidence: I know you won't repeat what I say. I saw Betty Fell this evening. She and Jock can't find a house of their own and they don't want to start married life with the old folks. Betty asked me could she and Jock come here to live for a while and look after the house for me if I needed anyone."

"Well, I never did!" exclaimed Mrs. Ramsden. "I'd never have thought Betty'd be so bold. Asking to come here, and me still in the house and all. Though you might do worse. She's a good worker is Betty. And they've been courting, for long enough, her and Jock. Time they got wed, I reckon."

"I reckon so, too," said Gilbert, and she sniffed.

"Oh, well—provided you know. They'll look after the house all right. Jock's a good honest lad, I'll say that for him. Maybe it'd suit. One thing I do know, if you kept this house empty you'd be pestered by folks coming after it. Miles round they're talking about it. It's a very good house is Aikengill, and your uncle he made it right comfortable and homely." She sighed. "Now it seems I can go away and live with Alice at Dent, I just can't bear the thought of leaving here."

"Well, you haven't got to make up your mind in a hurry," replied Gilbert. "I didn't make any promises. I just said I'd think it over. So it's for you to decide, Mrs. Ramsden. I realise it's lonely for you here, but even though I do decide to retire and come and live here, it can't be for a year or more—and I may decide to sell the house after all."

"I can't see you doing that," she said. "Well, thank you very much, Mr. Woolfall. I'll think it over." She stood with her arms akimbo for a moment, and then added: "I wouldn't ha' thought I could ha' been so silly. Telling you I wanted to go and then turning round and saying I can't bear the thought of leaving."

"It must be something about the place," he said, laughing a little. "I'm just the same as you are. I know it's common sense to sell the house, and yet I don't want to. But if I don't sell it, I shall always be wanting to come back to it. There's just something about it."

"You're just like your uncle," she replied indulgently.

CHAPTER II

I

GILBERT WOOLFALL SAT DOWN IN A COMFORTABLE ancient chair before a good log fire in Uncle Thomas's sitting-room. It was the middle room in the long house; beyond it, to the south, lay the entrance hall and the study: to the north lay the dining-room and the kitchen. Owing to the peculiar way in which Aikengill had been built, the different sections of it were almost soundproof. Sometime in the early sixteen hundreds, a John Woolfall had built a small stone house which he mentioned in his Will as "My little mansion which lieth to the north of mine house." His "little mansion" consisted of a sizeable kitchen, living-room and two bedrooms above it. His heir had built other rooms on to the gable end, one up and one down, cutting doorways through the thick stone outer wall of the original house to give access to the new rooms. And so the house had been added to, century after century, each additional room complete with stone gable and chimney. The consequence was that the walls were so thick and the doors so sturdy that each room was sealed off, as it were, from sound made in other rooms.

Sitting by the fire, his legs stretched out comfortably, Gilbert rejoiced in the silence and the profound peace of the house. Until he came to Aikengill it had never occurred to him that a house could have a character capable of influencing those who lived in it. But this house had some quality apart from its comeliness. It was beautiful, inside and out, with the beauty of right proportion, of good stone work; its mullioned windows and beamed ceilings were gracious as well as enduring. Yet it was something apart from architectural rightness which made Aikengill a good house. It had serenity, a quality of enduring happiness, which Gilbert sensed while he could not account for it.

Sitting there, relaxed and content, he regretted that he had shortly to entertain a guest; what he would have liked to do was to get out his uncle's papers and continue his leisurely study of bygone Woolfalls, together with the deeds and other documents which told how they had acquired their land and built their homes throughout the centuries. When the bell jangled at the front door, Gilbert got up and admitted Mr. Tupper, greeting him with a courteous apology that he had been put to so much trouble and delay.

"Well, I've been wanting to see you for some time," said Mr. Tupper.

He was an elderly man, on the small side, his ginger hair greying rather patchily, his face lined, or rather puckered, in a way which gave him a querulous aspect, like a prematurely aged infant. His voice always had a complaining or admonitory note, and Gilbert had never seen Mr. Tupper looking really happy. A small man in build, the Rector aimed at increasing his dignity by wearing very correct clerical black and a high dog collar which Gilbert suspected was very uncomfortable.

Settling his visitor in an easy-chair, dispensing a whisky and soda (despite a half-hearted refusal from the Rector), Gilbert sat down again with his own drink, prepared to be bored with a good grace for an hour or so.

Mr. Tupper spoke a few words of formalised condolence on the death of Thomas Woolfall, and Gilbert, sensing the note of condescension in the Rector's voice, replied:

"Thank you for your kind thought, Mr. Tupper. I had a great regard for my uncle. He was a lovable man when you got past his cloak of shyness and reserve. Moreover, he had fundamental integrity and a very wide charity. I was deeply sorry that accident should have deprived him of the happy years he had hoped to spend in this peaceful place."

"Perhaps it was for the best," said Mr. Tupper. "He was an old man, and he would have found it irksome here as his powers of locomotion failed. Indeed, his death was due to some such weakness, I gathered. The extreme cold and the frozen roads were too dangerous for a man of his years." He broke off, sipped his whisky contemplatively, and then turned to Gilbert, his face puckered more than ever, as though conscious of making a considerable effort.

"You mentioned Mr. Thomas Woolfall's wide charity: indeed I have always heard of him as a very kindly man. It was on that account that it came as a shock that he did not remember the Church in his Will. But perhaps I am misjudging him. He may have left some instructions that you, as his heir, should see to it that the Church of his fathers was not omitted in the benefactions, which I gather he bestowed on certain charities."

"I am glad that you have raised that point, Mr. Tupper," said Gilbert quietly. "I think that my uncle would have wished me to explain to you the reason that he did not leave any money to the church here. The omission was not due to forgetfulness on his part——"

"You surprise me," said Mr. Tupper, "but if you mean me to understand that the Church is not to benefit in any way, there is no more to be said."

"But I think there is," said Gilbert, "and I hope that you will listen to my explanation. I would not like you to think that my uncle was either ungenerous or unjust. His reasons were based on certain facts, and the facts are these. In the year 1690, an ancestor, one Martin Woolfall, who lived in this house left a bequest to the Church of St. Kentigern in High Gimmerdale, to ensure a stipend for a perpetual curate who was to reside in this hamlet and minister to the spiritual needs of its residents——"

"And what on earth has that to do with me?" protested Mr. Tupper. "Really, Mr. Woolfall, if you must indulge your own fancy for local history, I can only beg that you will excuse me. It is with the current difficulties of an inadequate stipend that I have to battle, not with events of ancient history."

"Not so very ancient," said Gilbert gently. "I am sorry if my prologue seems irrelevant to you, but such is not really the case, and I would ask for the courtesy of your patience while I explain the matter. The terms of the bequest I have mentioned were carried out until the year 1904. The last perpetual curate actually lived in this house: he died in 1904. The then Rector of Ewedale-with-High Gimmerdale persuaded the farmers of Gimmerdale that a resident parson in such a sparsely inhabited chapelry was superfluous, and that it would be expedient for the church here to be served by the Rector of Ewedale, to whom the stipend derived under Martin Woolfall's Will was from thenceforth allocated."

"An eminently sensible and expedient arrangement," said Mr. Tupper. "While I have no knowledge of the facts you mention, I will not at present dispute them, but I maintain that they are entirely irrelevant to the present day. Since the date you mention—1904, was it not?—the whole fabric of clerical stipends has been reorganised by the Ecclesiastical Commissioners. Livings which once had very comfortable stipends have been cut down to provide for the needs of the many new incumbencies in expanding towns. If you are under the impression that I live in the lap of luxury on the proceeds of your ancestor's will, may I assure you that you deceive yourself?"

"I don't imagine anything of the kind, Mr. Tupper, but you have put your finger on the very point which my uncle made to me. He said that he could see no object in leaving funds to benefit the church at High Gimmerdale when there was no guarantee that the said funds would not, in the course of time, be put to other uses than those he had intended."

"Really, the whole supposition seems to me quite preposterous," said Mr. Tupper indignantly.

"Not really," said Gilbert patiently. He was a conscientious fellow, and he wanted the Rector to understand the point at issue. "You must remember that my uncle was a traditionalist. The past was very real to him, as it is to those other people who live in Gimmerdale. In order to understand them at all, you've got to allow for their preoccupation with the past."

"I have only been incumbent here for five years," said Mr. Tupper acidly. "You, Mr. Woolfall, have been acquainted with Gimmerdale for as many months. I hardly think that you are the person to interpret my flock to me."

Gilbert laughed a little ruefully. He was trying very hard not to get irritated. "I'm afraid that I'm arguing my brief very badly," he said. "Let me try again. My uncle was immersed in the history of this place, particularly with the history of his own forebears, who had lived here for centuries. He knew that one of his ancestors had left property for two clearly defined purposes: one was to ensure that a minister of religion should reside in this place, one to ensure that a Grammar School should be kept in being here for 'the education and enlightenment of the youth of High Gimmerdale.' Of course the little Grammar School turned into an Elementary School when the Education Act of 1870 came into force, and the Elementary school was closed when transport was provided to take the children down to Kirkholm school—all very sensible, I've no doubt."

"But what has all this to do with me?" asked Mr. Tupper plaintively. "Education Acts, and the policy of County Education Committees is not my responsibility."

"Of course it isn't," agreed Gilbert, "any more than you are responsible for the fact that the funds left to pay a stipend for the curate in charge of High Gimmerdale were snaffled by the Rector of Ewedale while you were still a schoolboy."

"I protest, sir! I protest most vehemently," said Mr. Tupper, getting very pink in the face. "The word you have used is most improper. It suggests that there was some sort of sharp practice involved in the transaction. I have told you that I am ignorant of the facts in question, but if there was ever any financial readjustment in the matter of stipends, the whole transaction would have been carried out by the Ecclesiastical lawyers on behalf of the Diocese."

"Of course it was," said Gilbert cheerfully, feeling pleased rather than otherwise by the other's indignation. "But that's not the point. What I am trying to explain to you is the reaction of the people here to the 'financial readjustment.' It happened within living memory, you know. The older inhabitants of High Gimmerdale remember the event. They wouldn't use the word 'snaffled' to which you took exception, but the word they would use might offend you even more."

Mr. Tupper put down his glass—which was now empty. "I think there is no object in continuing this conversation," he said stiffly.

"I hope you will let me finish my explanation, Mr. Tupper," said Gilbert. "The last thing I wish to do is to be discourteous to you, personally, but I do know that you have commented to other people on my uncle's omission to leave a bequest to the church, and I want you to receive the same explanation which I shall give to others whenever I hear such comments."

Very pink in the face, Mr. Tupper interjected: "It appears that I have been misrepresented——"

"Perhaps you have," said Gilbert easily, "but I won't have my uncle misrepresented. That's why I am inflicting you with this explanation."

I I

"As my uncle reconstructed the matter, this is what happened," said Gilbert. "In 1904 the then Rector of Ewedale—Dr. Evan Rees-Williams—was an accomplished, scholarly, and persuasive person. No one living in High Gimmerdale at that date was educated, in your meaning of the word. There were some competent sheep farmers, but they were very far from being well informed or even very practical over affairs outside their sheep farming. The two churchwardens were very easily persuaded by the Rector that it would be for the good of all concerned if the spiritual needs of High Gimmerdale were attended to by the Rector of Ewedale, and that the stipend left for the perpetual curate should be merged with that of the Rector of Ewedale. It was a very simple transaction. The stipend in question was derived from the rent of Lambsrigg Hall Farm, and this farm was sold, by agreement of the churchwardens, and the capital vested in the Ewedale endowment."

"A perfectly legal and businesslike arrangement," said Mr. Tupper.

"Perfectly legal," said Gilbert. "Don't imagine I'm suggesting it wasn't. Dr. Rees-Williams was far too able a man to have permitted anything in any sense illegal—but local opinion takes no heed of legality. To my uncle's mind, an accomplished and scholarly cleric took advantage of the ignorance and dilatoriness of slow-thinking farmers, and deprived High Gimmerdale of its rights to a resident minister. That was his opinion, and I concur in it. Frankly, I think the transaction was a very shoddy one."

"You cannot not expect *me* to concur in that judgment,"

said Mr. Tupper stiffly. "Neither, until I have had opportunity to examine the data, do I accept your facts."

"The facts are plain enough," said Gilbert easily. "I have a copy of Martin Woolfall's will. I will have it transcribed for you. And the conveyancing of the land will be detailed in your diocesan records—as well as in the deeds held by Mr. Herdwick whose father bought Lambsrigg Farm. You will find that the facts are as I have stated. Of course, my Uncle Thomas was not living here at the time when the stipend was handed over; in 1904 he was a young man of twenty-five, making his way in the Yorkshire wool trade. He was very indignant when he heard the facts of the case, and his indignation did not abate with passing years." Gilbert smiled across at the flushed and ruffled Rector. "I don't want to renew a dead and gone controversy, Mr. Tupper, but I should like you to answer a question. Don't you think my uncle had a reason for resenting the fact that a benefaction made by one of his forebears was diverted from the use for which it was left? After all, the intention of Martin Woolfall who died in 1690 was laudable: he wanted to ensure that a minister of religion should live in this remote settlement, and by his counsel and example keep the people of Gimmerdale in the traditions of the Established Church."

Mr. Tupper flushed even more uncomfortably. Gilbert had got him into a corner, for church-going was a habit that had nearly died out in Gimmerdale. Mr. Tupper was ruffled and uneasy, but he had enough intelligence to see the pitfalls ahead; and, as Gilbert surmised, Mr. Tupper kept in mind the fact that it was Mr. Thomas Woolfall's heir who was talking.

"With regard to your question," began Mr. Tupper

carefully, "while I cannot agree that the transaction referred to was other than justifiable and reasonable, I remind myself that Mr. Thomas Woolfall was an old man, a traditionalist, as you say, to whom change was abhorrent. I am far from wishing to be censorious, and I will admit freely that, *to him*, his reasoning was justified. You, who are a realist, and very fully acquainted with the complexities of modern economics, will, I am sure, regard the matter in the light of present-day economic conditions. The Church is having the utmost difficulty in weathering the adverse conditions of to-day. Let us not, I beg of you, mar our acquaintanceship by shadows of outdated controversy. I had greatly looked forward to meeting you, Mr. Woolfall. Indeed, it is only the difficulties of transport which have prevented me calling on you before. My car is a very ancient vehicle, and your rough roads and steep hills are too arduous a journey to be attempted as often as I could wish."

"Yes. These roads are very hard on the tyres and wearing to engines," agreed Gilbert. "You'll find all the farmers agree with you there."

"But the farmers can afford good cars, and I cannot," said the Rector plaintively. "Nevertheless, High Gimmerdale is a most beautiful locality, and this house, if I may say so, is a most delightful residence. Your uncle did a great deal to modernise and...er...embellish it."

"Yes. He made it his hobby, along with local history," said Gilbert easily, concealing his own amusement as he guessed the trend of Mr. Tupper's remarks.

"Might I inquire if you plan to reside here permanently yourself?" went on the Rector.

"I'm afraid I can't tell you," replied Gilbert. "I have got

exceedingly fond of the house; I find it very comfortable and very peaceful."

"Indeed, I can fully realise those advantages," went on the other, "but of course it is a long way from your professional interests. You are still a young man in the sense that retirement from business cares must seem very remote."

"I am fifty-five, and I don't call that young in any sense of the word," replied Gilbert. "As to my future plans, I don't know them myself."

"Quite so, quite so," said Mr. Tupper hastily, "but if you do intend, at any future time, to dispose of Aikengill, or to let it, I hope you would notify me. I could advise you of some very deserving tenants, or buyers, as the case may be."

"Thanks very much," replied Gilbert, "but at present I am retaining possession of the house myself. I want to work through my uncle's papers at my leisure. While he was a methodical and businesslike man, his sudden death caused his historical research papers to be left in such a state that patience is needed to decipher them."

"Quite so, quite so: it is an act of piety on your part to expend the time and labour for their elucidation," said Mr. Tupper. "Now I must not take up any more of your time. It has been a real pleasure to meet you, Mr. Woolfall."

CHAPTER III

I

JUST AS GILBERT WOOLFALL WAS SAYING GOOD NIGHT to the Rector in the porch of Aikengill, another visitor opened the garden gate and came striding up the path. Gilbert swore silently to himself as he realised that his hopes of a peaceful solitary evening were to be further deferred. The newcomer was a big burly figure in farmer's rig, and Gilbert recognised Daniel Herdwick, the owner of Lambsrigg, who also farmed the two hundred acres or so which went with Aikengill. Herdwick had been Thomas Woolfall's tenant for the grazing ever since the latter bought back Aikengill.

"I hope you'll forgive me intruding, Mr. Woolfall," said the farmer. "I've been wanting a word with you, and I know it's a case of here to-day and gone to-morrow with you. Evening, Rector. Those tyres of yours don't look fit for our roads up here, if you'll excuse me saying so. Hope they'll get you home all right."

"If they don't, you'll have to play the part of good Samaritan, Mr. Herdwick," said the Rector plaintively.

"Not for the first time, eh?" chuckled Herdwick.

Woolfall led the farmer into the house: not into the sitting-room, where the cosy fire might induce Herdwick to settle down for hours, but into the study, at the south end of the house. He switched on an electric fire (Uncle Thomas had had the whole of Aikengill wired for light and power) and Mr. Herdwick said:

"By gum, you're comfortable here, Mr. Woolfall. A right good job your uncle made of this old house."

"He did that," agreed Woolfall. "Sit down, won't you."

"Thank you kindly. I'll ask you to excuse me coming in my working clothes, but I'm going out again up t' fell to see the lambs are safe. We've been having a mite of trouble with them."

"I'm sorry about that," rejoined Woolfall.

"Ah well: we have our bits of bother, but I didn't come here to worry you with my troubles. It's a matter of repairs to that barn of yours up top I've come about: Woolfall's barn we always calls that, and Woolfall's intak the land it stands on. The bostings just about rotted through."

"The bostings?" queried Gilbert Woolfall. "I'm afraid I'm out of my depth. What is the bosting?"

"The timber supports that hold the hay loft above the shippon and the timbering that divides the shippon from the barn floor—the threshing floor it used to be. The baulks aren't safe. Then there's trouble with the roof of the barn, Mr. Woolfall. The flagstones have shifted and let the weather in. Likely as not that's what rotted the timbering. I told your uncle about it and asked him to have the flagstones cemented over, right over the whole roof. He wouldn't do it: said it'd spoil the look of it, and he'd see about getting it reflagged."

Gilbert sat and considered a moment. "That will be a fairly costly job," he said.

"Aye. That'll cost money, that will. Not all profit being a landlord these days, Mr. Woolfall."

"It certainly isn't," agreed Gilbert. "It'll cost me a year's rent of the land to reflag that barn, if my guess is worth anything."

Daniel Herdwick nodded his grizzled head. He was a considerably older man than Gilbert, a big hulking slow-moving fellow, but with something impressive about his weather-beaten, rugged face.

"Aye. All of that," he responded, "unless you'd care to settle things another way."

"How so?" asked Gilbert.

"Well, I've farmed Aikengill land these six years. I've put a lot into it, in labour and till. If you're prepared to sell, Mr. Woolfall, I'd think of bidding for it. Tisn't everybody's land, but I can make more of a do of it than most. I've got my own steading and buildings to help out, and I know the land. Over fifty years I've worked in Gimmerdale and my father before me."

"Yes. Half a century's a long time," said Gilbert. "But I don't think I want to sell, Mr. Herdwick. You see, my uncle was very proud and happy because he managed to buy back land that had been in our family four or five hundred years, and I don't think I want to let it go again as soon as he's dead."

"Well, that's for you to decide, Mr. Woolfall, though I don't see what the land means to you seeing you're not likely to farm it, no offence meant. And if you're going to put those buildings to rights, it'll cost you more than you'll see out of it for a long time to come."

"Doesn't that apply to you, too, Mr. Herdwick?"

"No. It doesn't. Me and my lads, we're used to old buildings. We know the way of them. If that barn were mine, I don't mind telling you we could fettle it up ourselves. Who builds up the dry-stone walls when the frost brings them down, eh? We do. Who built that stone house for the car? We did. We're used to handling stone, Mr. Woolfall. You're not. I'd work on t' barn if 'twere my own. Not when I'm only paying rent for it. That's reason."

"Certainly. I see that all right. And I'd like to say how much I admired the skill with which you built that garage. It's a grand job. It belongs to the other buildings and looks all of a piece."

"Aye, it's none too bad. Well, having gone so far, I might as well say the rest I'd got in mind. Four hundred acres I've farmed, with rights of fell grazing three miles up t' valley. Right hard work that's been and I'm not so young as I was. I've got a nephew sheep farming up Kendal way. He'd like to come south a bit. Reckon he'd come in with me and farm Lambsrigg if he could get a house."

"I see," said Gilbert, and he couldn't help the gleam of amusement that showed in his eye. Daniel Herdwick saw it and allowed himself a quiet chuckle.

"Aye. Happen you do. A house is a house these days, what with their licences and all. I shouldn't be surprised if the Reverend mentioned the house, eh? Your uncle made a tidy job of Aikengill: very snug it is, and all modern-like with water laid on and the electric and that. But when all's said and done, Aikengill's a farm house, Mr. Woolfall. That's what your folks built it for in the long ago, before they went making their fortunes wool-broking instead of wool-raising. It's a rum thing, you know: my folks came from the cities—Liverpool my grandfather was born and my dad, too. They came out to the country and took to farming. Your folk left the country and went to the towns."

"I'm interested to hear you say that, Mr. Herdwick. I've been reading through the local history my uncle wrote, and I noticed that your name doesn't appear in the Gimmerdale registers before the eighteen-eighties, though Herdwick's a likely name for these parts. It's a remote part of the country-side for Liverpool folk to settle in."

"Aye, happen it is. Maybe my grand-dad came here for the same reason that yours left."

"How do you make that out?"

"I'm no scholar, Mr. Woolfall, not like your uncle and your grand-dad. Woolfalls, they always had a name for learning like, my dad said. Maybe that's why one of them founded the school here all those centuries ago. We've no family history to write, but my dad knew things in his own way—not a scholar's way, just the hard facts life'd taught him. 'Twas in the eighteen-seventies that cheap meat began to be imported into England—live-stock from the colonies that was. And then mutton began to come in from New Zealand and wool from Australia. Reckon your grand-dad knew all about that. Maybe he said to himself, 'If I stay here, I'm ruined. Better sell and get out.'"

"Perfectly true," said Gilbert, getting more and more inter-ested, quite contrary to his anticipations.

"Aye," went on Mr. Herdwick leisurely, "and because the prices of English mutton and lamb dropped, the price of sheep-land dropped too. My grand-dad—Nathaniel Herdwick—he hadn't a penny. He worked as hired man, and he saved enough to lease some fell land up at Ramshead—right up in t' hills. Maybe you've seen the steading he lived in—what's left of it. I wouldn't put a pig in it these days. But Nat Herdwick made out somehow, and left some brass to my dad, who got the tenancy of Lambsrigg, aye, and bought the freehold before he died. That's my family history, Mr. Woolfall. Hard work and precious little schooling."

"It's a jolly interesting family history, and one to be proud of," said Gilbert warmly. "Starting right up in the fells at Ramshead and buying Lambsrigg in two generations through sheer hard work and skilful farming."

"We worked right enow," said Herdwick, and there was dourness in his voice, but he added proudly: "And don't you forget, I've been working Aikengill land along o' Lambsrigg, too."

"I haven't forgotten," said Gilbert, and the other added with a chuckle:

"And don't you go selling this house to some fancy friends of the Reverend's, who'll use it for a country cottage, like as not, aye, and keep pet dogs that'll worry the sheep. We liked your uncle living here: he was a Woolfall, all said and done, and he'd got country ways in his bones, for all he was town bred. But I don't like seeing farm houses go to town folks and that's a fact."

"I see your point, Mr. Herdwick, but I haven't made up my

mind about the house. I've got fond of it, you know. I might come and settle down here myself."

"And farm your own land, eh?" chuckled the other, and Gilbert replied:

"I don't think I'm likely to do that. What was it you said— 'make a do of it'? I think you get more out of the Aikengill land than I could, and that's what counts, these days. The man who's skilled at farming the land is the man to have the use of it."

"That makes sense to me," said the other.

Gilbert made a sudden decision. "There's a matter I should like to have your opinion on, Mr. Herdwick. Mr. Tupper is feeling sore because my uncle did not leave a bequest to the church."

"Aye, so I've heard," replied Herdwick, "though for why I can't see. A man can do what he likes with his own."

"True enough, but the reason my uncle didn't leave money to the church was on account of the transference of the stipend left under the Woolfall will of 1690."

"Aye. I've heard tell on that right enow," replied the farmer. "My dad, he was one of those agreed to that bit of business, and without any disrespect to your uncle, Mr. Woolfall, I reckon 'twas plain common sense. The Reverend Curtis, him who lived in this house, was the last curate in charge. He was an old man when he died—close on eighty, and no one wanted to disturb him. But what did he do? How many steadings were there in High Gimmerdale fifty years ago? How many souls in the chapelry? Can you tell me that?"

"No. I can't," replied Gilbert, "not exactly."

"Then I'll tell you. There was Aikengill, Lambsrigg,

Ramshead, Ramsthwaite, Fullerby, Fell Cock—farmsteads, those were, each with holdings of fifty to two hundred acres of land. And there were three cottages for shepherds or hired men. Beck Cottage, Aikenhead, and Summerfold. In t' old days all these had families living in them. In 1900, Ramshead, Lambsrigg, and Aikenhead—that's your old cottage out yonder—was all being farmed by Herdwicks—four in family. Aikengill land was farmed by Flockton of Fullerby, and he had the Fell Cock grazing, too, such as 'twas, right up on fell top there. Aikenhead cottage was a ruin and Ramshead no better. Old Adam Theave, the shepherd, lived by's self in Beck Cottage. There were four Herdwicks, six Flocktons, old Adam Theave, and Flockton's shepherd and his wife—Aaron Tegg and Martha and their boy, up at Summerfold. Fourteen souls in all, counting four children. And if four folks came to church on Sundays, 'twas a marvel. D'you see what I'm getting at, Mr. Woolfall?"

"Yes. I suppose I do," replied Gilbert. "You're telling me that the population of Gimmerdale was smaller in the early nineteen hundreds than it was in 1690."

"And that's a fact," said Herdwick. "You see, in the old days 'twas small holdings and what was called subsistence farming—make enough to live on, food for man and beast and fuel when you could gather it. They bought nought. I tell you up to my grand-dad's day they made their own candles from tallow and twine, and the women used their distaffs and spindles and the weaver still made up their cloth. 'Tis a far cry from that to electric light and tractors. We got them by farming more land—bigger acreages. So there's fewer small holdings and fewer folk. And how's a parson to fill his time with only fourteen souls to care for? Parson used to teach in school—that was all set down in that will of Martin Woolfalls. 'A sufficient person to teach Latin' he arranged for. Latin, by gum. Well, maybe there was enough children in school then and enough folks in church. But times is changed."

"Yes. I see that—but I think High Gimmerdale was the loser by that transaction, all the same."

"Maybe—but I remember what my dad said, and old Mr. Flockton, too: 'we'll never get a parson with a wife and family to come and settle in Gimmerdale. No woman save a farmer's wife'd have come—too far away from anywhere and too much work. That'll mean a young parson, and single. More likely to get in mischief than not.'" Mr. Herdwick chuckled. "I can hear 'em saying it. You see, the Reverend Curtis, who lived here, he had old Aaron Tegg to clean and cook for him—if you can call it cleaning. And then Mr. Curtis, he'd an income of his own. Nay, I reckon they did the wisest thing, all said and done. Rector, he promised our church should have its services proper on Sundays, and Rector from Ewedale comes up for the marryings and buryings. Not that Ewedale didn't do nicely out of it, and Mr. Tupper, he's no call to expect more from Woolfalls."

Gilbert sat thinking for a moment. "The money left to the church here was in the hands of trustees, wasn't it?"

"Aye. The trustees was elected afresh as each died off or gave up. Your folks was always trustees until they left in the seventies. In 1898, there was old Mr. Flockton and his son John, my dad, and Rector as chairman. All in order 'twas— and I reckon they did the sensible thing. Dr. Rees-Williams was Rector then. He died in 1905, and then Mr. Walters was

Rector till 1930. A good man, he was. Never had one so good since. This Mr. Tupper now—no gumption he's got. A silly piece, if ever I did see one. But then they're hard put to it to get parsons at all, so I'm told."

Gilbert nodded. "True enough," he said. "Well, I've been very much interested to have your opinion about this matter, Mr. Herdwick. Possibly I was too much influenced by my uncle's views. He was an old man, and perhaps he was biased by his preoccupation with the past."

"Maybe he was, but there's no reason why he should have left aught for the Reverend to play about with," said Herdwick. "Well, I must be getting along. You'll bear that matter of repairs to the barn in mind, Mr. Woolfall?"

"I certainly will. I'll get Williamsons out from Kirkholm to report on it. I'm sorry you're having trouble with the sheep. Is it sickness?"

"Nay, they're healthy enough. It's thieving, Mr. Woolfall. I've lost three or four this past month and I'm right worried."

"Sheep-stealing? That's bad. I've never heard of that happening up here before."

"Never had times like this before, Mr. Woolfall, with a meat ration you can't hardly smell. Sheep-stealing's on the increase. Only last year there were scores of sheep stolen on Whernside. Rounded up at night, they reckon, and carted off in cattle vans."

"It's difficult to realise how it was done," said Gilbert wonderingly.

"Two smart fellows and a couple of good dogs can round up a flock faster than you'd believe," said Herdwick. "It can be done all right. It wouldn't be so easy on these fells—there's

none but the one road fit for a van, and no way out at t' head
of valley, but it's not impossible. So we're trying to watch
out a bit."

"You've told the police about it?"

"Aye. They know all right, but they can't be everywhere at
once. If you want a thing done, do it yourself's a good motto.
Mr. Lamb of Fullerby, he's taking turn and turn about. The
trouble is, we reckon there's always some local chap gives
information when these sheep-stealing gangs do a big job—
and that's a thing I don't like to think on."

Gilbert looked startled. "But surely, you don't suspect anyone in High Gimmerdale of co-operating with sheep-stealers?"

"Not in High Gimmerdale maybe, but down the Gimmer
valley there's some I'm not so sure on. Some of these young
chaps back from the Forces find it hard to settle down to farm
work and no gallivanting. Easy money and a bit of excitement
may seem better value." The old farmer saw Gilbert's sceptical face, and then added: "You don't believe me, do you, Mr.
Woolfall? Well, I'll tell you this. If our sheep's rounded up and
stolen one of these nights, you'll find it'll happen at a time
when no one's on the watch. They choose their times, these
gangs. Men who're working all day can't watch all night—and
them devils gets to know when the coast's clear. How do they
know? Eh. . . that's what I'd like to know."

"It's a dastardly business," said Gilbert. "I feel I ought to
do something to help. If it's a case of watching the road to see
if a van comes by, I could do it as well as anyone else."

"Well, that's a right neighbourly offer, Mr. Woolfall. If we
want a hand I'll remember what you say. Reckon a charge of
shot into their tyres might do a power of good. But there we

don't want to get you mixed up with this business. 'Twouldn't be fair when you come along for a bit of peace and quiet like to work through your uncle's papers." The old man got up stiffly. "I'll be off now. I've been keeping you from your work. 'Twas in this room your uncle did all his studies. Many's the time I've been in here, and him trying to make me remember what my grand-dad did before I was born!"

Gilbert laughed. "Yes. He always tried to get his facts at first hand, and he wrote things down just as they were told him. He was a very methodical old chap, and he'd got all his papers filed very carefully. I'm trying to read them all through before I destroy anything. It's quite a job."

"Reckon it is. Rather you than me, Mr. Woolfall. Reading's real hard work to me. I haven't read a hard-backed book more'n once or twice in my life. All the reading I do these days is those dratted government forms. The chaps who write 'em go out of their way to tie you up in knots."

I I

After Mr. Herdwick had gone, Gilbert Woolfall went back to the fireside, but he found he made little headway with the file of Uncle Thomas's papers he had meant to read. He found himself thinking of the Herdwicks and what they had succeeded in doing in three generations: the grandfather, old Nathaniel, had been born in Liverpool in 1840 and had come to High Gimmerdale about 1870 and worked as a hired man, living up at Ramshead in that ancient stone hovel which was now almost in ruins—a hard life, and Nat Herdwick must have been a stubborn worker. Nat's son, Timothy, had been born in 1860 and was ten years old when his parents had left the city to come to the fells. Daniel Herdwick, the present owner of Lambsrigg, was born in 1882. Between 1870 and 1904 the three generations of Herdwicks had saved enough money to buy Lambsrigg—an amazing example of success. Gilbert Woolfall knew the way some of the farmers worked and saved, putting every penny by, working from dawn to sunset, watching shrewdly for the chance of a bargain. Of course the sheep farmers were in clover to-day, in comparison with times past: wool, which had sold for twenty-seven pence a pound in 1864 and dropped to as low as sixpence or ninepence a pound in the early nineteen hundreds sold for over a hundred pence a pound in 1952, and the price of sheep and lambs had fluctuated correspondingly. With the price which they commanded to-day, it was easy to see how tempting it was to sheep thieves to round the beasts up from the lonely fells and sell them in some distant market.

The fire was warm, and Gilbert was tired. He put away Uncle Thomas's MS. and brooded sleepily over the ups and downs of sheep farming, over rural populations and the decline of church going, over the fors and againsts of selling Aikengill. Then he suddenly remembered Betty Fell and Jock Shearling, and his sleepy face brightened. "I'll let them come here and see how it works out for a few months," he decided. "Then I can come here, on and off, and have time to make up my mind what I really want to do about it." Of one thing he was certain. He wouldn't sell either the house or the land for a year or two—and perhaps not at all.

CHAPTER IV

I

"FIVE THOUSAND POUNDS SEEMS A LOT OF MONEY TO
pay for a fifty-acre farm," said Robert Macdonald meditatively.

There had been occasions when Macdonald—Chief
Inspector, C.I.D.—had assured harassed witnesses that detectives are only ordinary men, having their own personal likes
and dislikes, their own hobbies, preoccupations, worries,
attitude to life, and hopes of peace and quietness—sometime.
The majority of those whom he sought to reassure in this way
seldom believed him. A senior officer of the C.I.D. must, of
necessity, be somewhat alarming to those whom he interrogates. But when Macdonald pondered ruefully over the
cost of a small dairy farm in Lunesdale, he was very far from
alarming anybody. In fact he was as near to being bullied as his
independent nature allowed. The circumstances were these:
a fortnight's leave and a comfortable legacy from a thrifty
Scots uncle had brought Macdonald up to Lunesdale. He had

taken advantage of a long-standing invitation from Giles and Kate Hoggett to stay with them at Wenningby Farm for the duration of his leave, and he had confided in them concerning his legacy (about £7000 when death duties were paid) and his ambitions about investing it.

"Some day I shall retire," he said. "Not just yet. The police force is under strength, and I haven't the conscience to walk out on them at the moment—but some day…"

"Quite right," said Giles Hoggett. "Everybody should retire while they're still adaptable enough to develop other interests."

"What will you do?" asked Kate Hoggett, who was of an eminently practical turn of mind.

"What you do. I want to farm," said Macdonald.

"But you haven't got a wife," said Giles.

"What's that got to do with it?" demanded Macdonald.

"A lot. A farmer needs a wife," said Giles, but Kate put in:

"Don't be obstructive, Giles. Let him say what he really wants to do." She turned to Macdonald. "You mean you'd like to buy a farm in a few years' time, when you retire?"

"No. I mean I'd like to buy a farm as soon as I can find what I want—a small dairy farm, enough land to carry a dozen milking cows, with a reasonably good dwelling-house and the necessary buildings. Then I thought I could get a competent young married couple, the man to run the farm in my absence, the wife to look after the house and cook and do for me when I come up to stay. Don't you use the word 'hind' up here for the sort of farm manager I'm thinking of?"

"A hind. That's right," agreed Giles, but he spoke without enthusiasm. "This needs thinking about," he added.

"I *have* thought," protested Macdonald. "I've thought quite a lot. I want to put my legacy into farm land. I like hill country. I like Lunesdale. I like you and your wife, Hoggett. I did think of buying some land where my own folks came from, but Inverness is too great a distance from London. Lancaster is less than six hours' train journey from London. I could come up here for week-ends and short leaves, and get to know about things to some extent. Then, later on, when I do retire, I shall have a house ready to live in, work to keep me busy, and an abiding interest for the rest of my life."

"I think the idea of your buying a farm in Lunesdale is an excellent one, and we shall be happy and proud to have you for a neighbour," said Giles, "but I think it'd be much more satisfactory if you came and settled down on your farm as soon as you got possession of the land. No hired man will ever put the amount of work and thought and effort into the farm that the owner would do——"

"Look here," interpolated Mrs. Hoggett, "I think the first thing to do is to make it quite clear to Macdonald that it's all too easy to lose money over farming. Even quite small farms cost an enormous amount now: £5000 is an average sum for a fifty-acre farm, and some smaller holdings have changed hands recently at that price and over. Good milking cows cost more than they ever did, and if you lose a cow at calving or from disease it's a big money loss. And so many disasters can happen to cows."

"Not more so than in times past," argued Macdonald, "and if cows cost a lot, the price of milk is high. A four-galloner earns ten bob a day for her owner, less the price of fodder, and four gallons isn't an ambitious yield..."

This brought Mr. Hoggett back into the debate with his own experience of milk yields, and Mrs. Hoggett let off broadsides over the cost of concentrates, until eventually all three of them were talking simultaneously and with animation, until (being mannerly persons) they all apologised for interrupting one another.

"I'm sorry if I've been over-emphatic," said Kate Hoggett, "but I do want Macdonald to realise all the snags. I should hate it if he put his legacy into dairy farming and lost his money."

"He seems to have read a lot about the subject," said Giles. "He knows you feed a cow at least three and a half pounds of concentrates for every gallon she gives."

"I'm sure he'd make a very good farmer, because he's got a sense of detail. He'd take the trouble to do milk-recording," she added to Giles (who still refused to record his yields). She turned to Macdonald again. "Are you determined to do dairy farming? Why not buy a nice stone house with a few acres of land, and keep pigs and ducks and geese? It'd be much safer."

"I like cows," said Macdonald. "I used to milk my grandfather's cows in the school holidays when I was a kid. He kept Ayrshires."

"Look here. I've got an idea," said Giles. "Someone told me that house of Thomas Woolfall's in High Gimmerdale is probably coming on the market."

"But that's a sheep farm," said Kate. "He couldn't possibly take on sheep."

"Of course he couldn't," agreed Giles, "but the fell grazing is let to the owner of Lambsrigg. I know there's some cow pasture and meadow land down by the river. It's grand hill country———"

"Where is High Gimmerdale?" asked Macdonald. "It's not in Lunesdale, is it?"

"Oh, yes, it is," Giles assured him. "Not in the valley, of course. It's up in the hills across the river, not far away as the crow flies, but you have to go round by Gressingham to cross the Lune and then through Kirkholm and up into the hills. It's a place you ought to see, Macdonald. It has a character all its own, a bit like the Lakeland fell country, because it's so steep. I've always thought I could live in Gimmerdale, and I can't say more than that."

"Take him there to-morrow. It's a lovely drive," said Kate, "and I believe that house of the Woolfalls' is really beautiful. Are you sure it's for sale, Giles?"

"No, but I think it will be," he rejoined. "Thomas Woolfall left it to his nephew, and the latter's a business man from Leeds or Bradford or somewhere in Yorkshire, and he's not likely to live there. The house is called Aikengill—it's about as old as this house, or older, and I believe Thomas Woolfall modernised it inside. He was a fine old man. Woolfalls lived in Gimmerdale for centuries—as long as the Hoggetts have lived in Wenningby."

"What was that story Richard Blackthorne was telling you about Gimmerdale?" asked Kate, and Giles's eyes brightened.

"Why, yes. Sheep-stealing!" he exclaimed. "Macdonald ought to hear about that."

"I don't want to hear about sheep-stealing," said Macdonald, "or any other sort of stealing. I want to hear about a nice dairy farm, fifty acres or so, with sound buildings, good fences, not too far off the high road, and accommodation for a dozen milking cows, a few calves and some stirks. But I should like to see Gimmerdale if Hoggett will drive me there. Can't you get to Slaidburn over those fells?"

"Aye, you can. You've placed it all right," said Giles. "There's no direct motor road, but if you go right to the head of Gimmerdale there's a track over the fells. It's a grand walk—though I admit it's forty years and more since I walked it when I was a lad."

"Woolfall of Gimmerdale," said Macdonald thoughtfully. "It sounds familiar, somehow. Did someone of that name publish an article on sheep farming through the centuries? Not in The Countryman, but some other paper. The Dalesman, was it?"

"Quite likely," said Kate. "Old Mr. Woolfall was quite a historian, I believe he did a lot of research into local history. I always meant to go over and talk to him, but there's such a lot to do here I never found the time. I know you'd be interested in Gimmerdale. It's such a secret place, hidden away in the high fells there, and you get perfectly glorious views of Ingleborough and Whernside."

"The police never found out who stole all those sheep from Whernside last year," put in Giles. "They were absolutely stumped. You remember Bord, at Carnton? He's just been made a chief inspector, by the way. I had a word with him when I was passing through Carnton. He was one of the officers who co-operated in the investigation, and he still feels sore about it. I told him you were coming to Wenningby for your leave, Macdonald, and he said he hoped he'd see you while you were here."

"Did he? Then I'd better drive over and have a crack with him before he makes up his mind I'm fishing for corpses in

Lune," said Macdonald. "I always have the feeling that Bord thinks I'm a cross between a poacher and a bird of ill-omen."

"Nothing of the kind. He has a great regard for you," said Giles firmly. "He heard about your visit to Kirkby Wentworth last year, and he was most disappointed you didn't step off the train at Carnton and pay him a visit."

"It's my opinion that he's always hoping to work with you again on another case," said Kate, and Macdonald groaned.

Giles put in: "They ought to have got you up here over that sheep-stealing business, Macdonald," but Kate said:

"Oh, rubbish, Giles! The one thing the local police do know more about than Scotland Yard can possibly know is sheep. The whole thing was tied up with local usages and skills: with the training of sheep dogs, the movement of cattle vans, with local cattle markets and slaughter houses and the hangers-on at markets."

"Perfectly true, all of it," said Macdonald, "and may I remind you both that I am not concerned with sheep-stealing or cattle-rustling or regulations about pig-killing or any other official business whatever on this occasion. I'm interested in the price of cow pastures and meadows, and in the margin of profit on a thousand gallon cow with concentrates costing about £40 a ton."

"I know," said Kate, "but if you do take to farming you'll be very interested in sheep-stealing. We were, although we haven't any sheep. The police posted notices about the Whernside thefts on our barn door, and we were all agog about it." She paused and studied Macdonald in her characteristic way, half analytical, half amused.

"Well?" he asked defensively. "What have I done now?"

"Nothing. I was just wondering if you're really as single-minded as you're claiming to be. If a theft occurred in Wenningby while you're staying here, if Richard Blackthorne's sheep were stolen, or even if Giles's ducks all vanished in the night, would you say you weren't interested?"

"Of course I shouldn't," said Macdonald. "I should rush unasked into either case—and make a proper mulock of it, as you say up here, because, as you've pointed out, I haven't the necessary information. I was only trying to persuade you that I do want to buy a farm, in spite of all your warnings. I don't believe you're really taking me seriously about it, Mrs. Hoggett."

"Oh, yes, I am," she retorted. "It was because I could see you were really set on it that I reminded you of all the snags. I should feel awful over it if you bought a farm on our advice and then your cows got mastitis or contagious abortion and had to be slaughtered. You'd be miserable, and we should be miserable——"

"Cheer up, Kate," said Giles. "Don't out-do Cassandra. Remember the man who said on his death-bed 'I've had a lot of worries in my life, but most of them never happened.' I like the idea of Macdonald coming to settle up here, but I'm glad he's driving over to see Bord at Carnton."

"Why?" asked Macdonald suspiciously.

"Because it'd be a very good thing if you took an interest in this sheep-stealing business in Gimmerdale. All the farmers would be favourably impressed; they'd see your heart was in the right place. If you solved the case and the thieves were arrested, it'd make a wonderful début to settling down here as a farmer."

"And if I didn't solve the case?" asked Macdonald.

"It'd be more popular still, maybe. They'd say, 'He did his best, but he's no'but a Londoner and he's got to learn country ways.' Anyway, mention to Bord that I'm taking you over to High Gimmerdale to-morrow, and see if he opens up."

"All right, I will," said Macdonald. "I'll also tell him I'm thinking of buying a farm and see his reaction to that one."

I I

It was just after tea that Macdonald set out for Carnton. He had to wait patiently before he could back his car out of the barn where it was standing, because the milking cows were coming in. It had been a glorious April day, and the cows had been out at pasture in the sunshine, though they came back into the shippons for the nights which were still chilly. Giles Hoggett stood by his fold yard gate and watched Edmund Troutbeck's Friesians go by. Macdonald in turn watched Hoggett. The years had treated him kindly: Giles's hair was quite grey now, but he was just as straight-limbed and spare as he had been when he did his famous run over the dales after his "Iron Dogs" had been stolen. Macdonald chuckled a little bit to himself—that had been a good case, with Hoggett supplying all the information. "Iron dogs, a salmon line, a chaff sack, Mrs. Hoggett's washing line and Uncle Henry's spectacles," those were the items stolen, and what detective could have improved on them as basic evidence?

Macdonald was still chuckling as he backed his car out neatly into the narrow road and drove up the hill to the high barn, where he halted a moment or so to pay homage to the Wenningby sky line. It was a clear sunny day: to the east was the great limestone rampart of the Pennine Chain, Ingleborough, Pen-y-ghent and Whernside, sunlit, cloud-flecked, clean-cut against the azure sky: at their feet, it seemed, nestled the village of Kirkholm, castle and octagonal church tower rising above the trees, with the blue line of the River Wenning shining across the flood plain to join Lune. To the south the fells of Claughton and Clougha shut in Lunesdale in untroubled serenity. Looking back over his shoulder to the west, Macdonald saw the great curves of the river far below—Crook o' Lune, as lovely a stretch of water as a man might wish to see. Suddenly a thought flashed across Macdonald's mind: somewhere, high up in the fell country to the south-west, Gimmerdale lay hidden. High Gimmerdale and sheep-stealing—and Crook o' Lune. To a policeman's mind there was something apposite about the juxtaposition of the words—sheep-stealing and a crook. Not a shepherd's crook, but a human crook, the type of gentry Macdonald spent his life in chasing. He drove on along the switchback road, his mind busy with the theme: in the old days (good or bad, according to your social background) sheep thieves had been hanged. A brutal sentence, but it told of the hard necessities of hard times. Sheep had to be left to pasture on hillside, fell, or down, and any thief could steal one by night. Sheep farmers and wool trade had had to be protected, and thus sheep-stealing had been punishable by death.

It was odd to think that modern times provided stringencies which encouraged the re-emergence of the sheep-stealer, pondered Macdonald, and even as he thought it he realised that this crime constituted a challenge to the guardians of law and order, and an exciting challenge at that. In place of the house-breakers' and safe-breakers' tools was the skill of a fellsman and the training of his dog: it was like poaching on a large scale, only the quarry had to be removed in cattle vans. In spite of all his assurances to Mrs. Hoggett, Macdonald's mind began to play with counter manoeuvres: the great thing would be to be on the alert at the outset…and then he had to brake suddenly as a couple of stirks bolted out from the hedge and across the road. "Somebody's fences want looking to," he thought. The stirks were Friesians—nicely marked black and white beasts. "I'd rather have Ayrshires," thought Macdonald, and his mind went back happily to his project of fifty acres and a dozen milking cows.

CHAPTER V

I

MACDONALD CAUGHT BORD JUST BEFORE THE LATTER was leaving the police station at Carnton. Bord had just finished reprimanding a very young police constable. "What you've got to learn is the importance of detail, my lad. When you report I want all the facts, not only the ones which strike you as interesting. So you go back to the scene of this incident and take your measuring tape with you, and you can show me your plan again to-morrow morning, with every detail properly noted."

Flushed and perspiring, the constable saluted smartly and retired with evident relief as Bord came forward to greet Macdonald. "This is a real pleasure," he declared.

"Very kind of you to say so," replied Macdonald, "especially as I generally seem to land up here when there's a spot of trouble around. I hope this is the exception which proves the rule."

"I can't say we've got anything interesting for you," said Bord. "Mostly traffic incidents at the moment—some silly juggins trying to pass a tractor outfit on a road which isn't wide enough, or farmers failing to maintain fences and letting cattle stray on the high road. Now that was an interesting case which brought you up to Kirkby Wentworth last November. I'd been hoping to have a word with you about that."

They sat down in Bord's office and Macdonald regaled Bord with the details of the Rodney Bretton case.

"Amazing business," said Bord. "Not my cup of tea. Mathematicians are beyond me. Give me agricultural regulations or the Highway Code, and I know where I am."

"I don't think mathematics had much bearing on the case as a whole," said Macdonald. "In any case, I always remember the immortal dictum, 'Mathematics cannot lie, a truth which does not always apply to mathematicians.' If I were to generalise at all, I'd say that criminals and crooks are activated by identical impulses, no matter whether they're academic or illiterate. The profit motive is the most general basis of activity, whether the crime be blackmail by a learned man or sheep-stealing by an unlettered one."

"Ah, sheep-stealing," growled Bord. "I reckon you'd have heard of that. It was a proper headache, and they got away with it. Still makes me hot under the collar to think about it."

"I'd like to hear about it if you're willing to talk, Bord."

"Talk? Aye. I'll talk. Funny—I thought of you while we were on the job—though whether you'd have made any more than we did I can't tell." For the next ten minutes Bord spread himself on the problem of tracing thieves who got away with sheep by the score and vanished before the unfortunate farmers had realised their loss. On this occasion he was eloquent enough and he finished up: "And they may be at it again. A farmer in High Gimmerdale has reported losses, but the devil of it is you don't know if it's a case of theft or sheer bad luck. It's real hill country there—hard for the most experienced shepherd to search. There's been cases of sheep worrying by dogs. The ewes may take shelter in clefts of the rocks and die there: they may be driven for miles and join another flock. Whatever it is, I reckon they've not been got away in a cattle van this time. There's only the one road fit for a van out of Gimmerdale, and the Kirkholm chaps have been watching that all right."

"What about the head of the valley?" asked Macdonald, and Bord nodded.

"Could be—but it'd take a good fellsman to drive a bunch of sheep that way. Ever been up there?"

"No, but I'm hoping to go to-morrow," said Macdonald. "Isn't there a house up there which might come on the market?"

"A house?" queried Bord, staring at the C.I.D. man in astonishment. "Not coming to settle in these parts, by any chance?"

"Not yet, but some time in the not too remote future," said Macdonald. He outlined his idea of buying a dairy farm to Bord and saw the latter look more and more astonished.

"But could you settle to it—after the life you've lived in London?" he asked.

"I don't want to live in London after I've retired, and I don't want to chase London crooks till the day I die," rejoined Macdonald. "I think I could settle here all right. I only hope I shall have the chance."

"Well, if that's the case, so do I. It'd be fine to have

you up here to have a crack with—and a lot of peace you'd get…" chuckled Bord. "Anyway, see here, if you do go out to Gimmerdale to-morrow, you leave your car at Lambsrigg and tramp over to the head of the valley. It's a grand walk, that is."

"I don't mind if I do," replied Macdonald, "and if I see anything which strikes me as interesting, I'll report when I come back."

I I

Mr. Hoggett was of necessity an early riser. The milk lorry arrived about eight o'clock, and the milk lorry was the unofficial dictator in Wenningby: the cows had to be milked, the milk cooled and strained and poured into the milk kits by the time the lorry pulled up. The time of its arrival varied a little; if Mr. Thorpe of Farrintack had been slow over his milking it meant that the lorryman was delayed and much heat was generated, but if the driver was in good time he generally gave any odd bits of news he had picked up during his earlier visits.

Mrs. Hoggett was a little terse if her husband dallied with the lorry driver: she liked her breakfast at eight to the tick, and her fragrant coffee was poured out to the B.B.C. time signal with a punctuality which betrayed her urban origin. On this particular morning, Wednesday, April 16th, breakfast was a little delayed: Giles was still outside talking to the lorry driver at eight o'clock, and Macdonald was at the telephone, answering a call which Kate Hoggett viewed with some apprehension. She liked Macdonald and she enjoyed having him as a visitor and she was afraid this early telephone call might mean that he would be recalled to London before his leave was half over. Having poured out the coffee, she went outside to call Giles in, peremptorily. She had a theory that he tended to become over-fond of a leisurely gossip as he grew older.

"Giles, I've poured the coffee out," she called, and Giles hastened in, his expression eloquent of important tidings.

"Sorry, Kate, but a most remarkable thing's happened. There was a fire in High Gimmerdale last night. Thomas Woolfall's house was half-burnt out."

"What a pity," said Kate. "I believe it was a lovely house. How did it happen? I thought it was empty."

"So it was. The housekeeper had gone back to her own folk at Dent. She went just before Easter," said Giles. "It's a very queer business."

"What's the queer business?" inquired Macdonald, coming into the room and apologising to Kate for being late. He knew her punctual ways.

"Come and have your coffee," said Kate. "I do hope that telephone call didn't mean you've got to rush back to London."

"No—and thank you for the kind thought," said Macdonald. "It was Bord, speaking from Carnton." He turned to Giles and the latter hastened to tell his news.

"A very odd thing, Macdonald. It was only yesterday evening I was telling you about the Woolfalls' house up in Gimmerdale."

"And it caught fire in the night," said Macdonald.

"How on earth do you know that?" demanded Giles. "The driver of the milk lorry has only just told me about it."

Kate Hoggett was more on the spot than her husband. "Bord must have told Macdonald about it," she said. "Does he want you to go and help him find out why an empty house caught fire in the night?"

"Bord asked me if I'd care to go up there and join in their consultation," rejoined Macdonald. "You see, I'm afraid the lorry driver had only got half the story. The house wasn't empty. The housekeeper came back there yesterday to fetch some of her belongings and it was believed she'd gone away again before evening. Unfortunately, she stayed the night in Aikengill and they found her body this morning. She was suffocated in her sleep by the smoke."

There was a moment's horrified silence and then Kate said: "How wretched! I'm so terribly sorry. I wonder how on earth it happened."

"That's what Bord is wondering," said Macdonald. "Well, he's asked me to go and give them my opinion, for what it's worth, so the only thing I can do is to go."

"Of course," she agreed, "though I'm very sorry—in every way. It seems bad luck that you can't have a holiday when you've earned one."

"I'm having a very good holiday, thanks to you and your husband," rejoined Macdonald, "and there's this to it. Imagine that Giles had come up to London last year—Festival year—and gone to the South Bank Exhibition. If he'd done so I'm certain he'd have gone to see the Agricultural Section—they had some beautiful Ayrshires there at one time. Well, if the cowman at South Bank had needed a hand for some reason, wouldn't your Giles have leapt forward with the utmost enthusiasm to help the cowman?"

"Of course he would—and ruined his best suit in the process," said Kate.

Giles's comment was characteristic. "Kate is really suggesting that if you go to investigate the origins of a fire you ought to borrow some old clothes and not spoil the good ones you've got on, Macdonald. Incidentally, I think your analogy is very cogent. A busman's holiday is not without appeal, but if I had offered to help with the exhibition cows—or were they Festival cows?—well, all cows are pleasant creatures. But a fire—and a death caused by fire—nobody can say they can be a pleasant experience."

"'*Chacun à son métier et les vaches seront bien gardées*,'" said Macdonald. "I apologise for inflicting my French on you at breakfast, but the proverb is 'cogent,' to quote Giles. Both fires and corpses pertain to tragedy, as suffering and disease do, but the underlying causes of suffering and disease are of profound interest to physicians. It's not the fire as a fire, nor the corpse as a corpse, which will take me to Gimmerdale, but the reasons which caused the house to catch fire and resulted in a death. And if I can do anything to help ferret out the cause, then I shan't feel I've spent an unsatisfactory morning."

"What I like about Macdonald is his common sense," said Kate. "I often wonder if it's because he's so sensible that he's such a good detective."

"It can't be only that, because I'm sensible but I'm no good at detecting," said Giles. "Perhaps specialised training has something to do with it, as it does with cows. I remember reading somewhere that detection has something in common with translating a Latin unseen. You have to ferret out the verb first—"

"Is the verb analogous to the corpse?" inquired Kate. "Anyway I don't think it works, because Giles was good at unseens—once—but it didn't make a detective of him."

She turned to Macdonald. "Is Bord coming to fetch you?" she asked.

"No. I said I'd find my own way up to Gimmerdale," he replied. "I don't think Giles would enjoy close inspection of reeking ashes. The immediate aftermath of a fire is a melancholy experience."

"It must be horrible," agreed Kate. "If Giles wants to go and stare he can go when it's all cooled down. I'm terribly sorry about the housekeeper, and I do hope the house hasn't been altogether destroyed. It was such a lovely house, and a very interesting one historically."

"I believe only one room is burnt out," said Macdonald. "They got the fire brigade up there. I heard the siren—it was just after two o'clock. It's funny how long habits last: I was out of bed before I was really awake, groping for a tin hat and a gas mask, although it's seven years since I heard an air-raid siren."

"I know. That siren they use for a fire-alarm still makes me feel a bit sick," said Kate. "I wish they could use some other noise for warning the men who make up the fire service in the valley. We've heard too many sirens ever to forget them."

"Did you wake up when the siren went, Kate?" asked Giles.

"No. Neither did you," she replied. "That shows the difference between Macdonald and us. He's conditioned to wake up if things happen in the night. We're not."

"But I wake up if the cows make a noise," said Giles, and Macdonald said:

"One day I shall be like that—I hope. The cows will be the only things that matter."

I I I

It was a glorious clear day in the valley, but when Macdonald reached the high barn, whence he expected to see the Pennines and the fells above Claughton, he found the hills were shrouded in mist, as though the clouds were sitting on their summits. The mist was a sign of fair weather, but Macdonald wondered if High Gimmerdale had been swathed in mist throughout the night: it might have made a difference to the time the fire was first observed if the mist had been heavy.

He crossed the Lune by the narrow bridge at Gressingham, drove through the pleasant stone village of Kirkholm and was soon driving up into the hills by the same route which Gilbert Woolfall took when he drove to Aikengill. There was a young police officer on duty by the cattle grid but he saluted as Macdonald pulled up and told him that Chief Inspector Bord had already gone on to Aikengill. "It's a very steep hill down to the bridge, sir, and an awkward turn, but you can get right up to the house without any difficulty."

As Macdonald drove on along the unfenced road, the sun began to come through the mist and he was able to get an idea of the sort of country he was in, steeper and wilder than anything he had previously seen in Lunesdale. It was not until later in the morning, when the mist had quite cleared away, that he was able to see the great stretch of fell country as it really was but even in the white shrouding of misty air

Macdonald delighted in Gimmerdale. It seemed a world of its own.

Driving carefully down the steep drop to the bridge, he did not see the grey length of Aikengill until he was almost at its gate, but the sour smell of burning hung in the air and smoke still sullied the whiteness of the now sunlit mist. Seeing the beauty of long flagged roof and graceful mullioned windows Macdonald could only echo Kate Hoggett and say "What a pity." This house had a character all its own and it was sad to see the cracked glass and blackened stone-work at the gable end.

I V

"Well, I reckon this was where it started," said Bord.

He and Macdonald were standing on some steps which led down to a cellar immediately below Thomas Woolfall's study. Bord explained the structure of the house. "This was originally a farm house, of course. Its barn and the main shippons are across the road there. You can see the house is built on a fairly steep bank; this cellar here used to be the shippon and it had an entrance from the road before the ground was banked up and levelled to form the garden; those two rooms—the study and bedroom at the gable end—were built above the old shippon."

"Yes. I see that," said Macdonald, "and I don't wonder they built other shippons and stables—the approach to this one would have been steep and awkward."

"You're right there," put in Daniel Herdwick's voice. "It'd have been right awkward here, but Mr. Bord's quite correct in his facts. It was a shippon in the old days before these two rooms were added."

Macdonald looked down the short steep flight of steps which led to the cellar from the garden path where they were standing. "Is there an entrance to the cellar in the house itself?" he asked.

"No. There's never been one," said Herdwick. "The only entrance to the cellar is by these steps. I know that, because I've had many a crack with Mr. Thomas Woolfall—him that died—about the way this house was built. He was trying to worry out for himself what the house looked like before those two rooms were added on to it, and if the shippon had a lean-to roof against the old gable end. But if you want to know any more about the cellar, you ask young Jock Shearling. He's been in it of late. I haven't—and I've forgotten what I knew, which wasn't much, anyway," Herdwick turned to Bord. "If there's anything I can do to help you, Mr. Bord, I'll stay here and welcome, but if not, I'd like to get up on the fells Gimmerhead way and see to my sheep."

"You get on, Mr. Herdwick," said Bord. "It's been very good of you to spare so much time. I know you're worried. You go and check up and let us know later if everything's as it should be."

"I'll let you know all right," said the other, and hurried off.

"Mr. Herdwick was out on the fells last night with old Tegg," said Bord. "They saw the glow of the fire from upper Ramshead just after midnight, and Herdwick's bothered in his mind in case the fire was a put-up job to get him away from his sheep. But one thing at a time. First things first—and I'll tell you why I reckon the fire started in this cellar. It was packed with dry kindling and split logs. And that door was never locked."

The cellar door had been burnt away, only its long iron hinges remained, hanging from a massive door post. Bord went down a couple of steps. "It's not fit to go inside yet," he said, "but you can see all you want to see from here. There was never a plastered ceiling or anything of that kind. Just rafters, and the joists and floor boards of the room above were laid on the beams of the cellar roof."

"The surprising thing is that the whole house didn't burn," said Macdonald.

"It's the way it was built," said Bord. "There's the solid outer wall of the original house shutting off these two newer rooms. Now you notice there's a window in the cellar, just at ground level as the ground is to-day. That might have been another entrance to the shippon in the old days, but the reason I'm telling you about it is that the light of the fire shone through that space before the room above it was ablaze. Herdwick and old Tegg reckon that was what they saw from Upper Ramshead, and it was because they saw it and came hurrying back that they got the fire under before it got out of control." He came back up the steps again. "Now you've seen the cellar, let's go along to the other end of the house—the kitchen end. It'll be pleasanter to talk there."

CHAPTER VI

I

BORD TOOK MACDONALD THROUGH THE HOUSE BEFORE they settled down to talk, and explained the way Aikengill had been built during its three centuries.

"You can think of it as four houses made into one," he said. "There are actually three stone dividing walls, each with its gable going right up to the roof tree. Look at the thickness of the walls where the doorways were made, over eighteen inches thick. Good solid doors, too."

"It's good and solid right through," said Macdonald. "I was told it was an interesting house, and a beautiful one, too, but it's even more attractive than I'd imagined. Somebody took a lot of thought and trouble to make this house as it is to-day."

"That was old Mr. Thomas Woolfall, the present owner's uncle," said Bord, as he led the way back from the blackened, smouldering study, through the entrance hall and sitting-room which showed hardly any signs of damage by fire. "The old man was a real antiquarian, I believe. He died last winter: went up the fells during the great frost we had in January. He must have slipped on the ice-covered rocks. They found his body in a snowdrift."

They went into the kitchen, at the north end of the long house, and Macdonald said, "I agree with you the fire started in the cellar. The thing you want to decide is how it started."

"That's it—and it's not going to be easy," said Bord. "You see, anybody could have got into that cellar. The door was never locked. But we'd better start with the housekeeper, who was alone in the house."

Bord stated the facts he had learnt clearly and tersely. A week ago Mrs. Ramsden had left Aikengill and gone over to Dent to nurse her cousin Alice who had had influenza. Mrs. Ramsden had told her neighbours in Gimmerdale that she wasn't leaving Aikengill for good: she was coming back to look after the house until Mr. Woolfall had made other arrangements. She had come back to Gimmerdale yesterday (Tuesday) to collect some more clothes, and also to clean and air Aikengill. She had been given a lift by a neighbour in Dent who was driving to Lancaster, and she had been put down in Kirkholm, and had got Jack Daleham at the garage there to drive her up to High Gimmerdale. Mrs. Ramsden, a thrifty north-countrywoman, saw no sense in spending money on taxis if she could avoid it, and she had inquired in Kirkholm if there were any chance of getting a lift back from Gimmerdale to Kirkholm that evening. The grocer generally went to Gimmerdale on Tuesdays; maybe he could bring her back if he wasn't too late.

"Well, you never know what time he'll get up there," Jack

Daleham had said. "Tell you what. I'm taking the Rector up to see old Mrs. Hodges at Beck Cottage. His car's off the road, gear box gone wrong. I'll be bringing him back at half-past five. If you can walk down to the gate leading to Hodges, I can bring you back here after I've left the Rector at Ewedale."

Mrs. Ramsden had said that would suit her very well, and she had told Betty Fell and old Tegg, whom she saw over the garden wall, that she had only come to Aikengill for the day and was going back to Dent that evening. "And that's what she meant to do, but she must have lost sight of the time," said Bord. "Jock Shearling saw her walking down the old lane towards Hodges, and he reckons it'd turned half-past five then. When Jack Daleham told the Rector he'd promised to take Mrs. Ramsden back, Mr. Tupper was very short. 'I've got to be at a meeting at six o'clock and I can't wait,' he said. 'If you want to drive Mrs. Ramsden you'll have to come back and fetch her. I don't see why she should have a free drive at my expense and keep me waiting into the bargain.'"

"He sounds a charitable sort of chap," said Macdonald.

Bord nodded. "Yes. I hope he'll take it to heart. If he hadn't behaved like that, I reckon Mrs. Ramsden'd be alive now. Not that he meant any harm—he was just being uppish. Mrs. Ramsden was a Nonconformist and hadn't shown the Rector the respect he considers his due. However, that's how it happened. I supposed she realised the car had gone without her and decided she'd go back to Aikengill for the night and go home in the morning."

"What about Daleham, the taxi man? Why didn't he go back for her?" asked Macdonald.

"He said he reckoned she'd wait for the grocer's van. If

she'd wanted a taxi she could have phoned. Old Mr. Woolfall had the phone put in at the same time Mr. Herdwick did."

"Well, that's clear enough," said Macdonald. "We can assume she decided she'd stay the night at Aikengill, although the neighbours thought she'd gone back to Dent as she'd said she was doing. It's a point worth bearing in mind—it was supposed this house was empty. And now about the fire. Any ideas?"

"The obvious one to begin with," said Bord. "When she got back here the kitchen fire was out. She'd have been careful to see that it *was* out before she left. She went down to the cellar to get some kindling and struck a match to see what she was about—and dropped it."

"Well, you don't need me to list all the objections to that as a theory: you can see them for yourself," said Macdonald.

"Maybe I can, but you put them forward and I'll try to bowl you out."

Macdonald got up and went and opened the oven door in the kitchen range. "Just what you'd expect from a sensible country woman," he said. There was a neat pile of split wood and some small faggots in the oven. "They nearly always put some kindling to dry ready for laying the fire in the morning. Mrs. Ramsden would have seen to it that she'd left some kindling ready for her next visit. She wouldn't have needed to go down to the cellar for sticks. And even if she had, would she have needed a match? Presumably it was still daylight when she returned here, and there's plenty of light in the cellar with the doorway and the window. And wasn't it wired for lighting? I noticed a switch just inside the door."

"Perfectly true," said Bord, "but there's this to remember: the electric meter and the control switches are in that cellar. Mrs. Ramsden would certainly have turned off the current before she left the house. When she came back, she'd have gone down to the cellar to turn the current on again, because if she was staying the night she'd have wanted a light. There's a chance she lit a match to see what she was about."

"Yes. I suppose that's possible," agreed Macdonald. "What sort of body was she?"

"She was a woman of about sixty, highly respected hereabouts, and reckoned as a very competent housekeeper. She'd worked for old Mr. Woolfall for five years and he thought very highly of her. He left her £500 in his will."

"Do you really think she was the sort of woman who'd drop a lighted match in a cellar where the kindling was stacked and not notice what she'd done?" asked Macdonald.

Bord answered that one without hesitation. "No. I don't. But can you tell me how we're to prove she didn't? I think the probability is that she'd have gone down to the cellar to turn on the current again. The main switches are in the corner, to the left of the door. It's darkish there. She might have lighted a match…"

"If we accept what seems the obvious assumption—that Mrs. Ramsden came straight back here after she'd realised the taxi had gone without her—it's also to be assumed she got back here by seven o'clock at latest," said Macdonald. "If she went down to the cellar to switch the current on she'd have done it immediately she got back: which means that if she'd dropped a lighted match in the kindling at seven o'clock she had the whole evening to smell the smoke coming from the wood burning in the cellar. And she obviously did not smell it."

"That's about it," said Bord. "Why didn't she smell it?"

"You'll have to wait for the results of the P.M. before you can make a guess about that," said Macdonald, "but at a first glance the fire seems more likely to have been caused by arson than accident."

Bord nodded. "I agree. Well, I'd better get around and talk to the neighbours. Would you care to come with me?"

"No. I think you'll do better by yourself—a stranger would only put your witnesses off," said Macdonald. "I should like to wander around and get to know the lay-out, where the house is overlooked from and so forth. But just give me a list of the folk who live nearby."

"That's easy enough," said Bord. "There's not so many. Here in High Gimmerdale there's Mr. Herdwick and his daughter Maggie and a maidservant living in Lambsrigg Hall—that's the house on the left as you go on up the hill. There's old Aaron Tegg, living alone in that cottage on the fell above Lambsrigg; Tegg's the shepherd. Will Hodges and his old mother live in Beck Cottage, down by the stream. Then in Low Gimmerdale, about a mile away that is, there's Mr. Lamb and his wife and family at Fullerby House, and the Shearlings at Eweshead. Mr. Shearling works for Mr. Lamb. He's got two sons: Jock works for Mr. Herdwick: Len has a tractor and gear and is a free lance, so to speak. The only other family are the Fells at Ramsthwaite, but their farm is on the borders of Ewedale, nearly three miles away."

Macdonald made a note of the names and then said: "Well,

you'll be busy for some time interrogating the folks round about. I'll wander round and get the feel of the place."

"Right," said Bord. "We phoned Mr. Woolfall, and he expects to get here about midday. Maybe you'd like to hear what he has to say."

"Yes, I should," rejoined Macdonald. "I'll be back here about twelve o'clock."

I I

When Bord had left him, Macdonald strolled into the garden of Aikengill and considered the lie of the land. There was about an acre of garden, hedged in with clipped beech. The house was built on a hillside, the ground highest to the north, falling to the south. The builders had compensated for this by building the ground-floor rooms at different levels: from the kitchen and dining-room at the northern end, a step led down to the sitting-room, and two more steps led down again to the hall room and further steps led to porch and garden level. In the garden the ground had been levelled into terraces: the upper lawn, bounded to the north by a deep hedge bank, was perfectly level: steps gave on to another big stretch of grass which still sloped a little to the south, and another slight drop led to the beech hedge and containing wall. The latter was only two feet high on the garden side, but six feet high on the outer side, showing that the garden had been banked up.

Macdonald had learnt from Mrs. Hoggett that all the old steadings in this part of the world were built on sites which ensured a water supply. Even without that information it was obvious that the slope of the land at Aikengill must

ensure some underground becks to carry off the drainage of
the hill land above. It seemed to Macdonald that the cellar
below old Thomas Woolfall's study must inevitably be very
damp. The probability was that in wet weather, when the
drains and becks had more water than they could carry,
something like a stream would run down the cellar steps
and away by some ancient drain to join the River Gimmer
in the valley below. This point interested him, because it
had been a wet springtime, and from his own observation
of the ancient stone buildings of the locality, the dropping
of a lighted match would not produce a conflagration in
any cellar resembling the Aikengill one. Kindling stored
there would be out of the rain, but not therefore dry. In
this humid climate, the kindling would need a lot of dry-
ing before it would kindle. In other words, the dropping
of one lighted match would have been quite inadequate
to cause a fire.

Leaving Aikengill, Macdonald strolled up the road
until he came within sight of Mr. Herdwick's house—
Lambsrigg Hall. The length of Aikengill faced east and
west, its gable ends north and south, the north end having no windows. Lambsrigg Hall, higher up the hill than
Aikengill, was to the north of the latter and faced north
and south. Lambsrigg was tall and gaunt, built of dressed
stone, obviously not such an ancient house as that of the
Woolfalls. To its west (the weather side) Lambsrigg was
sheltered by a wind-break of close-planted pine and ash,
wind-stunted but sturdy. The juxtaposition of the two
houses interested Macdonald: it was customary to find
two substantial steadings built close together in a remote

place like Gimmerdale. They had afforded one another protection in lawless days when armed forays might occur. It was also characteristic that they were built in such a way that they did not intrude on each other's privacy. Owing to their siting, and to the close pine trees, they obtained no view at all of each other.

As he wandered round and spotted the scattered cottages which made up High Gimmerdale, Macdonald found that none of them had a view of Aikengill. That ancient house, in common with the other dwellings of Gimmerdale, was built on the northern slopes of the valley so that it enjoyed the sun from the south: there was no house opposite to it on the southern slopes. Tegg's cottage, Summerfold, was screened from Aikengill by the Lambsrigg barns. Beck Cottage, down by the river, had a steep coppice of hazel and birch and pine immediately above it. The dwellings in Low Gimmerdale were right out of sight, hidden from Aikengill and Lambsrigg by a bend in the valley. Noting these facts, Macdonald saw that Aikengill might have burnt to its roof tree without being observed by its neighbours, save for the chance of Mr. Herdwick and Tegg being out on the fellside that night. Going back to Aikengill, Macdonald went to the window space in the cellar wall and looked up at the slopes of Ramshead, mistily blue against the south-western sky. It was an uninterrupted view. The little window must have glowed like a beacon when the wood in the cellar was ablaze, but Ramshead fell was some miles away. By the time Herdwick and Tegg had got down the fellside, the blaze in the cellar had reached the unplastered beams and the room above was well alight.

I I I

Macdonald and Bord met again outside Aikengill just before midday. "I've been checking up on what folks were doing yesterday evening," said Bord, who was enjoying having Macdonald to talk to. "The chaps who work for Mr. Herdwick are Hodges and Shearling, full-time, and old Tegg, who's been shepherd on Lambsrigg all his life. Tegg's nearly eighty now, and he doesn't work full time. He lends a hand when he's needed, at lambing, clipping, and dipping. Hodges is a cowman, though he helps in all the other jobs, like most of the hired men do hereabouts."

"So Mr. Herdwick keeps milking cows as well as sheep," observed Macdonald.

"Aye. He's got a dozen milking cows—a T.T. herd. Friesians they are, and a very good lot I'm told. There's some good cow pastures and meadows down in the valley—Mr. Woolfall's land that is, leased to Mr. Herdwick. Well, I told you that Jock Shearling saw Mrs. Ramsden walking down to Hodges just after half-past five. Shearling had finished his own jobs, and he went to lend Hodges a hand with milking and mucking out the shippons, so that Hodges could get back home a bit earlier than usual as his mother's so poorly. So between 5.40 and 6.30, Shearling and Hodges were busy in the shippons behind Lambsrigg. Mr. Herdwick was having his tea and Tegg was in the paddock back of his cottage, skinning a dead lamb and tying its fleece on to another lamb to make the ewe take to it—you know the trick they play. I just got those facts clear because it explains why nobody saw Mrs. Ramsden when she walked back to Aikengill."

"What about the grocer's van?" asked Macdonald.

"He never got up here. Had a puncture in Roeburndale. Shearling went home just before seven. Hodges had his own meal to cook and his mother to see to. Mr. Herdwick stayed in the house and snoozed over the fire until ten o'clock; and Tegg did the same, because they'd settled to go up to Ramshead at ten. They went up the fell and round the head of the valley. They didn't pass Aikengill going that way, but they said they didn't notice aught amiss. It wasn't a clear night, of course. The mist hung in the valley after sundown. Maggie Herdwick went in to Mrs. Hodges about half-past nine and she said it was misty down below but fairly clear on top. Well, that's how folks spent the evening, but Tegg's got a story that may be relevant, if he's got the rights of it. You know that Mr. Herdwick's missed some of his sheep?"

"Yes. I'm bearing that in mind all right," said Macdonald.

"Mr. Herdwick told Mr. Woolfall about it and the latter offered to help them patrol. Mr. Herdwick said no to that—Mr. Woolfall doesn't know the land well enough. But one day last week, out towards Ramshead, Mr. Woolfall met a stranger, a rough chap, he said, and asked him his business. A young chap, Tegg said, and one of the dumb sort. Just said, he was out walking, and of course there is a track over the head of the valley. Mr. Woolfall spoke to him pretty sharply—warned him off, as it were. Tegg's got it into his head that this fellow started the fire out of spite."

"He'd have to be a pretty bad lot to do that," said Macdonald, "but the story may well have a bearing on the fire. It seems to me that the fire might have been started to cover a theft. I've known that to happen before. This house has been empty for a week or so, and empty houses are always an invitation to thieves."

"That's true enough of towns, but we don't get many thieves in a place like this," objected Bord. "It's too far away from main roads, and thieves are always aware of the danger of dogs barking in farm property. They've all got their own dogs round here—have to have 'em in sheep country. Hodges and Tegg and Mr. Herdwick have all got dogs chained in their yards, and they'd raise a proper racket if a stranger passed the steadings at night… Ah, that's Mr. Woolfall's car. I reckon he'll be properly upset about this."

CHAPTER VII

I

GILBERT WOOLFALL WAS CERTAINLY UPSET. HE WAS both sad and angry: sad on account of Mrs. Ramsden's death, for he had a warm regard for her, and angry because he was convinced that the fire which had originated in the Aikengill cellar could not have been due to accident.

Macdonald liked Gilbert Woolfall at sight. Giles Hoggett had described him as a "business man from Leeds," and Macdonald had expected to meet a typical Yorkshire wool merchant, forthright, very certain of himself, stout, hectoring perhaps, in town clothes and a bowler hat. Gilbert Woolfall did not look a countryman, certainly, despite well-worn tweeds and good country shoes. He was tall and dark and pale, and reminded Macdonald more of a bookish fellow than a business man—a don in a small university perhaps, or a legal man. His voice was quiet, and he had no accent by which he could be placed, and his manner was diffident rather than hectoring.

Gilbert's first reaction to the news had been to blame himself for Mrs. Ramsden's death. He said that he ought not to have left her living alone at Aikengill. "I did suggest she should have a relative to stay with her until I'd made up my mind what to do with the house," he told the two officers. "But she wouldn't hear of it. She laughed at the idea of being nervous at nights. There were neighbours near at hand, and she'd got the telephone—and what was there to be nervous about anyway? As for her having started a fire through carelessness, I just don't believe it," said Gilbert. "She was the most careful and conscientious of women, and as sensible a person as you could meet."

"About this cellar, sir," put in Macdonald. "We haven't been inside it yet—it isn't safe to do so—but am I right in assuming that it wasn't what you'd call a dry cellar, so far as the floor was concerned?"

"You're perfectly right, Chief Inspector. Dry? It was practically a watercourse in rainy weather. When my uncle came to live here five years ago, he had a small reservoir made in the hillside above the house and piped water brought to the house. The old well, which used to supply water, was sealed off—in theory. But you can't seal watercourses on land like this. Drain as you will, some of the small underground streams still evade you. You can see the water run across that cellar floor after heavy rain, and it's not surface drainage, it's a runnel following its own course."

"So the kindling wouldn't have been dry?"

"Very far from dry," rejoined Gilbert. "It was stacked in the cellar after it had been brought in as a matter of convenience, but every week a load was taken up to the old wash-house to dry off, and after that a day's supply was put in the kitchen oven. The idea of starting a blaze in the cellar by dropping a lighted match is absurd—unless petrol or paraffin had been spilt over the kindling."

"Very much what we argued, sir," said Bord, "but we've got to consider every possibility. Have you any idea if there was either petrol or paraffin on the premises?"

"Certainly no petrol. Mrs. Ramsden had a horror of it because she'd seen an accident caused by carelessness with petrol used to clean some clothes. There's a can of paraffin in the wash-house to fill the lamps in case of a failure or cut in the electricity supply, but the wash-house is locked at nights."

"It's still locked now," observed Bord. "The next thing we ought to consider is the possibility of theft. Chief Inspector Macdonald suggested the fire might have been started to conceal the fact that the house had been broken into by way of the study windows."

"Was there anything valuable in the house, sir?" inquired Macdonald; "I mean valuable in the sense of having a cash value for a thief?"

"No. Nothing," replied Gilbert. "My uncle left some Georgian silver, spoons and forks and so forth, and one or two goblets, but I sent the silver to the bank. My uncle was not a wealthy man, you know. He spent some hundreds of pounds on the house, repairing the fabric and putting in electricity and piped water, but his income was only about £500 a year after tax had been paid. The folks round here knew he wasn't wealthy. He had no car, he neither drank nor smoked, and he chose a housekeeper who was a thrifty soul. If you ask the neighbours round about, they'll tell you that Mrs. Ramsden *was* thrifty: there was no money wasted in this house. There was comfort, admittedly, but no show of wealth."

It was Macdonald who spoke next.

"You have told us that you don't believe the fire was caused by an accident, sir, in so far as Mrs. Ramsden was concerned: it doesn't seem likely that there was any report of valuables in the house to attract a thief from farther away. Since the electric wiring was new, I think it's very improbable that a fault in the wiring could have caused a fire—"

"I'm pretty certain of that," said Gilbert. "The work was well done and carefully tested. Responsible electricians see to it that wiring is properly insulated these days."

"Then have you any suggestion at all, sir, as to how the fire could have started?"

"Only deliberate malice," said Gilbert. "I don't see there's any likelihood of accident."

At that moment Bord's attendant constable knocked at the door (they were sitting in the dining-room of Aikengill) and said that Mr. Herdwick was asking for a word with Bord. "He doesn't want to come in, sir, he's been up on the fells and his boots are pretty mucky."

"All right. I'll come and see him," replied Bord.

Left alone with Gilbert Woolfall, Macdonald said: "As you know, sir, I have no official standing in this case. In other words, I'm not on a C.I.D. job."

"Of course not, but that's of no moment to me," said Gilbert. "I know you are a C.I.D. officer of distinction and repute, but if you'll be kind enough to give me the benefit of your experience I shall be exceedingly grateful. I feel there's something wrong here: something that shouldn't have happened in the normal course of life in Gimmerdale, and I shan't have a moment's peace of mind until I've found out what did happen. I'm profoundly shocked and grieved at Mrs. Ramsden's death. She was a good faithful soul and I feel that her death is my fault."

"You've no reason to feel that, sir," said Macdonald. "In as much as she had not intended to sleep in the house last night her death *was* accidental."

"The fact that she came back here was due to the impatience and self-importance of that despicable cleric," said Gilbert indignantly. "It was deliberate, of course. He disliked Mrs. Ramsden because she was a Nonconformist and because she was too forthright in her speech. She thought he was always out for what he could get, and I don't think she was far wrong."

"I'm prepared to admit that the reverend gentleman behaved with marked lack of consideration, to say nothing of the Christian charity which he professes," said Macdonald, "but to get back to a comment you made a moment ago, sir: you used the word 'malice.' Do you know of anybody who felt malicious about Mrs. Ramsden—who held a grudge against her?"

"She was liked and respected by all her neighbours—except that pernicious parson. And talking of grudges, Mr. Tupper had a grudge against me and against my late uncle, because no bequest was left to church or incumbent in my uncle's will."

"Let's get this straight, sir," said Macdonald. "Are you suggesting that the Rector may have gone off his head and committed arson to square his grudge?"

"No, of course I'm not," said Gilbert, "but I admit I'm so incensed against him that I could wish someone else might inspire a rumour to that effect."

"If they do anything of the kind they will certainly be proceeded against for slander," said Macdonald. "I think there's another aspect of the case we ought to consider. Mrs. Ramsden's death might have been accidental, in the sense that there was no intention of causing her any harm—in which case the malicious act was aimed at you, sir. But we can't afford to ignore the possibility that Mrs. Ramsden was deliberately murdered."

"But why on earth should anyone have murdered her?" protested Gilbert. "It seems crazy to me. She was a peaceful, sensible, middle-aged body, who had worked hard all her life: she was liked and respected by all her neighbours around here. She wasn't quarrelsome or interfering. The only person who ever spoke an unfriendly word about her was the Rector, and that was mainly because she was a Nonconformist. The arrogance of some of these C. of E. parsons is unbelievable."

"If you'll forgive what may seem an irrelevance, sir, was your uncle a member of the Church of England?"

"No—not a practising member, anyway. He was baptised in the Established Church, but the older he grew the less tolerant he became of organised religion. He disliked dogmas and deplored the dissensions of Christendom—but that doesn't mean he wasn't a better Christian than most churchgoers. He was not only fundamentally honest and truthful, he was also charitable and generous."

"Did his charity and generosity run to kindly tolerance so far as the Rector was concerned?"

"My uncle disliked the present incumbent intensely—but he held his tongue over it. I think he made a rule of never discussing the Rector with any of his neighbours." Gilbert turned to Macdonald with a half smile: "I don't know what you're getting at, but even such an anti-clerical as myself isn't prepared to believe that a parson would commit a crime. I may dislike the majority of them, but I think their errors are all committed within the law of the land."

"I quite agree," said Macdonald. "What I'm trying to get at, by a devious route, is whether anybody had a serious grudge against Mrs. Ramsden, or any cause to fear her."

"Why on earth should anybody have feared her?"

"Because she knew something to their discredit. I've asked about the Rector for this reason: if it were known that he disliked her he might have been confided in by others who had reason to dislike her. I shall be seeing the reverend gentleman, and I wanted to know his attitude to this household. I gather he was not any more amiably disposed to your uncle than your uncle was to him."

"True enough, but that didn't prevent Mr. Tupper from complaining all round the neighbourhood because my uncle didn't leave any money to the church."

"But he did leave some money to Mrs. Ramsden, I believe?"

"Yes, but she hasn't got it yet—his estate hasn't been wound up."

"Nevertheless, that five hundred pounds was due to her and will become part of her estate. We can't afford to overlook anything in a case like this, sir."

Gilbert Woolfall's face showed his distaste for this line

of thought. "Of course you've got to consider every contingency, I know that, but Mrs. Ramsden's folk are good country stock. You won't find anything shady there." He paused, and then added: "I'm asking for your advice, Chief Inspector, and I don't want to obtrude my own ideas, but isn't it more probable that Mrs. Ramsden's death was an unintentional consequence of the fire rather than murder? Nobody knew that she was in this house. Even Mr. Tupper wouldn't have assumed she would come back and stay the night here because he'd done her out of a lift."

"On the whole I agree with you," said Macdonald, "but long experience has made me rather wary of accepting easy assumptions in cases of unnatural death. You say 'Nobody knew that she was in this house.' That is an assumption, not a proven fact. We don't even know what it was caused her to stay the night here. It may have been some reason quite unconnected with the fact that the taxi didn't wait for her."

"But she was seen walking down to Hodges at half-past five."

"Wouldn't she have gone to tell Daleham she'd changed her mind—if she did change her mind? I'm not trying to obscure the issue, sir. I'm only saying that in detection you can't afford to accept anything as proven until you've got proof. It's worth remembering that anybody who saw a lighted window in this house would have known the house wasn't empty."

"Yes. I'd thought of that, but the house isn't overlooked by any of the neighbours. You could see the windows from across the valley, or from the bridge, if you happened to pass that way—" He broke off, his sensitive face puzzled and unhappy. "I just can't believe that anybody would have killed her deliberately," he said.

It was at that moment that Bord came back into the room.

I I

"Well, sir, Mr. Herdwick says there's a score or so of sheep missing from his flock on Ramshead Fell," said Bord. "I think there's more than a chance that the facts are connected. You see, it was the sight of the fire here that brought Mr. Herdwick and Tegg back when they'd meant to watch out on Ramshead."

"It's a dastardly business, but I'd rather believe that than think Mrs. Ramsden was murdered," said Gilbert. Bord went on:

"Now, sir, I want to know about this man you saw out on the fells last week—a stranger, you told Mr. Herdwick."

Gilbert nodded. "Yes. I was here for the week-end before last, and stayed over the Monday. In the afternoon I went up the fells towards the head of the valley. As you know, the road doesn't continue for more than half a mile beyond Lambsrigg, but there's a good track. It was a bridle path, I believe, and it's still plain enough to follow right up to Bowland Forest. If you don't mind a stiff climb you can get over Croasdale Fell and on to Slaidburn. It's only fair to remember that it is a track, marked on the Ordnance Survey, and anyone who likes walking has a right to use it. It's magnificent country, with the fells rising to thirteen hundred feet. I didn't get right up to the head of the valley. I stopped at the shepherd's shelter on Hawkshead Fell—I'd had about as much climbing as I'm good for, and I sat down in the lee of an outcrop to recover my wind. The chap I saw was coming down the fell, as though he'd come over from Slaidburn. He was quite young, not more than twenty I should think, and he looked a roughish customer at a first glance. He'd got a stubble of beard and his hair wanted cutting. He was wearing an old raincoat and clogs—the sort of rig the farmers wear. I don't think he saw me until I called to him, because I was well back from the track. I've never seen a lad look more startled. It was that which made me suspicious. He looked properly rattled." Gilbert Woolfall paused here, as though he were visualising the unkempt lad, startled at the presence of another human being in that immense solitude of wild hill country. "I asked him where he came from," he continued, "and he answered, 'What's that to do with you?' I knew from his speech he wasn't from these parts. I told him that it was still lambing time up in the hills, and the farmers weren't keen on strangers over their land. He replied, 'It's a footpath, isn't it? I came from Slaidburn, and I'm tramping to Ingleton.'"

"Ingleton?" put in Macdonald. "Isn't that a mining town?"

"They've given over mining, but there's some quarrying still," replied Bord, "and of course there's navvying work near Slaidburn with the pipe-line for the Manchester waterworks. Was this lad you saw a labourer of the navvy kind, sir?"

"I don't know. I shouldn't have thought he'd the physique for it," said Gilbert. "Seen at close quarters he was thin and weedy looking. I was puzzled about him because I couldn't place him. He wasn't a farm lad, and he didn't strike me as being a likely labourer. Neither was he the cadging type of industrial ne'er-do-well. He didn't ask for a cigarette, or try to cadge a couple of bob for a drink: he didn't ask how far he was from a village or a main road. I said, 'If you're going to Ingleton, you'd have done better to keep on a main road— why do a climb like this when you haven't got to?' and he answered, 'That's my business, not yours.' I replied, 'It is my business if people come over my land in lambing time. Get along with you, and be careful you don't go wandering off the track. The farmers will set their dogs on you if they see you on the fellside. They have trouble enough, without trespassers adding to it.' He didn't answer. He just walked on—and he walked quickly. He was out of sight in ten minutes, although I followed him." Gilbert broke off and then added: "I was puzzled. I couldn't place him at all. He spoke roughly, but his voice wasn't really an uneducated voice, and he wasn't north country bred."

"But presumably he didn't know who you were, sir?" asked Macdonald.

"Again, I don't know. But I do know that he didn't go down by the main track into Gimmerdale. He'd have been seen if he had, and nobody saw him, because I asked."

"Well, sir, for all you know he hid on the fellside until you passed," said Bord. "It'd be easy enough up there, in which case he may have watched you go down the valley and turn into Aikengill. Mr. Herdwick's got an idea that these sheep-stealing gangs have a look-out man, who passes the word which direction the farmers take when they go out of a night. If he's right, this lad you saw might be employed that way."

Macdonald had spread out his Ordnance Survey and found Hawkshead Fell, where Gilbert Woolfall had rested near the shepherd's shelter. "If he was walking from Slaidburn to Ingleton he went right out of his way. He'd have had a shorter tramp if he'd gone by Clapham. It seems to me that the only reason he could have taken this route is that it's so lonely and remote. There's very little chance of meeting anybody if you come over Croasdale and Hawkshead. So far as I can gather from the map there isn't a habitation for miles."

"Not for miles." Gilbert Woolfall spoke softly, as though the recollection of that upland solitude was dear to his heart. "It's five miles from Lambsrigg to Hawkshead at the top of the pass, and another five miles over Croasdale Fell down to the first houses in Slaidburn, and in all that ten miles you don't pass a single steading—you don't even see one. When people in the south say that the county of Lancaster is dense with industrialism and smoke-grimed cities, I should like to drop them on to Bowland Forest and let them sense those square miles of high moorland devoid of any habitation at all."

"True enough," said Bord, "but I'm interested in this chap who knew there is a track over Bowland. Most people don't know it—even the folks in Lunesdale."

"There's a reasonably good road—a motoring road—through Slaidburn," said Macdonald. "It connects up Long Preston in Ribblesdale with Clitheroe; that is, it connects the arterial roads A65 and A59. It also connects with the railway junction at Hellifield—that's the junction for your Kirkholm line."

"Aye, that's plain enough," said Bord, and Macdonald went on:

"If you think it out, there's a circular route, so to speak: Kirkholm to Upper Gimmerdale by road, Gimmerdale to Slaidburn over the fells by Hawkshead and Croasdale, and Slaidburn back to Kirkholm by rail. It seems to me there are possibilities in that route for your sheep-stealing gentry. Thieves always like a back-door get-away."

Gilbert sat up and joined in again. "I believe you're getting on to my idea: that the sheep-stealing is worked by driving the sheep up to the head of the valley and over by Croasdale to be picked up in a van on the Slaidburn side. I've never believed they'd risk taking them down into Lunesdale by the Kirkholm road. There's only the one road, and all wheeled traffic has got to go over the cattle grid. It's so easy to watch."

"What you're saying bears out what Mr. Herdwick believes, and what my chaps at the Kirkholm station believe," said Bord. "That road up from Kirkholm's been watched all right, and they've planted a booby trap or two, as well. If you think it out, that fire makes sense of a sort. It was visible from Ramshead: a fire'd bring any farmers down from the fell—they've got their beasts to think of."

"It sounds reasonable enough," said Gilbert, "but how much farther does it get us? We don't know who did it."

"That's our job, sir," said Bord. "This isn't only a sheep-stealing case. It's arson and manslaughter, if not murder. It's up to us to see this case through."

It was Macdonald who spoke next. "One's got to make a beginning, sir. This may be a long job, but Bord's right, we've got to see it through—and we shall have every police force and C.I.D. in the country working with us."

Gilbert Woolfall got up and went to the window, and looked out at the daffodils tossing on the grass outside.

"Yes," he said slowly. "But what a wretched business it is—and I loved the peace of this house."

"I sympathise with you there," said Macdonald. "I've never seen a house I liked better."

"It makes me so angry," said Gilbert Woolfall. "In a place like this, crime seems even uglier than it does in a town."

"It's ugly anywhere," said Macdonald, "but I admit I know what you mean."

CHAPTER VIII

I

It was after one o'clock when Macdonald and Bord left Aikengill: Bord drove back at once to Carnton, where routine duties demanded his attention, but Macdonald said he would stay in Gimmerdale and explore the nearby fells. The C.I.D. man was not at all surprised when he saw another car parked beside his own, and Giles Hoggett's long figure emerged from his battered and long-suffering Morris.

"Kate said she didn't see how you could get a meal up here," said Giles, "so she's sent you some ham sandwiches and apples, and there's some beer if you'd like it."

"God bless her!" said Macdonald. "I'd just decided not to feel hungry; now I haven't got to delude myself. Are you busy, Hoggett—have you got to get back to the farm immediately?"

"Not till milking time," said Giles. "The cows and stirks are all out at pasture and there's nothing pressing."

"I want to go up the fell yonder, as far as the road will take us," said Macdonald. "Shall I drive, or will you?"

"I will," said Giles. "My car's used to this sort of thing and yours isn't. It's a rough road, but we should be able to keep going for nearly a couple of miles: there used to be a cart track up to that tiny steading on Ramshead, and it's still negotiable if you don't mind bumps."

"Thanks very much. I'll eat when we come to a standstill," said Macdonald.

They got into the roomy old car and Hoggett set out up the steep road, above Aikengill, above Lambsrigg, above the gaunt little church. In bottom gear, rattling in all its loose bodywork, the fifteen-year-old car showed what sort of work had been put into its old engine: it plugged on without protest, without stalling, as the surface deteriorated from a metalled road to a rutted farm track with a gradient of one in six.

"That's about it," said Giles Hoggett at last. "I don't think we'd better go any farther. I'll just find some stones to put behind the wheels. The brakes are good, but it's rather an incline."

Macdonald helped man-handle some rocks behind the back wheels, and then the two men sat down on the fellside in the April sunshine. The mist had cleared away and the breeze blew softly through the lucid air: before them the ground dropped steeply to the river valley far below: behind them, and to the south, it rose in ridge after ridge of rock and heather and sedge. Far below them, Macdonald could just see the long grey roofs and stunted pines of High Gimmerdale, but to the south he knew the fell stretched for ten miles without a dwelling place.

"So much for industrial Lancashire," he observed, as he chewed some excellently solid ham sandwiches.

"There's the remains of a Roman road not far away," said Giles. "They must have been a persevering race. They were told to make a road due north, and they made one. No other people have ever made a road over Bowland Forest. To-day there are only roads round it."

"Long may it remain so," said Macdonald, and then went on: "How much have you heard about the fire in Aikengill, Hoggett?"

"More than you might believe," rejoined Giles. "It's wonderful how news travels in the country. I couldn't very well come to Aikengill myself, since you and Bord were in consultation there, but I wanted to know what had really happened. You've heard me mention my Uncle Henry, who used to fish from Wenningby Barns?"

"I certainly have: furthermore I've worn Uncle Henry's coat and heard about his spectacles and creel."

"Good," said Giles imperturbably. "When he was quite old, Uncle Henry lived in a cottage near Gressingham and had a housekeeper to look after him. After he died, this housekeeper—Mrs. Hornby—went to live with a married niece in a cottage near Ewedale, not far from Low Gimmerdale. Mrs. Hornby's an old lady now, and I sometimes go to see her and talk about old times: she's a great talker. I hadn't see her for some time, so I took the opportunity of driving over there to-day, and took her some apples. She's very fond of apple cake. I don't know whether the facts I've learned about the fire are the same as the facts you've observed at first hand, but I seem to have heard quite a lot, to say nothing of absorbing a lot of information about the inhabitants of Gimmerdale."

"You're one of the most co-operative men I've ever known, Hoggett," replied Macdonald. "First of all, the facts about the fire—as you heard them."

"Right," replied Hoggett. "I was told that the fire started in the cellar, the cellar being beneath old Mr. Woolfall's study, and the study being below the housekeeper's bed-room. The cellar, I was told, had been used to store logs and kindling, and the wood was stacked there by Jock Shearling. Jock was employed—in his own time, of course—by the late Mr. Woolfall to do wood-chopping, tree-felling, and hedging in the beech coppice which lies to the north of Aikengill."

"The facts seem substantially correct," said Macdonald. "Now who is Jock Shearling?"

"The Shearlings live at Eweshead, in Low Gimmerdale. The father—Edward Shearling—works for Mr. Lamb at Fullerby. Ted Shearling's been hired man at Fullerby for over twenty-five years; he's a first rate farm worker—a real all-rounder. Unfortunately he married an ill-tempered wife. She wasn't a local girl; she came from south Lancashire, and she's known as a quarrelsome mischief-making woman. Jock's the elder son: he works for Mr. Herdwick at Lambsrigg, and the younger one has his own tractor and gear and does contract jobs—ploughing, cutting, and all the rest." Giles Hoggett paused for a moment and then went on: "You've sometimes used the word 'contacts,' Macdonald, to describe those people who impinge on your cases. Well, Jock Shearling is a con-tact in this one, so to speak. I'm sorry to tell you that some ill-natured things are being said by some people, because I believe Jock's a good lad."

"In that case the best thing to do is to investigate the rumours and disprove them if they're wrong," said Macdonald. "Are people pointing out that Jock stacked the wood in the cellar?"

"It goes much farther than that," said Giles Hoggett. "Jock's been courting Betty Fell from Low Gimmerdale. They want to get married, but they don't want to start married life in the Shearlings' cottage. Mrs. Hornby says that Betty Fell went to Gilbert Woolfall and asked him if she and Jock could have two rooms in the old end of Aikengill—that's the kitchen and the room over it—after Mrs. Ramsden had left, of course. But Mrs. Ramsden didn't seem able to make up her mind about leaving Aikengill."

His slow deep voice broke off, and Macdonald said, "I see."

"I'm not sure that you do see—yet," said Giles Hoggett gravely, "but you will, in course of time. It's an abominable insinuation," he added, "and the only reason that's caused it to arise is that Mrs. Shearling, who is an ill-tempered nagger, is at loggerheads with another old dame who is a real termagant."

"What interests me is how the facts about the fire got round the valley so quickly," said Macdonald.

"It's simple enough," said Giles. "First, there was the milk lorry. It goes from farmstead to farmstead between 7.0 and 8.0 o'clock every morning, and every farmer is standing ready with his milk kits, to load the full ones and unload the empty ones. Every farmer will tell his wife and his hired man the news. Then there's the postman, who arrives in Gimmerdale about half-past eleven; he has a small-holding himself, near Kirkholm. Also, to-day is the day for the egg van: new-laid eggs are taken to the collecting station. You see, these days, no matter how remote the place, news is blazoned abroad with the velocity of the infernal combustion engine."

Macdonald laughed a little, but in his own mind he was appreciating afresh Giles Hoggett's ability to gather and to describe salient facts which were of value to a detective. Hoggett was now a farmer on a very modest scale, but his academic background still emerged in the simple clarity of his speech, and his ability to tell a story, while his countryman's sense made him aware of all the undercurrents of feeling among his friends and neighbours.

"What is the general reaction to the behaviour of the gentleman whom Woolfall describes as that pernicious parson?" asked Macdonald.

"The reverend gentleman has got an exceedingly bad press," said Hoggett. "At its simplest it is expressed in the words, 'He shouldn't ha' done that. 'Tis his fault Mrs. Ramsden died,' while the postman voices the majority verdict: 'You can't do nowt with a man like that: you can't do nowt with him.' The fact is, the Rector's generally disliked and he's also distrusted."

"Why?" demanded Macdonald.

Hoggett took his time over answering, and then said: "Folk around here have no enthusiasm for parsons in general: they are very conservative and when a new incumbent arrives in a living he's watched pretty shrewdly. The first thing that's expected of him is that he should take the trouble to get to know and to take a friendly interest in all his parishioners; next, that he should always abide by his word—say the same thing to everybody and not go back on a thing once he's said it. In both these matters, I've gathered, the Rector is found wanting, and because the country folk find that he doesn't satisfy their primary notions of parsonical behaviour, they tend to distrust him in all else. In actual fact I think he's said some very foolish things, uttering strictures which were based on his own opinion rather than on fact." Hoggett broke off, rubbed his grizzled head thoughtfully, and then added: "I think he's one of these chaps who doesn't know a fact from an opinion. It's a common failing, but a bad one in parsons who feel that their calling invests them with authority."

"Admittedly," said Macdonald, "but in most of my researches in country districts, I've found a certain measure of toleration for parsons. Even when they weren't popular, or regarded as friends, the attitude was, 'Well, he's parson. Doesn't do to expect too much.'"

"Yes. I know what you mean," replied Hoggett, "but in the case of High Gimmerdale I believe there's some story about 'having been done out of their rights.' Something about a transaction over stipends. I don't know the facts. Ask Kate. She's much more accurate over some things than I am. There's been some measure of hocus-pocus in the past, and it's left a distrust of parsons. But though the country folk are prepared to say that Mrs. Ramsden met her death because the Rector was high-handed and inconsiderate in refusing to wait for her, they're not suggesting that he set fire to Aikengill because he had a grudge against the Woolfalls: but I wouldn't say it's impossible that that suggestion hasn't entered anybody's mind." He broke off and turned to look at Macdonald, asking his first question since they had started talking. "Do you think that that fire could have started by accident, Macdonald?"

"No. I don't. But kindly observe that that is an opinion and not a fact. There's one thing I should like to know, if you can tell me. How did your Mrs. Hornby get to know that Betty Fell had asked Mr. Woolfall if Jock and she could come to live at Aikengill?"

"Oh, that's quite straightforward," replied Giles. "Mrs. Ramsden often came to see Mrs. Hornby, and Mrs. Ramsden told the latter that Betty Fell had asked Woolfall if there was any chance of herself and Jock living at Aikengill and house-keeping for Woolfall when he came to stay there. He's got very attached to the house, apparently."

"And what was Mrs. Ramsden's reaction to the request?"

"She couldn't make up her mind if she wanted to leave Aikengill, though she'd nothing against Betty. She talked it over with Mrs. Hornby and the latter tells me that their con-versation must have been overheard by Miss Wetherby—the thorn in the flesh of Ewedale. She's one of these eavesdropping rumour-mongers who do occur even in the most neighbourly of villages."

"And Miss Wetherby, being at daggers drawn with Mrs. Shearling, has weighed in with the suggestion that Jock Shearling started a fire in Aikengill in the hope of getting Mrs. Ramsden out of the way," said Macdonald. "It doesn't sound very convincing to me."

"No. It doesn't to me. But it's mischievous," said Giles Hoggett. "It'll start people talking." He paused, and rubbed his head as he often did when he was cogitating. "Gossiping in the country is quite different from gossiping in towns," he said. "Most of it's done indoors, safely away from other peo-ple—or perhaps unsafely is a better word. It's more tenacious that way. It's never forgotten. Folks may say in public that Miss Wetherby's nought but a sour old maid who makes trouble because she's got nothing better to do, but they'll remember what she said."

"Speaking as a detective, who can't afford to let simple faith in human nature bias his inquiry, I should like to add a rider to your comment," said Macdonald. "You're saying that mud sticks: it's an old adage, but in my experience mud is much more adhesive if it finds spots of itself to stick to." Hoggett stared at him.

"Is that your way of asking if Jock Shearling has incurred comment on a previous occasion?"

"That's about it," said Macdonald, "but it's a question which I must find the answer to on my own account. Let us do a bit of summing up. Mrs. Ramsden, as far as our information goes at present, was suffocated in her sleep by smoke. It was generally believed that she had gone back to Dent according to plan and that Aikengill was empty. Two people, at least, knew that her return journey had not gone according to plan, those people being Daleham the taxi-driver and the Rector, but there's no proof that other persons didn't have opportunity to observe that Mrs. Ramsden was in the house. It's only common-sense to assume that lights would have shown in the windows during the course of the evening."

"Yes, but Aikengill isn't overlooked by any other house in High Gimmerdale," said Hoggett, "so the lights wouldn't have been noticed by the neighbours unless they'd gone out of doors."

"Perfectly true," said Macdonald. "I see you've been making good use of your time. Now the most dramatic point which has emerged about the course of the night, apart from the fire, is that Mr. Herdwick has lost a score or so of sheep from his flock up on Ramshead."

Mr. Hoggett gave a prolonged whistle and his face lightened: he was very quick on this clue. "Herdwick and Tegg came pounding down from Ramshead when they saw the fire," he said, "leaving a clear field of action for the sheep thieves."

"That's it," said Macdonald. Hoggett hurried on:

"You've often said that if a crime is committed in any neighbourhood, you always try to find out if any other accident or unusual occurrence has happened there recently, because the odds are the two things may be connected. Well, here you have two crimes—arson and sheep-stealing. Wouldn't it be far more surprising if those two crimes weren't connected than if they were?"

"Yes," said Macdonald. "There I entirely agree with you."

"Good," said Mr. Hoggett. "You see I should be very sorry if Jock Shearling really came under suspicion. He's a good lad—hard-working and honest."

"How much do you really know about him?" asked Macdonald.

"Nothing," said Mr. Hoggett truthfully, "but I think Mrs. Hornby is a good judge of character and she speaks well of Jock. Country people have their own ways of assessing character. The fact that Jock is courting Betty Fell is a point in his favour. Betty Fell is a fine lass."

"But they can't get married until they get a house," said Macdonald. "What are the chances of their getting a house in High Gimmerdale?"

"None—until some of the old folks die off," said Giles, "unless Mr. Woolfall could get a licence to restore that old cottage by the barn. It must have been a good cottage once."

"The tense, like the cottage, being past historic," said Macdonald. "Thanks very much for all the news items, Hoggett, and please thank your wife for the best sandwiches I've had for years. When I get my farm I must certainly keep a pig and have my own ham and bacon. Now I think I'll walk up towards Ramshead and survey Gimmerdale from above. Perhaps to-morrow I might drive to Slaidburn and walk back here by Hawkshead."

"It's a fine walk," said Hoggett. "Well, I'll be getting back. Kate wants a hand in the garden."

I I

Having succeeded in reversing his car on a gradient which would have made most motorists feel sick, Giles Hoggett bumped back slowly and cautiously to High Gimmerdale. He pulled up before reaching the foldyard gate at Lambsrigg, because Mr. Herdwick and old Tegg were inducing a ewe, the mother of triplets, to go through the gate. One of the newborn lambs could walk and it tottered along beside its parent, lively for all its unsteadiness: the other two lambs were being carried by their forelegs, one each by Herdwick and Tegg. They seemed hardly alive until they were set down on the ground, just within the gate, and then they found their feet and cried in thin but surprisingly loud voices, and the ewe dashed up to them, followed by the third lamb. Herdwick shut the gate and raised his hand in salute to Giles Hoggett.

The latter let his car slip forward as far as the gate and spoke to the sheep farmer.

"Good day, Mr. Herdwick. I'm very sorry to learn of all the trouble here."

"Aye, Mr. Hoggett, 'tis a sorry business." He came forward and stood with one foot on the running-board of the car. "I hear that C.I.D. chap's a friend of yours."

"Aye. I've known him for some years, ever since that trouble we had at Wenningby Barns. He's on holiday here, but he'll be only too glad to lend a hand, as it were, in this case. He's a very able man at his job."

"I'm glad to hear it." Herdwick suddenly clenched his fist and shook it towards the fells. "By gum, I'm that mad!" he burst out. "The dirty rogues! It's all of a piece, this is. They were out after my sheep and they've done murder with it this time. Reckoned they was being smart, getting me and Tegg down here with that fire, leaving the coast clear for them to drive my ewes down Slaidburn way."

"You think that's the explanation?" asked Giles.

"That's it, Mr. Hoggett. That fire wasn't an accident, by gum, it wasn't."

CHAPTER IX

I

MACDONALD WALKED STEADILY UP THE TRACK WHICH led to the head of the valley and thence towards Hawkshead and Croasdale Fell. The rutted farm track had given place to a path which followed a twisted and erratic course dictated by the rocky contours of the ground: it went up and down, always steep, sometimes tricky, and with every bend and gradient it led into a wilder and more rugged solitude. After the first mile or so, Macdonald lost sight of High Gimmerdale altogether: the green of meadows and pastures and budding trees which marked the course of the beck disappeared first then the pine trees were lost, and last the steep gable of the gaunt little church. He knew he would see the steadings again as he got towards Ramshead Pike, because he had seen its rocky profile from Aikengill, but for some time he climbed in a world which showed no sign of human kind. Even the track he followed was now not much more than a clearly defined sheep track.

Turning an abrupt corner by a rocky outcrop, he was the more surprised when a sheep dog rushed at him with one short sharp bark. The dog did not spring at him, but crouched ready to spring, its lithe black body quivering, its eyes watching him with an expression which made Macdonald stop dead. He had every respect for sheep dogs, and if this one had been set to guard some of the fell sheep, it would be a poor look-out for any man who tried to pass it. As he stood there, watching the dog as intently as it watched him, he heard a clear short whistle: instantly the dog turned, raced a few yards back and then crouched again. Beyond, some twenty yards along the path, Macdonald saw the dog's owner: it was a woman, and she was sitting on the rocks beside the path. She whistled again and the dog raced back to her and dropped down beside her, its sharp collie nose on its black paws, its eyes still on Macdonald.

"It's all right. He won't touch you," called the girl.

Macdonald saw that she was quite young, a sturdy young woman in a belted raincoat, with a bright knitted scarf over her dark hair. He walked up to her and said:

"Good day. I ought to have expected that. He's a fine dog."

"He's a good dog all right. I shouldn't have brought him up here if he wasn't," she replied. "We can't do with untrained dogs lambing time." Her face was flushed with wind and sun, but her eyes were heavy and Macdonald realised she had been crying. She went on abruptly: "You're the London detective who came with Mr. Bord this morning. I saw you outside Aikengill."

"Yes. I'm a detective and I'm from London, but I'm not really here on duty," he replied. "My name's Macdonald and

I'm staying with Mr. Hoggett in Lunesdale. I was walking up to Ramshead so that I could see the view of Gimmerdale. Can I go on, or are the sheep dogs keeping strangers off?"

"There's no dogs up here save with their owners," she replied. "I came up here to find Mr. Herdwick's shepherd, and Laddy would find him before I could." She patted the dog's slender black head and its wavy tail thumped cheerfully, so that it looked a different creature from the fierce beast who had crouched so menacingly a few moments before.

"I'm so sorry about all the trouble down yonder," said Macdonald. "It's an upset for all of you."

"It is that." Tears welled up in her eyes again, but she went on resolutely: "You say you're not on duty—but you were there, with our police, at Aikengill."

"Yes. I was. Mr. Bord asked me to come and give an opinion about the fire because I've had quite a lot of experience of fires. When I said I wasn't on duty, I meant I hadn't been sent here by Scotland Yard." He spoke so easily and naturally that the girl took confidence.

"My name's Fell," she said. "Betty Fell. Maybe you're hearing about all of us."

"I've been learning people's names," he agreed. "In any police job witnesses play a very important part." He stood beside her, looking across the valley to the steeply tilted fells on the far side. Long experience of witnesses of all types had made Macdonald adept in recognising certain reactions. He could nearly always sense fear: he knew at once when a man or woman would take refuge in obstinate silence or simulated ignorance, and he could also sense the opposite reaction—a desire to talk. He knew that Betty Fell wanted to talk to him, and it seemed to him that he could never have a better opportunity of hearing her talk than on this far away fellside. It was her own ground: she had her dog with her; she wasn't afraid of him. He turned and looked down at her.

"You're worried, aren't you?" he said. "I don't know if you'd like to tell me what's worrying you. I might be able to help, though of course I can't be sure. But I can tell you this, from a lifetime's experience of police work, no innocent person need ever be afraid of telling the truth. More trouble and confusion is caused by innocent people concealing the truth than you can imagine."

"I'm glad you said that," she replied. "It's true I wanted to talk to you. I don't know why, but it's easier to talk to you who're a stranger than to someone who half knows us, or thinks they know us."

Macdonald sat down on the ground not far away from her; the dog was between them and he raised his head suspiciously, but the girl patted him reassuringly.

"There's something in that," agreed Macdonald. "A stranger can start at the beginning, without any background of what so-and-so once said. I think I'd like to tell you that my own folk—my grandparents—started as sheep farmers in country not unlike this. It was near Inverness. My father went to live in London, but I've an uncle still farming up there, and a niece who's very like you—just about your age and colouring."

She laughed a little. "That explains it then—why you look as though you belong here. I noticed it at once. You're more like us than Mr. Bord is." She took a deep breath, and then plunged on: "Maybe I'm wrong to talk about things.

I'm always dashing into this and that like a daft stirk, but I've got to do something. It's about Jock Shearling. You know about Jock?"

"I know he works for Mr. Herdwick and that maybe Mr. Woolfall was going to let the two of you live at Aikengill when you're married."

Betty Fell drew a breath of relief: the homely form of words gave her confidence and it seemed easier to talk now that there was no need for explanations about herself and Jock.

"That's right," she said eagerly. "When Mrs. Ramsden went to live with her own folk, Jock and I were to have the kitchen-end and look after the house for Mr. Woolfall. 'Twas me asked Mr. Woolfall if we could live there: Jock said I ought never t've asked, but we'd never've got a house just by wishing, and Jock's slow to ask anybody for anything. Folks got to know we were going to live in Aikengill and some weren't that pleased about it." She broke off, and then dashed straight at her point in a rush of words: "Now they're saying 'twas Jock set fire to the house, lit the kindling he'd stacked in the cellar and came away to let the house burn."

"Why do they say he did it?" asked Macdonald.

"'Tis all along of Mr. Herdwick's sheep being stolen," she replied. "He says the fire was lighted to bring him and Tegg down from Ramshead and that someone did it who knew they were going up there. It's not Mr. Herdwick named Jock— he'd never say ought like that—it's that Miss Wetherby who's always quarrelling with everybody. She doesn't care what she says just for spite, and she's got a down on Jock."

"It doesn't matter what Miss Wetherby says if she's only talking from spite," said Macdonald. "The only person she will get into trouble is herself. It's evidence that matters, not malicious opinions."

Colour came up hotly into the girl's cheeks, but she faced Macdonald steadily.

"She says she's got evidence. Jock was out yesterday evening: he was with me. You see, we never get a chance to talk when I'm at home: I've got two sisters and a young brother, and we only have the one fire to sit by. It's the same at the Shearlings. So sometimes we go for a walk in the evenings, so we can have a bit of time to ourselves like."

Macdonald watched the girl's flushed unhappy face, and when she stopped speaking he helped her out: he was quite sure where the young couple would have walked together.

"And you walked up to Aikengill and had a look at the house and thought how grand it would be when you lived there?"

She nodded, eagerly, and Macdonald went on: "Maybe you said perhaps Mr. Woolfall would let you have a bit of land later on, enough to graze a couple of milking cows and some stirks, so you could begin to get your own stock."

"How did you know that?" she cried, and Macdonald replied:

"Well, that's what I'd have thought myself if I were in Jock's shoes. It's making a start that's so hard, isn't it, with land the price it is?"

"Yes, that's it," she cried. "Wanting's one thing and getting what you want's so different. We haven't but a little money— what Jock's saved and I've saved."

"I know," replied Macdonald, but he went on: "Now you've started you've got to go on, haven't you? Tell me what time you set out, and exactly where you went."

"I'll tell you and thankful," she cried. "I'll be glad to tell you, because I feel somehow you'll believe me. I went out at half-past seven. Do you know where I live? 'Tis at Low Gimmerdale, that's three miles from High Gimmerdale. I said I was going to see Peggy Bentham to ask her about getting some day-olds—I keep some of my own hens. Peggy lives nearer Kirkholm and I did go there, but she was out. I knew she'd be out, 'tis W.I. on Wednesday evenings. I'd got my bike and when I left the Benthams I rode back to Low Gimmerdale and met Jock. About eight o'clock it was then, and I left my bike in the little foldyard just beyond Miss Wetherby's, and Jock and I walked up to Aikengill. It must have been nearly nine we got there, it's quite a step and it's hilly."

Macdonald interrupted here: "Was there a light in the house, in any of the windows?"

"We didn't see one, but Mrs. Ramsden would have been sitting in the kitchen, and you can't see the kitchen window from the road because of the beech hedge. It's thick, that is. We didn't go in the garden. We had a look at that ruined cottage across the road, because Jock thinks he might get the roof built up if he could only get the beams. Timber's hard to come by."

"Was it misty?" asked Macdonald, sticking to the matter in hand, for all his interest in the aspirations of the practical young couple who had debated ways and means on a cold spring evening.

"It was thick down by the beck," she said. "The mist always lies there, but the sky was clear, and I could see the gable ends of the church—it was above the mist. It was all quiet, never a soul stirring, but it was cold, so we went and sat in the porch of the church and talked for a bit and then walked home. I picked up my bike, and maybe 'twas then Miss Wetherby saw Jock. She often comes out of an evening with that blind old dog of hers."

"What did you do then? Did Jock walk home with you?"

She hesitated, and then said: "No. He didn't. I got on my bike and rode home fast because it was getting late, but Jock went straight home. I know he did."

Macdonald paused before he answered, and then he changed the angle of the conversation a little:

"About this sheep-stealing. Did Jock tell you that Mr. Herdwick had lost some sheep before all this happened?"

"Yes. He told me. He was a bit bothered like, wondering if he'd be blamed for not noticing enough. You see, he's not been at Lambsrigg that long—Michaelmas 'twas he came—and he doesn't know the sheep like you do if you've been through lambing with them. Once you get to know them it's like knowing people—they're all different and their faces are different, but it's at lambing you get to know them, when you handle them. There's lambing and clipping and dipping—when you've handled the sheep right through the year you know them all, but it's not so easy at first when there's hundreds of them."

"I'm sure it isn't," said Macdonald. "You can tell me a lot that will help over this job," he went on. "For instance, how often are the sheep rounded up, so they're reckoned as it were?"

"They round the ewes up in November, service time that is," she said, "but after that they're left on the fell till spring. If there's heavy snow the men go out and see they're not caught in drifts, but there's not much else they can do. At lambing time they bring them down from the high fells, and through the summer they're looked to, for maggot and foot rot and that, and the gimmers and wether lambs sorted out, and they mark and ear-clip them. Then there's shearing, June or July that is, and dipping in August. But the shepherds go around quite often and bring in any that's in trouble. They walk miles on these fells—it's a good life if you take to it."

"I'm sure it is," said Macdonald, "but you'd need to take to it young. Where was Jock Shearling working before he came to Lambsrigg?"

"At Stapleby: that's Whernside way, right up in the hills. He was hired man at Moorcock Hall, but he had to live in, with the family, and he didn't like it so well—always with other folks. So after he'd been there a couple of years he came back home, and Tegg was getting too old to do the job by himself and Mr. Herdwick took Jock on." She paused a moment or so and then hurried on: "You'll have heard about the trouble some of the farmers had on Whernside, with the sheep being stolen? That wasn't where Jock was—they didn't lose any at Moorcock." Then suddenly she cried out at him: "I've told you. Can't you see? Miss Wetherby's started reckoning it all up and soon everybody'll be talking. I know just how it'll be. Talk like that gets round."

The tears were running down her face now; the sheep dog, startled by the pitch of her voice, raised his long nose to her face and whimpered.

"Yes, I see," said Macdonald quietly. "Now look here, Betty: don't be sorry you've told me all this. I should have heard it all sometime, sooner or later, and I think you've shown a lot of pluck to tell me everything quite plainly. Now I'll tell you something. I don't think you need feel so bothered about what people say: I'm told that Jock's well thought of hereabouts, and so are you, so you needn't be afraid your friends will go back on you."

"I shouldn't, not for most things, but it's this sheep-stealing. It makes the farmers that mad they're ready to believe anything. And, you see, it all fits—I'm not such a fool I can't see it. They'll be saying Jock wanted money to buy a place for himself, so's we could get married: they'll think it all out—folks do when they're right mad."

"Now, look here," said Macdonald, "you wouldn't have told me all this if you hadn't been quite certain that Jock wasn't mixed up in any of it. If you'd been afraid he'd had anything to do with it you'd have said that the two of you walked down to Lunesdale instead of up to Aikengill. You say you're not a fool, and I quite agree with you. You'd the sense to tell the truth, and it does take some sense."

"It wasn't only that," she put in. "You said no innocent person need ever be afraid of telling the truth. Well, I believed you, and I've told you the truth."

"You're quoting me so I'll quote you," said Macdonald. "You said just now, 'they'll think it all out, folks do when they're right mad.' You're right mad now, aren't you?—so you use your wits and try to think it out. You know this place, you know the people here. You may think of something, no matter how small, that may give us a lead."

"I'll try—but I can't think who'd have been wicked enough to do it."

"It's a good thing you realise it was wicked," said Macdonald. "I'm not trying to frighten you, but remember that somebody has committed a serious crime. If you do think of anything that throws any light on it, don't tell anybody but the police: tell Mr. Bord or me—you'll see me about. But don't tell anybody else—not Jock or your own folks or anybody. Do you understand?"

She nodded. "Yes. I understand. I've had a sheep turn on me when it's frightened enough—and I reckon whoever did that is frightened by now."

I I

After he said good-bye to Betty Fell, Macdonald continued his walk. He left the track and went up through the dry heather towards Ramshead, wondering how the sheep could pick up a living at all on this bleak fellside. It was a stiff climb, but he did not pause for a breather until he caught sight of the steadings of High Gimmerdale again, far below him. The flagged roofs and the lighter stone of the barn walls caught the sunshine, so that Macdonald, who was long-sighted, could pick out the different buildings. On a cloudy day, he meditated, you would hardly be able to see the grey buildings against the grey hillside behind them. Aikengill was the long house, Lambsrigg the tall stark one, and above Lambsrigg was the little church. There was another stone building behind the church which Macdonald had not noticed from the road: that must have been the school building, he decided, small and squat and grey. He knew it was not used now, and made a note in his mind to go and have a look at it: a disused building is always of interest to detectives. Then he remembered having heard Giles Hoggett say that there was an abandoned steading somewhere up on Ramshead itself—a tiny ancient sheep farm where a family had once contrived to make a hard and comfortless living from their small flock.

It was some time before Macdonald spotted the place: the sun did not catch its lichened walls, and the stone of the little barn-like structure identified itself with its background. He walked up to the small piece of level ground on which it was built and marvelled afresh that men had had the courage and tenacity to build a home in such a spot. The flagstones had gone from most of the roof and lay broken on the ground: the building had two rooms, one up and one down, and a little lean-to shippon, which was in better condition than the dwelling-house. The front door was still there, surprisingly enough, though it was off its hinges and held in place by a piece of fallen masonry. Macdonald bent to move the stone and found it heavy: he rolled it away and the door promptly fell down on him. When he felt the door's weight he wasn't surprised that no one had taken it away: the thought of carrying it down the steep rough ground was enough to discourage any thrifty salvager. Getting himself clear of the door, Macdonald went inside into what had once been a farmhouse kitchen. He looked up cautiously at the rotting rafters and the sagging roof-tree above, where spaces of pale blue sky shone where the flagstones had slipped. The chimney was still intact, the chimney breast supported by a wide flat arch, curiously reminiscent of late Perpendicular architecture. It was a true arch, he noted, its keystone still in place, but even as his eye was taken by this evidence of the skill of the original builders, another sense overcame the visual one. As he had done in so many different places, Macdonald stood and sniffed, as a dog might sniff. The first thing his nose told him was that at no very distant time wood smoke had gone up that chimney and billowed out into the ruined kitchen: something of its resinous pungent quality still hung about the open chimney, though no ashes lay on the debris of mortar and fallen stones which cluttered up the huge hearth stone. It wasn't only wood smoke: somehow in the enclosed space where he stood there was the smell of human kind, something quite unlike the smell of rotting mortar and lichened stone, decaying timber and pungency of dry heather.

Standing quite still, Macdonald stared about him, seeking other evidence of occupation. The window spaces were mere slits, bunged up with dried grass and sedge: the floor was cluttered with broken masonry, mortar and remains of the wattle and daub which had once lined the walls, but there was nothing else: no bedding, no pots or cans, no litter of a later date. He stood still for some time, thinking hard. Then he went outside again and propped the door back in its place and wedged it with the stone block. Having done this, he walked back by the way he had come.

I I I

On his way back to High Gimmerdale Macdonald met nobody. If Jock Shearling or Mr. Herdwick were on the fell-side Macdonald did not catch sight of them, but he knew it was quite possible to pass within a few hundred yards of the farming folk and not see them, for their drab working clothes toned in with the drab fellside. Turning off the road by the church, Macdonald went through the churchyard to look at the disused school. It was built in stone and consisted of but one room and a solid porch. Over the door were the initials M.W. and the date—1845. It was easy to see in through the windows to the school room: the children's benches were still there, and the teacher's table and big Windsor chair. On the walls there hung a few faded posters: "Anti-gas...decontaminating measures," read Macdonald. He turned away with a sense of the futility of mankind in general: anti-gas activities in Gimmerdale struck him as at once ludicrous and pathetic. On impulse he went into the church porch and rummaged until he found the key, tucked away on a ledge. He opened the heavy door, which swung slowly and stiffly to his hand, and went and stood in the dimness at the west end of the tiny building. It had the same dignity and sombreness as the stone barns near at hand: the rough-hewn timbers of the roof were the same simple pattern as the barn roofs, but here was no fragrance of hay or living breath of kine. It was cold and still and silent: there was no decoration: a few wooden pews, a dark oak table at the east end, a dark wooden cross below the clear lancet windows above the table. And in its stark plainness the little church had a quality all its own, akin to the stark fellside around it, silencing criticism, compelling respect.

"It's Little Gidding," flashed through Macdonald's mind, and T. S. Eliot's words came back, inevitably:

> "...You are not here to verify,
>   Instruct yourself, or inform curiosity..."

He stood there for a few moments and then went outside, locked the door, replaced the key, and stepped into the pale spring sunlight again. In some obscure way he felt that he had learnt something more about Gimmerdale through going into its church. It was cold, undecorated, silent—but it was there, as it had been throughout the centuries: in a sense neglected, in a sense forbidding, it had the reticence and endurance of the folk who had built it. And to ignore it was to ignore something intrinsic to the people whose church it was.

CHAPTER X

MACDONALD GOT BACK TO WENNINGBY FARM JUST IN time for a large tea. Kate Hoggett made the tea as he came in, and said:

"Giles is talking to a young farmer who wants to buy two of his heifers: they'll probably go on talking for hours, so we might as well have our tea. You must be hungry. What did you think of Gimmerdale?"

"It's very beautiful and very impressive," said Macdonald, "but I think you'd need to be brought up there to get on to what I call 'farming terms' with it. When I came back to Lunesdale proper it looked so lush and green and rich after those stark fellsides. I can imagine the hill dwellers of old looking down on the wealth of your dales with bitter envy."

Kate laughed: "I've always imagined the Norsemen must have felt like that when they first penetrated into Lunesdale: after the poverty of their hill farms the herbage here must have promised wealth untold in terms of cattle. Did you meet some of the Gimmerdale farmers?"

"I had a word with Mr. Daniel Herdwick, and I met Betty Fell while I was climbing up towards Ramshead. She's a fine looking lass."

"Giles is longing to know if you went and interrogated the Rector," said Kate.

"No, of course I didn't. It's not my business to go and interrogate anybody," said Macdonald. "Bord asked me to go with him to Aikengill to give an opinion about the fire, but that was only consultative. It's true I stayed and talked to Mr. Woolfall, or rather he talked to me, but it's not my case, it's Bord's. I can walk around, as anybody else can, and make such observations as I like, but I've no status for domiciliary visits. Betty Fell talked to me, because she was so bothered she felt she must talk to somebody, but it was not on an official level. We got cracking in the first place because her dog nearly flew at me. If she hadn't called it off it would have been at my throat."

"A sheep dog?" inquired Kate.

"Very much a sheep dog. I'll have one of my own one day." Kate paused, filled Macdonald's cup and passed him the scones before she said: "But you're interested in what happened, aren't you?"

"I'm very much interested," replied Macdonald, "in the place, in the people, in Aikengill and the reasons for the fire. If Bord gets his chief constable to apply to C.O. for help, I shall be at the case with as much determination as Betty Fell's dog came at me, but for the moment it's not my job."

Then he suddenly grinned at her and the lightening of his eyes and the mobility of his lean dark face made him look suddenly young again. "I've got to say all that, to you and everybody else, because we do have rules about poaching and my own boss would be livid if I didn't live up to his ideas of decorum, but having said it—well, I'd trust you and Giles just as far as I'd trust myself. This, lady, is a prelude to a request for co-operation."

"Good," said Kate. "If you didn't want to talk about it, I'm as capable of holding my tongue as most people, but it'd be a bit hard, because Giles and I are bound to discuss it together. Anyway, I'll go and call him in, and then you can tell him what you want."

"Don't do that. He's referred me to you: he says you're much more accurate than he is—which is true, inasmuch as you don't go hurdling over facts. I want to know exactly what Giles means when he said there was some hocus-pocus over the Gimmerdale stipend."

"It wasn't hocus-pocus. It was a perfectly legal transaction, though we don't think it ought ever to have been done," said Kate. Very briefly and lucidly she told him the facts about the old Woolfall benefaction of 1690, and the transference of the stipend some fifty years ago. While she was still talking, Giles came in and listened until she had finished. Then Giles said:

"Very clearly explained, Kate. I'm interested to know that Macdonald is considering the reverend gentleman and his predecessors. I've an idea that the reverend isn't entirely unconnected with what's been going on."

"That's very moderately put, Hoggett: 'not entirely uncon-nected with'—a form of speech known as 'Litotes,' if my memory of Matriculation English is not at fault. So for once I'll agree with you," said Macdonald.

Turning back to Kate and ignoring Giles's portentous

whistle, Macdonald said to her: "Have your researches into local history led you to discover the local usages to obtain Probate of Wills—say in the late sixteen hundreds—in these parts?"

"I think so," said Kate, "because I got permission to examine some of the old Deeds relating to the inheritance and purchase of the Hoggett's land. I applied to the last Lord of the Manor in these parts—but do you want to know about wills in High Gimmerdale in the seventeenth century?"

"Of course he does," said Giles. "He's on the track of the hocus-pocus."

"There wasn't any, so don't be so foolish," said Kate. "The Diocesan authorities will proceed against you for slander if you're not more careful." She turned back to Macdonald. "High Gimmerdale is interesting in this respect: it was in the Manor of Kirkholm, until the Manor rights were dissolved early in this century. Kirkholm was a very important and powerful Manor in medieval times, and it had a Manorial Court, or Court Baron, for transacting business. This Court had considerable powers, because for centuries all those who held land in the Manor were Customary Tenants and had to pay Manorial dues and fines when land was 'alienated' as they called it—sold or willed away. The Court consisted of the Lord of the Manor, his heir, his steward, and his clerk, and they administered Probate, dealt with Intestacy, and the supervision and estates of Minors."

"So the original Wills would be held in the Manorial archives, or Muniment Rooms?" asked Macdonald.

"We just don't know," said Kate. "You see, Giles has got several ancient documents which appear to us to be the original

Wills of his forbears: the signatures of the witnesses are on them, and the seals. Of course it's possible there were two copies made, of which the Manor held one. But before Somerset House came into being, I imagine local usages held good, and you know how casual people were over ancient documents before local historians began to collect and publish records. So far as the Court Baron of Kirkholm was concerned, the safe keeping of bygone documents would have been in the hands of the Stewards, who might have been careful—or not."

"When were these Manorial Courts finally superseded?" asked Macdonald.

"Kirkholm Court Baron went on, though with diminishing powers, until about 1840, I think," replied Kate. "But if it's the Woolfall Will of 1690 you're considering—well, two hundred and sixty years is rather a long time, isn't it?"

"It certainly is," replied Macdonald. "Now I gather from what you have told me that Customary Tenants were equivalent to Freeholders, inasmuch as they could leave land to their heirs, or sell it, after paying Manor dues or fines, but in both cases the new Customary Tenant had to appear before the Manorial Court and pay his suit and acknowledge that he only held the land in accordance with the Customs of the Manor?"

"That's right," said Kate, and Macdonald went on:

"So when land was left by the Woolfall of 1690 to provide a stipend, the trustees of that benefaction would have had to appear at the Manorial Court?"

"Yes, they would," said Giles, interrupting with determination after several minutes of restlessness, "but for goodness' sake let's tell Macdonald the one thing he ought to know. In

1880, Kirkholm Manor was burnt to the ground. The present Manor House was built in 1885. So if it's ancient documents that Macdonald wants to get hold of—well, they were all burnt in 1880."

"That certainly cramps my style a bit so far as said documents are concerned," said Macdonald, "so let us consider another angle of the case altogether. Hoggett, you remember that there's an ancient steading up on Ramshead Fell?"

"Yes. But it hasn't been inhabited for years."

"It certainly hasn't. I went into it, and it's virtually a ruin, so far as the roof's concerned, though the walls and chimney are still sound. Now this is for your private information, but it's my own belief that someone has been using the place. I've no evidence but my own nose, but I could smell recent wood smoke and turf smoke in the chimney, and there was a fugitive smell of human kind. I can't describe it as anything except 'fugitive'—it was there when I went in, after having tumbled the door down. I knew someone had been in there, not long since, though there were no tangible signs of his occupation."

"Isn't it possible that some of the men from Lambsrigg might have sheltered there when they were out with the lambing ewes in bad weather?" suggested Kate.

"I thought of that, but dismissed it because such care had been taken to conceal the fact that it had been used," said Macdonald. "The ashes had been cleared away and the hearth stone littered over with mortar and fallen stones. No shepherd or farm worker would have bothered to do that."

"Quite true," said Giles. "It looks to me as though the place had been used as a meeting place by the sheep thieves. If they had to hang about on the fellside at night they'd have been glad of any shelter, and dry heather and turves make a good fire."

"But wouldn't there have been a risk of the firelight being seen?" objected Kate.

"No. I don't think there would if care was taken," said Macdonald. "The door is still intact and could be wedged tight. The window spaces are only slits and they are stopped up with sacking and dry grass. It's a big chimney, and a turf fire well at the back of it wouldn't give much light. The only place anybody would be likely to spot it from would be on the very ridge of the fell, above the roof of the cottage, that is, and even so there's enough of the roof and flooring left to screen firelight, unless it were a big fire."

"Did you search the place?" asked Giles.

"No. I didn't. I had a hunch that someone might be watching me," said Macdonald. "That's not so nebulous as it sounds: I believe Jock Shearling, or another of Herdwick's men, was out there on Ramshead, because Betty Fell had gone up there with her dog to find them. I don't want a story to get around that the place has been carefully searched."

"Then you are thinking that it may be used again?" queried Kate. "Isn't that very improbable after what's happened?"

"It depends who used it," said Macdonald. "Woolfall spoke of a lad he saw up there on Hawkshead. It's easy enough to assume that this lad was connected with the sheep-stealing, but we've no proof that such was the case."

"But if you think it's possible that this lad took shelter in Ramshead Cottage, what earthly reason could there be for his presence there except in connection with the sheep-stealing?" asked Giles.

"The only answer I can give you is guesswork," replied Macdonald. "I, in common with C.I.D. men throughout the country, know that there are plenty of fugitives from the law: not only men who are 'wanted,' as we say in our own jargon, but men of whose existence we are not even aware. There are still deserters from the army, and in addition to them are the young men who have evaded national service. Through fear, or laziness, or because discipline is intolerable to them, they leave their homes and live a fugitive existence. When Mr. Woolfall described this lad, quite young, unkempt, speaking roughly yet with something in his speech that suggested he'd been educated, I was reminded of one or two silly young fools I've happened across who were 'on the run,' as they call it."

"But can you imagine any lad living up there on Ramshead?" protested Kate. "How could he get food?"

"I didn't suggest he was living there, but it's possible he could have been using the cottage as an occasional shelter," said Macdonald. "Some of them are like tramps, they do a round from doss house to doss house. An unsuspected shelter is very valuable to them: somewhere where they can lie-up when they want to avoid notice. As for food, it's possible to buy enough unrationed food to live on—bread and meat-pies and tinned stuff, potatoes and rabbits to make a stew." He turned to Giles. "Woolfall said he saw this chap coming over Hawkshead presumably from Slaidburn. I've never been right into Slaidburn. What sized place is it?"

"It's what we should call a small township—bigger than our villages hereabouts, but smaller than a market town," said Giles. "Slaidburn's a prosperous looking little place, stone-built, ancient: a bit like Dent—you've seen Dent. There are one or two shops, including a Co-op. Slaidburn serves a very large area of fell farms in addition to the valley farms nearer at hand, and there's a certain amount of lorry traffic through it. I should think it'd be possible for a fellow to buy food without making himself too noticeable, because there may be some coming and going of labourers from the waterworks tunnelling scheme out on Bowland."

"Well, my idea is an idea and nothing more," said Macdonald. "I shall report what I noticed to Bord, of course. If he'd like me to look into it—well, I don't mind if I do, as you say hereabouts."

"What tactics would you employ?" asked Giles, who was beginning to get deeply interested.

"I'd like to come up from Slaidburn, at night. I've a feeling that if that cottage is still being used as a shelter, the inhabitant wouldn't expect anybody to come from that direction at night. Of course, if a good fellsman undertook to do a reconnaissance from the Gimmerdale direction and synchronise with me in a pincer movement, it might be very helpful."

"Look here," said Kate, before Giles had time to reply. "I know Macdonald too well to insult him by suggesting that the fells have gone to his head. I know he's always got his feet on the ground, but I think he might tell us a bit more what he's really got in mind."

"Fair enough," said Macdonald. "I know I've just been running ahead of all my data, but there's some sense behind it, all the same. That hut has been used. I know it has. I smelt it. It wasn't used by the shepherds or farm men. It wasn't used by Betty Fell and her Jock. They sit in the church porch to chat. So it was probably used by the lad Woolfall saw."

"That's all right so far," said Kate, "but why don't you agree with Giles that the lad was one of the sheep-stealing gang?"

"It's not that I disagree with Giles, but I'm aware there's likely to be an alternative. Either explanation is possible—a sheep-stealer or a shirker, evading national service. I'm inclined to the latter because I don't think one of the gang would have risked walking over from Hawkshead in broad daylight. But take the chance as fifty-fifty. If he was one of the gang, it's certain he won't go there again. If he's a fugitive, he may have taken a fancy to his hidey hole and he may go there again. Why shouldn't he? It's very doubtful if he's in the habit of talking to folks round about, and he's probably not heard what happened in the fire. You see, the basis of my argument is that he may have seen something—and if we can get him *before* he's heard that a death is involved, he may be willing to talk. In our job, it's ingrain to search for witnesses. Sometimes imagination helps you, sometime it doesn't. But in this case it's a fifty-fifty chance of something useful."

"I think that's a good example of considering a problem in the round," said Giles. "I admit I was looking at it in the flat. If Macdonald's alternative turns out to be well-founded, I agree there's a chance that this chap might have seen something of the sheep-stealing racket, but it's not very probable he'd have seen anything of the fire-raising at that distance."

"But I thought you were convinced that the sheep-stealers did the fire-raising," said Macdonald, "so isn't it the sheep-stealers who are our target?"

Giles grinned a little sheepishly, but his answer came quickly enough: "If the sheep-stealing has priority, what's the reason for your interest in Thomas Woolfall's Will of 1690?

What have Courts Baron got to do with sheep-stealing? And you did agree that it's possible the reverend wasn't entirely unconnected with the matter."

"Perfectly true: the reverend is an alternative trail," said Macdonald, and Kate put in:

"What I want to know is this. Are you and Giles going scouting out on Ramshead to-night? I can't say I've any enthusiasm for the idea, but if you're going, I should like to know what you're likely to do when you get there."

"Well, first of all it depends on Bord," said Macdonald. "I'm going over to see him at seven o'clock. If he agrees, I should like to tackle this part of the job. I think Hoggett and I could do it more easily than Bord and his chaps—and they've got enough on their hands anyway. My idea is that I drive to Slaidburn immediately after seeing Bord, and get one of the local men to set me on the right track. Then I shall walk up over Hawkshead and on to Ramshead. If I get to Slaidburn at nine o'clock, I should be back over Hawkshead between eleven and midnight."

"Then I'll drive as far as Aikengill and leave my car there," said Giles, "and walk up to the cottage—or within a few hundred yards of it—and wait for Macdonald."

"And then?" asked Kate.

"If the chap's there, my own belief is that he sleeps in the shippon," said Macdonald. "The shippon roof is intact, the house roof is in ruins. He could cook his supper on the fire in the big chimney, have a good warm, and then go and settle down for the night in the shippon on a bed of brushwood. There was no sign of any bedding in the old living-room, and it'd be no sort of place to doss down in, but the shippon would be reasonably weatherproof. Still, I don't know: so if Hoggett keeps an eye on the house door while I tackle the shippon, we ought to be able to prevent him bolting."

"Well, I hope he's not a gangster with a gun," said Kate.

"Somehow I don't think so," said Macdonald. "Gangsters keep to the cities. The only sort of lad who'd have the nerve to sleep in a place like that cottage is a boy who's used to hill country. He's used to walking, because he's had to walk miles to get food. Guns don't seem part of the picture to me." He laughed at Kate's sceptical face. "Don't look so disgusted. I've admitted I'm guessing, but an unofficial assistant investigator is allowed more licence than the officer who's handling the job."

"Oh, I can see your point," said Kate. "You feel there's a chance, even though it's a small chance, that you may get some first-hand evidence if you go up to Ramshead to-night."

"If I don't find anything it doesn't matter," said Macdonald. "You see on this occasion I'm not tied down to the everlasting exigencies of routine. Bord's doing all that. For to-night, at least, I can offer a hand as a free lance. Bord can take it or leave it."

"He'll take it," said Giles. "Once you've told him that cottage has been used, he's bound to have it investigated. And he'd rather you than himself. It's a long walk, Macdonald— and Bord's no fellsman."

"I thought something of the kind myself," agreed Macdonald.

CHAPTER XI

I

Apart from Driving Down to Kirkholm for a midday meal at the Manor Hotel, Gilbert Woolfall had been at Aikengill all day. In the afternoon a couple of young officers from the County C.I.D. had come up to take records of fingerprints throughout the house. Gilbert had gone round the house with them, conscientiously searching to determine that nothing had been stolen and nothing moved from its accustomed place. He had felt all the time that it was a futile proceeding, but he had fallen in with all the suggestions the police had made.

"This house is a very simple proposition from your point of view, officer," he said. "My uncle had a minimum of personal gear: after his death his clothes and footwear were all sent to a charitable organisation in Liverpool, where there is more real poverty than in any rural district. He had an old-fashioned gold watch which I have got at home, a double-barrelled shot-gun which is on its brackets in the hall, and a good pair of binoculars which are in my bedroom here. The gun and the glasses are both worth money, but they weren't taken. Apart from his papers and books in the study he left hardly any other personal possessions. There are some clothes of mine here, including a good raincoat and tweed overcoat and good leather shoes, any of which are worth stealing, but they haven't been stolen."

"Were there any rare books, valuable engravings, clocks, anything of that kind?" asked the detective.

"No. Nothing. Everything was valued for probate. The most valuable things in the house are the old furniture— dower chest, a court cupboard, old tables, and chairs, but they can hardly be described as portable. As for Mrs. Ramsden's things, I know nothing about them, but I'm pretty certain she didn't possess anything valuable. When she heard that my uncle had left her £500, she said it was the first time in her life she'd ever had any money of her own, apart from the wages she earned as housekeeper."

"You evidently don't believe in the theory that a thief was responsible for the fire here," observed the C.I.D. man.

"No. I don't, but what I believe is neither here nor there," said Gilbert, "so I'll leave you to get on with your job. I can see that it's important for you to find out if any stranger has been in the house; if you want to take my fingerprints, so that you can eliminate one lot, you're welcome."

"Thank you, sir. That will be very helpful."

The young officer got out his gear, and while he was taking impressions of Gilbert Woolfall's fingers, he asked: "Would you tell me who has been in the house recently, to your knowledge, sir?"

"I can only tell you about the times I have been in the house. I have had very few visitors. A fortnight ago the Rector, Mr. Tupper, spent an hour or so here in the evening: we sat in here, in the sitting-room. Mr. Herdwick, who leases the Aikengill farmland, came in about some repairs to farm buildings the same evening, but I took him into the study. I had Jock Shearling in to see me the following evening. He had been stacking logs in the cellar: it was a dampish evening and I asked him into the house because I wanted a word with him. Apart from those three people, nobody else has been to see me since my uncle died except the two men who valued for probate—one inspected the land and buildings, the other went over the house with me to value the contents. Of course Mrs. Ramsden may have had neighbours in, but they would have sat in the kitchen with her. She was a punctilious woman, and I'm sure she wouldn't have taken her friends into any other room than the kitchen."

"Thank you, sir. As you say, it looks as though we should have a straightforward job," replied the other.

Leaving the two officers in the sitting-room, Gilbert went and opened the door of the study for the first time since he had come into the house that morning. The sturdy oak door was charred black on the inner side and it was warped and blistered on the hall side, but it still swung on its hinges. The smoke and fumes had cleared away, and the heat of the smouldering wood had nearly died out, but the stench of fire and sodden ash remained, though the glass in the windows was all broken and the keen wind whistled between the stone mullions.

It was a hideous scene of desolation. On the side of the

room farthest from the door the floor was burnt out and some of the charred beams which had roofed the cellar below had collapsed. Into this black gap had fallen the heavy bookcase and writing table; half caught against the sagging beam, the remains of the oak knee-hole table hung in charred ruin above the reeking blackness of the cellar. Seeing it thus, Gilbert was amazed that the whole house had not burnt out. He knew it was the thickness of the stone walls which had saved it, and the fire-resisting qualities of the oak door, which had been farthest from the origin of the fire. The firemen had got their hoses and pumps into the deep pool in the river and played their hoses through the windows. Down below, the cellar was a foot deep in black malodorous water, for the drains were choked with ashes and debris.

Dragging the door to again, Gilbert went outside and stood in the garden to clear his lungs and blink the tears away: his eyes were smarting with the fumes, but tears of rage mingled with tears of discomfort as he stood in the sunshine. He went indoors again and walked upstairs to Mrs. Ramsden's bedroom: the floor was scorched, the linoleum blistered and cockled, the wooden wainscot blackened, but nothing had been consumed by fire. The bedding had been taken away from the iron bedstead and the curtains from the windows, lest they caught fire from the heat which rose from below, long after the fire had been controlled. The room was blackened under a film of soot, but the old-fashioned alarm-clock still ticked noisily on a table near the bed. Gilbert had once laughed at Mrs. Ramsden over her alarm-clock. Its alarm made so much noise that he himself could hear it in his bedroom at the far end of the house; he had said it was like the last trump. Mrs. Ramsden had not been in the least put-out. "Then it's the right clock for me," she had replied, "for my husband he did use to say I slept like the dead. Happen he'd got the toothache of a night, he had to shake me right hard before I'd wake up to see to him."

It had been the bell of the alarm-clock which had brought the firemen upstairs at six o'clock that morning. They had been told there was no one sleeping in the house, and yet through the heat and smoke and stench had come the loud ring of the clock upstairs. Up they had pounded, to find a room so dense with hot, suffocating smoke that they had been driven back again and again before they had reached the bed and found Mrs. Ramsden asleep in the sleep which has no earthly awakening.

I I

Gilbert Woolfall had determined to stay at Aikengill until the police had concluded their investigation or at least until the inquiry was through its early stages. Maggie Herdwick had suggested he should come and sleep at Lambsrigg, or go to the hotel in Kirkholm for the night, but Woolfall's innate obstinacy was not to be persuaded. "Thank you very much, but I'm going to sleep here," he had said. "My own room is at the far end of the house and it's not affected by the fire. It's very kind and neighbourly of you to offer me hospitality, but I shall manage all right."

Maggie—she was a big heavy woman of forty-five— looked at him unhappily. "I'm right sorry about it all, Mr. Woolfall. Me and Mrs. Ramsden, we didn't always agree, maybe, but she was a good soul and a rare hard worker. I wouldn't have had this happen for the world. Well, if there's aught I can do, tell me, and I'll do it and welcome."

Gilbert realised the effort Maggie Herdwick had made in getting out her sentence of condolence. She was no talker and work came more easily to her than words.

Even to himself, Gilbert could not explain the impulse which made him determined to stay in the sad reek of the fire-haunted house. An illogical feeling in his mind insisted "The truth is here, somewhere. If I stay I may realise the truth. If I go away I shall lose the chance."

It was just after tea that the telephone rang and Mr. Tupper's agitated voice expressed his profound sorrow at this "deplorable tragedy" in a nervous spate of words which exasperated Gilbert almost to fury. "I am deeply distressed," moaned the throaty and slightly falsetto voice.

"I also am distressed," replied Gilbert, "and I hope I am not unduly censorious in saying that a little patience and kindliness on your part yesterday might have been of more value than condolences to-day."

He slapped down the telephone, a little ashamed of the fact that he could gladly have hurled it at the clerical countenance had the speaker been within throwing distance. Then the back-door bell rang and Gilbert walked through sitting-room, dining-room and kitchen to the back door, thinking how odd it was to be in and out of Mrs. Ramsden's kitchen.

It was Betty Fell waiting at the door. Her face flushed and miserable, her eyes heavy, she burst out: "Mr. Woolfall, I had to come and tell you how sorry we are, me and Jock. We just can't bear thinking on it."

Something about the unhappy young face and spontaneous voice went to Gilbert's heart. He replied:

"Betty, it's wretched, isn't it? I feel as though it's my fault, having left the poor soul alone here. Come in a minute, won't you? I'd be glad to talk to you about her."

"May I ask Jock to come too, Mr. Woolfall? He's in the garden. He wants to talk to you that bad, but he's afeared you wouldn't let him speak. I made him come. You know they're saying he did it—fired the house?"

"What utter nonsense!" exclaimed Gilbert indignantly. "Of course Jock can come and talk to me. I'll go and call him myself."

He went outside and called, "Come along in, Jock. I'm glad you thought to come."

Jock Shearling was a big fair-skinned lad, with powerful square shoulders, long-limbed and lissom. His hair was auburn and his fair skin tanned to a warm freckled flush which made his blue eyes even bluer.

"Somehow you two are the only people I can honestly say I'm glad to see this evening," said Gilbert. "I've been talking to the police and answering endless questions. They're decent fellows, and the Yard man who came up has something about him which is likeable as well as intelligent, but I'm weary of them. Just before you came, the Rev. Tupper rang up to condole. I'm afraid I'm a bit of a heathen, but I could have thrown the telephone at him with pleasure."

"He's a nowt," said Jock impulsively, using the local term of contempt, and Betty suddenly flared up.

"He's worse than that. He's bad. He's said things no man

should say, parson or no parson. He couldn't even see Mrs. Ramsden was a good woman, good all through."

"Nay, 'tis no use repeating all that dirt," said Jock heavily, but Betty went on:

"I'll say it and be done. He says country folks don't know what morals mean—and I know what he means by that."

"If he'd be willing to forget his own self-importance, he might have learnt what neighbourliness means from country people," said Gilbert. "My uncle always said that the native population of this valley could all give the answer to the old question, 'Who then is my neighbour?' But I'm sorry that evil tongues are attacking you, Jock. Who started this rumour, Jock?"

"Reckon 'twas Miss Wetherby began it," said Jock, "but as things are, anybody'll believe anything. 'Tis this sheep-stealing has got the farmers in a state so that some of them'll say anything. I'd like you to know the rights of it, Mr. Woolfall. I'm not such a fool I can't see they've got a bit of sense in what they say, for all it don't add up to the truth."

"All right, Jock. You tell me the whole story," replied Gilbert.

"It all started because Betty and I came up here yesterday evening. We often go for a walk of an evening, to get a chance to talk on our own, and somehow with planning to come and live in Aikengill, maybe, it seemed natural to come up here and talk on't."

"I understand that all right," said Gilbert readily, "but did you tell anybody you came here?"

"No. That we didn't," said Jock, "but there's not much you do hereabouts folks don't notice. It's like that most times in a place as quiet as this: so few people living here that they can well nigh tell who's passing by the sound of the foot-steps. I've heard old Tegg say he always knows who's past his cottage without looking—'tis the way they walk. And with this sheep-stealing worry, they'll notice the more if anyone passes after dark like. Betty and me, we've come up here more'n once of an evening since you said maybe we could live in Aikengill. Why shouldn't we have come?" he cried. "Seemed natural like."

"Of course it did," replied Gilbert. "I'm interested in what you say about recognising people's footsteps. I shouldn't have thought of that because I live in a town where there's too much noise to hear anything like that."

"Well, they knew I came up here last night," went on Jock. "That's one thing. They know I stacked that wood in t' cellar, and 'twas I could have stacked dry kindling instead of green—dead heather and turves and brushwood that'd burn like matchwood. And there's this to it, Mr. Woolfall. If so be you wanted to light a signal fire hereabouts, where so safe as in that cellar? Once you're down yon steps and shut the cellar door behind you, who's to see what you're up to? 'Twas a right cunning thought, that was."

"That's true," said Betty. "You could fix it all ready with dry stuff and light it and be away easier than you could light a bonfire out of doors, where you'd be seen getting away as the light flared up maybe."

"Aye, that's how 'tis, and what Betty and I can see plain, why, so can other folks. But we know 'twasn't me who did it, Mr. Woolfall, but others don't."

"But why should you have done it?" demanded Gilbert. "You wanted to come and live here. Would you have set fire to the one house where you'd a chance to make a home? I'd as good as promised, hadn't I? It doesn't make sense."

"Some folks are making sense of it though, Mr. Woolfall," said Jock bitterly. "I'm minded of the way a fire spreads in dry bracken when we burn it off the fellside: tongues of flame this way and that—'tis human tongues and words that's creeping like flames in brushwood. My last job was up in the hills by Whernside. They're all remembering that, when scores of sheep was shifted and none found out who did it. 'Happen he was in that and they've got a hold on him.' That's what's some folks' saying now."

"It's just plain wickedness!" cried Betty, but Jock replied with a moderation that surprised Gilbert Woolfall.

"Tha's got to be fair, lass. If 'twere some other chap, not me at all, and we were trying to guess what happened like, wouldn't we add up all there was—him coming up here after dusk, him knowing t' cellar and stacking t' wood, him having had a job near where that gang rounded up t' flock and got away with it? We know 'tisn't true—but other folks don't." He turned to Gilbert Woolfall. "I wanted to tell you what some folks are saying because I'd rather you heard it from me than from them. And all I can say is—I didn't do it, Mr. Woolfall."

"And all that I've got to say is that I believe you," replied Gilbert Woolfall. "I know you didn't do it, and that's that. But Jock, who did do it? Do you believe that fire started by accident, because Mrs. Ramsden dropped a lighted match when she went down to the cellar to turn the current on again?"

"That it didn't, Mr. Woolfall. Inspector Bord asked me that same question, and I answered it straight, whether it told against me or not. The last lot of billets and clippings I stacked in that cellar wasn't only green, 'twas running with sap. You asked me to fell that young beech tree in t' coppice, and clear some of the alder down yonder by the stream where it fouled your casts. When I felled and cleared, I cut the stuff up and stacked it. Mrs. Ramsden, she fairly flew at me. 'That stuff won't be fit for kindling till the back end,' she said. 'It's sodden, that is. How'm I to light a fire with that?' and I told her I'd got some old posts that weren't fit for naught save burning and I'd split them for her and put them in the wash-house. They're there now, along with the last of the dry hedge clippings I brought her up from the cellar. That stuff in t' cellar never got burning without paraffin or petrol or such like. Once you've started a right good blaze anything'll burn, green or dry, but it's hard to get it going—and there's no draught in that cellar. As for smoke—well, you know how green wood smokes."

"Well, we all seem agreed about that," said Gilbert Woolfall. "Someone started the fire deliberately. The most probable thing is the suggestion that the sheep-thieves did it. But there are a few points want explaining before we can accept that explanation. How did they know about the cellar, and that it was stacked with wood?"

"That's not so hard, Mr. Woolfall," put in Betty eagerly. "You said you saw a strange fellow up yonder on Hawkshead Fell. If he'd been hanging around a bit, maybe he saw Jock bringing in those barrows of wood across t' garden. After dark, maybe, he went and tried t' cellar door and found 'twas left unlocked and looked to see if there was aught he could steal."

"Aye, that might be," said Jock. "I left Mr. Woolfall's hatchet down there, and an old bushman saw and some wedges. A chap like that, a tramp or such like, might have taken them. Then if he came back a few days later and found the house was empty, he might've told the others about it."

"Of course the house *was* empty those days Mrs. Ramsden was over at Dent," mused Gilbert. At the same time, he was conscious of the doubtfulness in Jock's voice. His "Aye, that might be" was spoken in a tone that had little conviction in it. "Have you any other suggestion to make, Jock?"

The lad hesitated, evidently thinking hard. "Nay, Mr. Woolfall," he said at last. "You see, 'tis this way. I know how it feels when folks get talking, and 'tis easier to say a thing than unsay it. I'm not going to get cracking without something to show for't. All this 'might have' is too easy to say."

Betty turned to Gilbert. "When I was up on Ramshead this afternoon I met this Mr. Macdonald you were talking about. I liked him: there's something decent about him. I told him what some folks was saying about Jock, because I reckoned 'twas better for him to hear it first than last. He said to me, 'If you've any ideas about what happened, if so be you think of anything that may help, tell it to the police, to Mr. Bord or to me: don't tell anybody else.' I reckon there was sense in that, and I've told Jock to remember it. If he thinks someone acted queer, why 'tis better to let the police sort it out than try to have it out with whoever 'twas—if you see what I'm trying to say."

"Yes. I see what you mean, Betty, and Macdonald's advice was sensible. The police will investigate any idea, and if they find there's nothing in it they won't get gossiping. Well, I only hope they'll clear it up, for it's a miserable business. I know I'm not going away from this place until they've found out what happened."

"But Mr. Woolfall, the house isn't fit to live in," cried Betty. "See, there's black on everything. If you're going to stay here, let me come and clean up for you. I'll do it and welcome, and I'll cook your meals too, if you'd like it."

"Well, that's a good offer, Betty, and I won't say no. The house has got to be cleaned somehow."

He broke off, and then added: "Look here. You two have been wanting to get married for months. Why not get a special licence and be done with it. Then you can both come and live here and look after the house when it's repaired, and folks'll see then that whoever else doesn't believe in you, I do. I trust you both and I'll be glad for you to come here."

"Well!" gasped Betty, her cheeks flaming, her eyes dancing, and Gilbert said:

"Talk it over and tell me to-morrow when you've made up your mind. And if Betty likes to come and clean up, I shall be only too glad."

Jock, crimson in the face, blurted out: "I don't know how to say thank you for that, Mr. Woolfall, for trusting us when thing's look so's nobody need trust me. We'll think it over and do what seems best. But let me do this—come and sleep in t' house to-night if you're set on staying here. I'd've been around somewhere, I tell you that straight. If so be folks aren't trusting me, I reckon I'm not trusting folks."

"If anybody needs a decent night's rest to-night, you do, Jock," said Woolfall. "You were fire-fighting all night. All right. You come along and sleep in the room above this one. And we'll look after each other and the house, too."

"I will and all," said Jock. "I'll see Betty safe back to Low Gimmerdale and settle so my own folks won't be bothering, and then I'll come back here, quiet like. 'Twouldn't be a bad idea at all if no one knew I was here, just for to-night. I reckon there's something wrong somewhere, Mr. Woolfall."

"Well, I feel that way, but what's wrong is past my wits to fathom," said Gilbert sadly.

CHAPTER XII

I

MACDONALD DROVE OVER TO CARNTON TO SEE BORD after his, (Macdonald's), consultation with Giles and Kate Hoggett. Bord welcomed the Yard man, if not with open arms, with a degree of satisfaction seldom put into words by those raised north of the Ribble.

"I'll be right glad to have a crack with you and get some ideas off my chest," said Bord. "If you hadn't been around, I'd have driven over to H.Q. to see our Super. There's some things I don't care to talk to the younger chaps about. And if it's not taking advantage of you while you're on holiday, I'd like to get our old man to ask for co-operation from the Commissioner—meaning getting you on the job officially. I've a feeling this job's wheels within wheels."

"No complaints from me," responded Macdonald cheerfully, "so we'll take it as fixed. So now let me hear your news before I tell you mine."

"Champion," said Bord heartily. "Well, to take things in order. First, Mrs. Ramsden. The surgeon's pretty well satisfied she died of asphyxiation and nothing else. No signs of violence, drugs, or poisoning. They'll get an analysis done, but the surgeon says that's by way of a formality."

"Good," said Macdonald, "that simplifies things."

"It does that. Now I've had a word with the Dentdale chaps. They know Mrs. Ramsden's folk well, and know her, too, and they're certain as can be there's no complications in that quarter. Steady elderly folks, comfortable enough in a small way, and no earthly motive for wanting Polly Ramsden out of the way. It was the other way about: they wanted her to settle with them for good."

"Had she any children?" asked Macdonald.

"She had two sons, one born in 1912, one in 1914. They were both killed in the war, one in the Merchant Navy, one in Tobruk. Her husband died in 1939, and she went to live with this cousin at Dent for a year or two, then took a job as housekeeper to a widowed farmer, and in 1947 became housekeeper to Mr. Thomas Woolfall. She was then sixty-three and glad of a light job, as she called it. She'd always worked hard. Her husband was a small shopkeeper, but times were bad in the 'thirties, and when he died there wasn't any money left. She was devoted to the Woolfalls, thought the world of this chap we saw this morning. It's a straightforward story, and it was a sad ending for her after a sad life, but she was very happy at Aikengill. I'm glad to think she passed on without knowing a thing about it—just died in her sleep. But I'd like to get the chap that did it, and by gum, we will."

"Agreed to that," said Macdonald. "Just one question. Did

she phone to her folks at Dent to say she wasn't coming back last night?"

"No, they're not on the phone, and they didn't expect her to send a message. She said she'd likely be back by evening, but maybe she'd stay the night, so they didn't worry. She wasn't one to use Mr. Woolfall's telephone for her own convenience. Very straight she was about it, they said."

"She seems to have been straight in all her dealings," said Macdonald, and Bord cut in:

"More than some of them are up there. I went to see a Miss Wetherby—she sent a message saying she'd got some evidence for me and I thought I'd better see what it boiled down to. And by gum, she's a termagant!" exclaimed Bord. "I had a few straight words with her before I left. Not that she hadn't got some evidence of a sort, but talk about malice, she's a snake if ever I met one. Well, her story was that Jock Shearling's responsible for all the trouble."

"I've been hearing something about this," said Macdonald. "I met Betty Fell when I was up on Ramshead this afternoon." He gave Bord a concise account of what Betty had said, and then went on: "I admit all those points have got to be considered, but why is this Miss Wetherby so bitter against Jock Shearling?"

"She's a sour old cat," said Bord, "but the reason she's got her knife into Jock is this. She's one of those females who reckons she's the special agent of the almighty for improving other folk's morals. I've met her sort before, and between you and me, I reckon they're enough to send any youngster off the rails. She says Betty Fell's in the family way, which is likely true enough, so Miss Wetherby takes it on herself not only to abuse Betty, but spread the story round. When Jock Shearling heard of it, he went and told Miss Wetherby if she didn't hold her jaw, he'd duck her in the river, same's they used to do with scolds in the old days—and he meant it. He frightened her, and she's been waiting for her chance to get back on him. Well, she reckons she's got it and she's playing it for all she's worth."

"What's your opinion of Jock Shearling, Bord?"

The north countryman took his time before answering. At last he said: "I talked to him after I'd seen this Wetherby dame. He's as fine a young chap as you could meet, and he was straight. He told me his own story in his own way and didn't try to find an easy way out. He swore the wood he'd stacked in that cellar didn't catch fire by accident: it was cut green, with the sap rising. He said he got home between ten and half-past last night, and that all his folks were abed by the time he got in and he'd no one to corroborate that he came in when he said he did, or that he didn't go out again. And yet—I don't know." Macdonald waited for him to go on, and after a pause Bord continued slowly: "You know how 'tis between Jock and Betty Fell. It's that way often enough hereabouts, but the lad marries the lass and no one's the worse and most often no hard words said. But it's difficult for young folks these days. Houses are hard to come by and land costs the devil of a lot. This pair don't want to start married life in either of their parents' homes. The Fells have only got a small house and it's full up already. The Shearlings—well, no bride wants to live with a mother-in-law like Mrs. Shearling. She's as quarrelsome as a Kilkenny cat."

"You're arguing that Jock's more likely to be tempted by a bribe than one might think," said Macdonald.

"Well—they've got to get married, and that's flat," said Bord.

"But wasn't Gilbert Woolfall going to let them live in Aikengill?" urged Macdonald.

"Aye—when Mrs. Ramsden left. Well, she's gone. And not more'n an hour ago Jock and Betty went to see Mr. Woolfall. I've got the place under observation and I know. He's a kind-hearted chap is Mr. Woolfall. D'you reckon he'll say 'you can't come here now'? I don't. He's more likely to say, 'Get married and come here.' After all, it must be damned uncomfortable for the poor chap: the house is filthy—and Betty Fell's a good housewife I'm told. You mark my words, that's how it'll be done. I'm a married man myself and I don't hold with goings on," added Bord, "but I'd find it easier to say 'yes' to Betty Fell than 'no.' She's got a way with her."

"I grant you that," said Macdonald, "but I'd have guessed she was straight. She told me that she and Jock came up to Aikengill together, but she made no attempt to cook up an alibi for him after she picked up her bike and left him. Now there could have been two reasons for her telling me that the pair of them were at Aikengill yesterday evening: either that she thought it was best to tell the plain truth and that she was glad to tell it, because she was worried to death, or else that she is subtle enough to argue that telling the damaging side of the story was good policy. In my opinion, Betty Fell isn't capable of subtlety. She's got plenty of common sense, but she's not clever. Personally, I'm disposed to believe her—until, or unless, evidence proves she's lying."

"I feel the same about the lad," said Bord, "but you can never be sure. Now for the rest of my report: I went to see the Rev. Tupper—and, by gum, he's nearly as malicious as Miss Wetherby—and I shouldn't be surprised if it's not for the same reason. You know I said she was frightened of Jock Shearling. Well, the Rector's frightened, too. He's frightened of what folks are saying about him."

"That may well be," said Macdonald. "Hoggett says they're saying quite a lot, and Hoggett's as sound a judge as you'll get so far as local feeling's concerned."

"Aye. He's sound along those lines," agreed Bord. "I reckon myself the Rector argues the best line of defence is attack, and so he took trouble to inform me about the deplorable state of morals in remote and—what was his word...half a jiffy—uncouth, that was it, uncouth country districts. By gum, I could have told him about 'uncouthness' as he calls it, in cities which no one calls 'remote.' 'Akin to the beasts of the field' he says. Not only Betty Fell, mark you, and her a decent lass, even though she should ha' been married before now, but Mrs. Ramsden, too. The things some folks'll believe! I reckon Miss Wetherby got some of her poison in that quarter, and the silly old fool believed it—and him a parson!"

Bord was red in the face with indignation, but Macdonald chuckled. "I've met the same sort of thing before, and a man's a human being before he's a parson. What you said about his being frightened is probably the truth, and fear's a bad counsellor. But look here, Bord: do you think there's the least likelihood that the Rector knows anything at all about this business? Had he any reason to fear that Gilbert Woolfall might unearth anything prejudicial to himself in the papers which old Mr. Woolfall had collected, and the researches he had made into the history of the parish and chapelry?"

Bord gaped in astonishment. "I can't swallow that one, Chief. I'd say no, definitely no. Maybe I've been letting my tongue run away with me. I was disgusted at the way the man condemned folks whom he knew nothing about: he made me very angry with his high and mighty pillar of virtue attitude, but when all's said and done, I suppose he regards himself as a chosen vessel and it's his job to rebuke sin, as he sees it—just as it's yours and mine to run in law-breakers. But he's respectable to his measly bones. Mean he may be, and malicious, too, I reckon, but he'd no more commit a crime than he'd pinch pennies out of the collection plate. What are you getting at?"

"The fact that it was old Woolfall's study which was burnt, with all his papers. It may be irrelevant, of course."

Bord cogitated a moment. "It's true the reverend went up to see Mr. Gilbert Woolfall and created a bit because there wasn't a bequest for the church, but I can't see him going to extremes to get his own back. No. I'd wash that one out."

"Right. Then let's get on to the next," said Macdonald. "I walked up to that old steading on Ramshead Fell this afternoon. There's an ancient dwelling-house there, with the flagstones off the roof for the greater part. It's been used as a shelter by somebody, or I'm greatly mistaken. I could smell turf smoke in the chimney, and the smell of sweat and human dirt. It's not the shepherds who've used it, because the ashes were cleared from the hearth stone."

"By gum, that's more like!" exclaimed Bord. "Where is the place exactly?"

Macdonald pulled his Ordnance Survey sheet from his pocket and spread it out on the table.

"It's here," he said. "It's marked all right. As you can see, it's a tidy step to get there. If you want me to come in on this job, what about me going up there to-night? It's a slim chance— but I'd be sorry not to take it."

"You do as you think, Chief, and if you want any help, say so. But what's the chances of finding aught? They've done their job, damn them: got the sheep away and fired a house into the bargain. They won't oblige by paying another visit."

"Well, we don't know who used the place, Bord. There's that lad whom Woolfall saw: it's only an assumption that he was one of the sheep-stealing gang." Seeing the other's sceptical face, Macdonald added: "I said it was a slim chance: there's so little in it that I wouldn't suggest you losing a night's rest over it, but I'd like to go myself."

"You'll go up there after dark?"

"I thought of driving to Slaidburn: if you phoned through, maybe one of their chaps would set me on the way back over Hawkshead. I'm told the track's clear enough, and there'll be moonlight to help—it's not much past the full. I'll come over Hawkshead and down to the cottage about midnight."

"It's the heck of a rough walk, Chief—all of ten miles."

"I don't mind that. Hoggett said he'd drive up to Gimmerdale to collect me. He might be useful in more ways than one. If he hadn't been a very law-abiding chap, I reckon he'd have made a first-rate poacher. He can move quietly on the fellside, he's in good training, and he did as neat a tackle as any bloke I've seen when he played rugger."

Bord looked a bit scandalised. "What about regulations, Chief?"

Macdonald laughed. "I'm not regulation myself—not till

to-morrow. This is my last night on leave. I wouldn't have done it without consulting you, but if you're agreeable, I'll cock a snook at the rest."

Bord began to laugh, too, a wholesome roar of laughter that set his stout person all aquake.

"I get you. Well, you'll be doing overtime without extra pay, so to speak. I hope you enjoy the tramp—rather you than me."

"Is there anywhere I can get a bite in Slaidburn? I can set out straight away and drive through Trough of Bowland. I should get there in about an hour."

"Aye, that's about it. There's a good inn at Slaidburn, the Hark to Bounty. I'll get them to keep a meal for you."

"The Hark to Bounty," echoed Macdonald. "That's a good heartening name. Well, I'll let you know how I fare."

"And don't you go on the casualty list yourself," said Bord. "It'd be a rum go if we had to take a search party over Hawkshead Fell looking for you."

"A rum go it would be," grinned Macdonald. "Without boasting, I'm prepared to say I've never yet needed a search party to pick me up when I've gone playing a lone hand. Still, it's nice to know you'll look for me if I come a cropper."

I I

It was a clear light evening when Macdonald set out on his drive, the western sky deep gold behind the fells. He crossed the Lune at Caton and turned south-west through Quernmore, driving past the rich pastures and meadowland of Lunesdale for some miles, until he turned sharp left round the angle of an old stone house which had once been an inn and was still known as The Dog and Partridge. From here on he drove up into the hills: on his left the fells stretched away to the summit of Bowland, to his right the ground dropped to the valley of the Wyre, and in front the fells were a dark rampart against the faint pallor of the evening sky. It was a magnificent drive and Macdonald enjoyed it to the full: mile after mile of moorland with never a habitation in sight. His only regret was that the twilight closed down on him and he soon had to turn his headlights on to enable him to see the moorland sheep who nibbled industriously on the verges of the unfenced road and occasionally bolted across it. By the time he reached the steep declivity of Trough of Bowland it was too dark for him to be aware of anything save the steepness of the fells which dipped down to form the trough, and his attention was at stretch to negotiate the sharp gradients and angles of a road which demanded all a driver's attention. It was dark when his headlights picked up the pointer to Slaidburn, but he knew he was clear of the hills, driving between fields again, with occasional farmhouses whose windows showed homely gleams of lamplight. Driving slowly now, he reached the main street of Slaidburn, whose stone houses were built on the roadside without any intervening gardens, and at length he saw the long stone-built inn with its big painted sign THE HARK TO BOUNTY—the pleasantest name for a hostelry which Macdonald had met in years. Here he found a sergeant of the Yorkshire County Police awaiting him, and suddenly remembered that he had crossed the county boundary and was no longer in Lancashire but in the West Riding. The Yorkshireman, looking very smart and regulation, was highly entertained at meeting a C.I.D. officer whose name was a household word in every police force in the country, none the less so because Macdonald said firmly he was still on leave and out to enjoy his evening in his own way. They had a good meal together within the hospitable walls of the inn—which did not belie its name.

I I I

Shortly before nine o'clock, Macdonald set out on his return journey, afoot this time, in company with a retired policeman who now had a small holding and a few cattle on the verge of the moor. This worthy—by name William Blackburn—knew the fell tracks like the back of his own hand, and saw nothing out of the way in a "young chap" (for so he regarded the lean, dark-haired C.I.D. man) walking over Croasdale and Hawkshead after dark. "Many's the time I ha' done it," he said cheerfully. "When I was courting and my lass lived in Roeburndale, I'd go over Hawkshead many an evening, aye and back too. I'd take me bike with me, ride as far as I could, push it the rest and down t'other side. 'Twas forty years ago, mind you. No cars for chaps like me those days. We used our legs—and did us a power of good. Half the lads these days don't know how to use their legs."

They left Slaidburn by road, and the road went on for a couple of miles up into the hills. It was a clear night, and surprisingly light. As they began to climb the fell, Macdonald saw the last of the small steadings—stone buildings, their walls lime-washed, so that they showed up surprisingly light against the shadowy background. Blackburn had heard about the events in Gimmerdale: it was the sheep-stealing which interested him, and Macdonald was amused to find that the old man blamed the new roads which had been made to take workmen and materials to the waterworks tunnel.

"These days them road's alive with lorries," he said. "No end to them. Puts ideas into folk's heads. In the old days they wouldn't ha' dared take vans oop in t' hills—they'd 'a been spotted, for sure. Nowadays who's going to notice what happens? Thrang them roads is, thrang like."

"Thrang." He meant crowded, pondered Macdonald. The word was certainly not applicable to the solitude in which they walked—or climbed. The empty fellside stretched all around them, mile upon mile of hill land: two sheep could subsist on one acre on ground such as this: five hundred acres, a thousand sheep—but even the sheep were rarely seen.

The old man walked sturdily with Macdonald for two hours. Then he said: "You can't miss it. T' track goes on, oop yonder: stick to t' track and you can't go wrong. 'Tis clear as daylight all t' way. That do you?"

"Aye. Does me fine, thank you very much," said Macdonald. "I'm very grateful to you for your trouble. When I come back to fetch my car, may I come and see your stock? Maybe you can give me some good advice if I take to a hill farm myself."

"Come and welcome," replied the other. "'Tis a good life. Quiet like, but always something doing. Well, I'll wish you good night. You can't miss it now—'tis a good clear night."

He turned back and Macdonald tramped on towards the summit. He could see the last ridge dark against the sky, and soon he realised that the gradient had changed. He had topped the ridge—the crest of Bowland Forest; around him was an immensity of moorland, and behind him the moon

shone white: below a faint mist curdled white in the moonlight, and somewhere, far below, lay the cottage on Ramshead,
and below that again the valley of High Gimmerdale.

I V

As he stood on the crest of the ridge for a breather, it suddenly occurred to Macdonald that it was a pity he hadn't
had an impulse to do this tramp last night: it must have
been some time between eleven o'clock and midnight that
Daniel Herdwick's sheep were driven up to the head of
the valley of High Gimmerdale and over the ridge where
Macdonald now stood. It was the only way they could
have been driven: the sides of the valley were too steep
for the men and dogs to keep a flock under control and
the outcrops of rock would have helped the sheep to break
back to their own ground, bolting round and round the
rocks and thus defeating the dogs. But they could have
been driven sedately up the track, with the men behind
and the dogs circling their charges. It would have been a
wonderful sight, pondered Macdonald: in that immensity
of shadowed ground, the compact flock of sheep, their
fleeces strangely whitened in the moonlight, would have
looked like ghosts, and the ever-watchful dogs would have
swept round and round the huddle of ewes, the long slender
collie bodies, lithe and flattened, running at thirty miles
an hour as good sheepdogs do.

"And what the devil could I have done?" thought
Macdonald. "I might have spoilt the party so far as sheep-
stealing was concerned, but the dogs would have downed me."

He remembered Betty Fell's dog crouching that afternoon, ready to spring. "Losh, that would have been a party, that would," he chuckled, as he set out, over the watershed, down to Gimmerdale again.

CHAPTER XIII

I

GILES HOGGETT SET OUT FOR HIS RENDEZVOUS WITH
Macdonald shortly after ten o'clock. He felt a bit vague as
to what was likely to be his own contribution to this excursion, but when Macdonald had phoned from Carnton, after
seeing Bord, Giles had said he thought that when he himself
drove to High Gimmerdale, it would be wiser if he left his
own car "on top," and did not drive it down to the bridge and
park it by Aikengill. "On top" meant on the stretch of high
fell between the cattle grid and the hill leading down to the
bridge. Macdonald had agreed at once, and Giles had added
that he himself would walk on, past the steadings and the
church, and take the track which led up to Ramshead, arriv-
ing there between 11.30 and midnight. In his own shrewd
but cautious mind Giles Hoggett did not believe that there
was the least chance that Macdonald would find anything
or anybody at the ruined cottage, and the excursion would

probably end in the comfortable anti-climax of a stroll in the moonlight and a return drive to Wenningby. But—and Giles admitted it was a good "but"—when Macdonald had had hunches in the past, he'd quite often put up a fox.

Giles's suggestion about leaving his car on top was a concession to the possibility that there might be someone on Ramshead Fell who could watch comings and goings in the valley: if that were so, to drive a car over the bridge would be to give notice that somebody was approaching Gimmerdale at an hour when all hard-working country folk were in their beds. The headlights of a car can be seen for miles in hill country and the sound of its engine may carry for miles, and Giles had no intention of driving down Gimmerdale with his engine and headlights switched off— that would be driving to perdition and done with it. He had remarkably good eyesight, and he was quite prepared to drive up to the cattle grid with only spot-lights—or with no lights at all if the moon shone bright, and leave his car on the fellside, clear of the road, where it was not likely to be an obstruction.

He drove through the peaceful night, along the familiar switchback road which all Wenningby folk regarded as "their" road, down Gressingham hill and across Lune, then through the silent stone street of Kirkholm, where the cottages shone white in the moonlight, and on up into the hills. As he approached the stiff hill up to the cattle grid, he switched over from headlights to spot-lights, but as he reached the level he was called to halt and a flash-lamp was shone straight at him. Giles put his feet down on clutch and brake as a voice shouted "Police here," but a moment later the same voice said quite amiably, "All right, Mr. Hoggett. You can carry on—but you'd better put your headlights on again before you cross the bridge."

Giles recognised Sergeant Berry of Kirkholm, whom he knew quite well, because the sergeant was a bee-keeper.

"I thought I'd leave my car up here, Sergeant. If I get it off the road I can leave it without the lights on, can't I?"

"Yes. That'll be all right. I'll come along with you and see where you park and then we'll be able to keep an eye on it for you. If you find some red paint on your tyre to-morrow, don't be surprised. We've been checking cars on this road at night for some time—and you're our only catch so far."

With the sergeant on the running-board, Giles bumped his long-suffering car on to a reasonably level stretch of grass and pulled the handbrake on hard, leaving the car in gear as he always did on an incline. He suppressed a desire to quote "In yon straight path a thousand might well be stopped by three," and said prosaically: "Well, I'll be getting along. It's a fine night."

"Aye. Lucky for all of us," said Berry.

Giles walked on, thinking how peaceful it all was. The moon gave plenty of light to see the road, though there was a swaddle of mist below by the river. Before he started descending the steep hill, he stopped and listened. The only sound was the murmur of the beck chattering on over the stones. He knew he was in view of Aikengill and Lambsrigg, but no glimmer of light showed in any of the steadings. It was peaceful with the profound peace of hill country and Giles Hoggett found it difficult to believe that nefarious doings had interpolated themselves into the orderly rhythm of life in this secluded, little-known spot.

He walked down the rough road conscious of a keener chill in the air as he entered the mist which swathed the valley bottom. This would be a "frost pocket" he meditated, the type of hollow which collects all the cold air rolling down the hillsides, a site to be shunned by fruit growers. He crossed the bridge, up past Lambsrigg and the church, where the gable end and belfry stuck out oddly, clear of the mist, and finally into moonlight again as he mounted the track where he had driven Macdonald that afternoon, expecting any moment now to see the C.I.D. man swinging down the hill towards him.

Giles Hoggett walked on steadily for an hour: he was drawing near to Ramshead now, and though the fellside was as peaceful as ever, Giles was less easy in his mind: he knew that Macdonald was an uncommonly fast mover in hill country, and it was now past midnight. Rather uneasily, Giles pondered over the fact that though the moonlight made walking easy enough, it wasn't much of a light for searching the fells—and there was a perishing lot of ground to search. He paused for a while to get his bearings: before he set out he had been quite certain that he knew the position of the ancient steading: you had only to keep to the track until you rounded an outcrop of rock whose craggy summit resembled the head of a primitive lion, complete with mane and gaping jaws, and then you struck up the fell to your left, finding the overgrown track which had once marked the easiest approach to the cottage. But in the moonlight it was very difficult to tell an outcrop of rock from a ridge of heather or clump of bracken, both of which assumed all too easily the form of prehistoric beasts. Then he remembered that the track swung sharply to the left round the outcrop he was looking for and he went on again more certainly, because he was quite sure that he hadn't taken any sharp turn since the rutted road had petered out into the track.

When he did at last reach the outcrop of rock—which was quite unmistakable even in the hazy moonlight—Giles rounded it with a sense of satisfaction: he would have felt exceedingly foolish if he had lost himself on a fellside, which, he had assured Kate, he had known from the time he was a boy. "Up yonder," he knew, was the old steading, and probably Macdonald was up there already, waiting for him.

I I

What made Giles turn he was not sure: one second he was striding deliberately up the sharp slope, his feet brushing through dry heather and dead bracken, the next he had swung round and was standing with knees flexed, arms at the ready, his scalp prickling and pulses thudding. There, flat against the rock, was a man's figure, less than a yard away.

"Steady on: it's only me," said Macdonald's voice, in placid anti-climax. "I heard you coming, but I thought I'd let you get past in case both of us took a header down yonder. It's quite a good spot for a tumble."

Giles Hoggett took a breath of relief. "It must be the moonlight," he said. "I was just going to tackle you. Have you been up to the cottage?"

"Aye. There's no one there—but there has been someone there, not long ago. The shippon door's open. Someone's been lying up there, on a nice bed of dry bracken. I've been standing here wondering what's happened to him, and my guess is that he's taken the header you and I might have taken if we'd been dunderheaded enough to mistake one another in the moonlight."

"But why should he have taken a header?" demanded Giles.

"I don't know, but I think there's something odd about that open door," said Macdonald. "A chap who's hiding in a place like this doesn't forget to shut the door behind him: the place is only of use to him if nobody suspects it's being used."

"Perhaps he heard you coming and did a bolt."

"He didn't hear me coming," retorted Macdonald, his voice very low but quite positive. "I may not be the sprinter I once was, but I've learnt how to be quiet when I want to be quiet. My guess is that he heard someone else coming: in other words I'm not the only person who wondered if the chap in there could give some damaging evidence."

"I see," murmured Hoggett, and turned to stare down the steep slope which fell away like the side of a ravine to the valley bottom. "You mean you want to go down there and make sure?"

"That's it," rejoined Macdonald. "Since we're here, it's worth while finding out. I'll walk back about fifty yards and you go down from here. Then we can beat along the valley bottom for a hundred yards or so."

Without another word, Giles Hoggett began the descent, crabwise: the ground was steep but not in the least dangerous. In daylight he wouldn't have considered it worthy of any particular caution, but in the moonlight it was impossible to see the clefts or loose rocks which could easily result in a trip or a broken ankle. Soberly and carefully he traversed the slope and arrived at the rocky bottom with only one thought in his mind: "If the chap's here, how do we get him up?" Going down, unimpeded, was one thing: climbing up that rough gradient with an unconscious man to lift would be quite another. It wasn't any of Macdonald's arguments that had convinced Giles Hoggett that the man they sought would be lying somewhere on the rocks in the chattering beck, it was the visualisation of the open shippon door where the man had sheltered. Giles agreed with Macdonald—the chap would never have left that door open: it was open because something had prevented him going back to close it.

It was when he had worked back to a spot immediately below where he and Macdonald had met that Giles found the body: it was lying prone, and the drab clothes looked very much like the stones among which they were lying, but the bare head shone flaxen in the moonlight. Oddly enough that fair head gave Giles a shock. He hadn't visualised the chap they were looking for as a fair-haired slip of a lad, nor thought of anyone as thin and unsubstantial-looking as this lanky form lying athwart the beck.

Bending down, Giles satisfied himself that the lad's face was not in the water: then he waited. First aid was not his long suit, and he decided that Macdonald had better do the moving of the body. It was only a few moments before the C.I.D. man was bending over the lad, running his hands over head and neck and limbs. Then he stood up and turned the beam of his torch on to the ground beside the beck. "There's a level bit here," he said. "We'll lift him and lie him on his back. He's not dead by a long chalk, though he's broken some bones and got a bonny bash on his forehead. You take his legs—just enough to prevent them dragging as I lift him."

Easily and skilfully Macdonald raised the thin body and they got the casualty neatly on his back among the bracken. Macdonald took off his own Burberry and jacket, saying to Giles, "I'll have your raincoat, jacket, and pullover, please. You're going to do a spot of exercise, so you won't need them."

Obediently Giles stripped off his coats and shivered as the cold air cut through his shirt.

"I'll stay here: we can't move him without a hurdle," said Macdonald. "You go along to Aikengill by any route you like, and wake Woolfall. Then get one of the chaps from the farm and bring back a hurdle and blanket. We shall have to carry him along the valley bottom, it's too steep to carry him up the fellside. Tell Woolfall to phone a doctor to come out to Aikengill, and then come back here with a couple of helpers. It's going to be quite a job."

"Right," said Giles obediently. He gave one look at the boy's white face. "He's only a kid," he said sadly.

Macdonald nodded. "That's all. He'd have been safer in the army—poor silly lad."

I I I

Giles went up the slope at a pace which set his heart thumping, and regained the track: he could have gone along the valley bottom of course, keeping to the beck, but he didn't know the ground and doubted if he could have made much speed in the confusing light. Once he had regained the track he could jog-trot down it and recover his wind as he went.

Giles was a hefty fellow, and there was nothing the matter with his heart or his legs, but he didn't do much running these days and he found himself puffing like a grampus after his rush up the fellside. "I'm getting old," he thought resignedly—and then remembered the boy's white face in the moonlight. He had looked very dead indeed, but Macdonald had said he was alive—and he was a very young-looking weed of a lad. The recollection helped Giles to keep going and not stop for the breather which was due to his years. It didn't occur to him that he looked a very odd sight in the frosty moonlight, a long, lean, grey-headed man in blue shirt and corduroy breeches, running with a long lolloping action which still showed the skill of a one-time runner. As he ran he got his second wind and ceased to lament his advanced years, so that by the time he jog-trotted down the hill past the church he was beginning to enjoy himself and even to use his wits again. Macdonald had told him to go to Aikengill first, and rouse Gilbert Woolfall: then telephone the doctor: then rouse Lambsrigg, get a hurdle and guide the helpers back to Macdonald.

When he stood in the porch of Aikengill, ringing the bell, Giles Hoggett's mind was too full of his errand to spare any thought for his own appearance, but when the door was opened and the light glared out, Gilbert Woolfall stared at his odd-looking visitor with a jaw-dropping amazement. Giles Hoggett still contrived to speak with some measure of dignity.

"There's been an accident higher up the valley, Mr. Woolfall. Chief Inspector Macdonald has found an injured man below Ramshead. Will you please telephone for a doctor to come out here, and then come and help get the lad back?

We shall want a hurdle and a blanket, and straps of some kind. By the way, my name's Hoggett. You don't know me, but Macdonald's staying at my home in Wenningby."

"'Tis all right, Mr. Woolfall. That's Mr. Hoggett right enow."

It was Jock Shearling who spoke. Clad in unusual splendour in a pair of Gilbert Woolfall's brightly-striped pyjamas he looked as odd to Mr. Hoggett as Mr. Hoggett looked to him, and the unspoken thought was in both minds: "What the heck's he doing here, anyway?"

Gilbert Woolfall was the first to recover from his shock of surprise. "I'll phone Dr. McTay at Kirkholm. Jock, go and get some clothes on—quickly—and fetch a light hurdle. I'll get a blanket and straps and come along to help. Mr. Hoggett, there are some coats in the cupboard under the stairs. Help yourself, you must be damned chilly."

Giles found himself a coat while Gilbert was at the telephone: the latter called to Giles: "McTay wants to know the nature of the injuries."

"Broken bones and a broken head: the chap took a toss down the fellside. He's unconscious but not dead. Better ask for an ambulance to be sent out."

Gilbert finished his telephoning and hurried upstairs to get some clothes on: Jock Shearling had already dragged on trousers and braces and came downstairs again pulling on his coat: he hastened outside to collect a hurdle and then another voice spoke from the garden:

"Is aught amiss? I heard someone running past the house and then t' lights from here all shone across t' garden—"

"Nothing wrong here, Mr. Herdwick," replied Giles.

"There's been an accident up the valley and I came here for help."

"And what's Jock Shearling adoing here at this time o' night?" demanded Herdwick suspiciously.

Gilbert Woolfall came running downstairs. "Jock stayed the night with me here in case there was any further trouble," he explained quickly. "I've just telephoned for Dr. McTay to come here. If you're prepared to help, Mr. Herdwick, would you wait here until the doctor comes, and maybe see there's a fire going—there are plenty of logs in the sitting-room."

"Ay, I'll do that—but who's the man you've found and where is he?"

"We don't know who he is," replied Giles. "Chief Inspector Macdonald and I found him up the valley. He's badly hurt and we shall have to carry him back—the sooner the better."

"It beats me what's going on in t' place," said Herdwick. "I'd better come and lend a hand."

"Thanks very much, but you're going to do nothing of the kind," said Gilbert. "You were up all last night, fire-fighting, and you've been working hard all day. You stay here. There'll be four of us, that's quite enough."

"Have it your own way then," said Herdwick. "I'd come and willing, but if I'm not wanted I'll be glad enough to stay here. The whole set-out's plain daft."

"Plain daft just about expresses it," said Giles, as the three set out together. Jock and Giles carried the hurdle between them and Woolfall had the blankets over his shoulder. "It'll take us an hour to get up to Ramshead and a great deal longer to get back. Jock, what's the going like in the valley? We can't carry the chap up the fell, it's too steep."

"It's rough like, Mr. Hoggett, but I reckon t'would be the best way. The fell's right steep below Ramshead. Do you know how't happened?"

"I've not the least idea," said Giles. "Maybe the chap fell, maybe he was pushed over. All I know is that he's there and we've got to get him back, and it's going to be a tough job for all concerned."

I V

A tough job it was—just that. Taking turn and turn about, ten minutes a shift, the four men negotiated the improvised stretcher along the rough ground beside the beck, helped by the beam of Macdonald's torch and the misty moonlight. "Not a drum was heard, not a funeral note," quoted Giles Hoggett, as he stumbled uncomplainingly over the rocky ground.

They knew now that the lad they carried was the young man whom Gilbert Woolfall had spoken to on the fell. Jock believed him to be one of the sheep-stealing gang and suggested that he had fallen down the fellside the previous night.

"He wouldn't have been alive by now," said Macdonald. "He's unconscious and he'd have died of cold. He hadn't been there long when we found him. He was still warm."

"Isn't it quite likely he just slipped—lost his footing in the moonlight and went crashing down?" suggested Woolfall. "If he'd been sheltering in that cottage, he might have wanted some water to make tea in his billy-can and climbed down to the beck to get it, and slipped on the way."

"If he did that he was right daft," said Jock. "There's a spring of water close to the old steading. There's always water nigh to them old steadings. They'd never've built them else. And as for slipping, why should he've slipped? If he's been staying up there, he must be used to t' fells, and 'tis light enow with the moon near full. Nay, I reckon 'tis a case of thieves falling out. Likely he knew too much."

"That seems the most likely thing to me," said Macdonald. "I'll go up there when it's daylight and see if I can find any traces. Change over now—it's my turn for a stretch."

Jock and Giles Hoggett took one stretch, Macdonald and Gilbert Woolfall the other. The two who were not carrying the hurdle went ahead with the torch, trying to find the easiest way for the bearers. While Woolfall and Macdonald were leading, the latter tried to find out about the events of the evening from Gilbert Woolfall.

"Jock offered to come and spend the night with me," said Gilbert. "Quite honestly, I was glad to have him. The house seemed quite incredibly miserable, and I like the lad. He came along about eight o'clock, after seeing Betty home, and we had supper of sorts and got to bed by nine. Jock was dead tired—he'd been up most of last night—and I was tired, too. I took a book and a supply of candles to bed with me, as the electric cable hadn't been repaired yet—it was burnt through. I didn't read for long. I think I was asleep by ten."

"And you didn't hear anything after that?"

"Not till Hoggett rang the bell. Actually I didn't hear it, Jock did. He came and woke me and we both went downstairs, expecting anything except, perhaps, Mr. Hoggett in shirt and breeches. I was just about taken aback. Stout chap, isn't he?"

"Champion, as they say hereabouts," said Macdonald.

"Well, it's about time we took over again. How are you feeling? This sort of thing can't have come your way much."

"Oh, I'm bearing up. I'm pretty tough. I did ambulance work during the blitz, so I'm not so green at it as you might expect."

Giles and Jock went ahead, and Jock said, "We're through the worst now, Mr. Hoggett. There's a bit of a path as the valley widens out, and 'twon't be so hard going."

"I'm glad to hear it," said Giles. "It's surprising how one can go on, but once or twice I've felt I'd like to be a stretcher case myself."

"Don't blame you. I reckon I'd as lief be on the stretcher meself. Reckon it's one damned thing after another for me. You're all right—but who's to prove I didn't come out and bash yon chap on the head? I could ha' done it, easy enow, so far's the time goes. We turned in early, Mr. Woolfall and me. Over three hours 'twas between t' time we went to bed and you knocked us up."

"Provided you didn't do it, I shouldn't worry about that," replied Giles. "I suppose I might have done it myself so far as the time's concerned."

"All very well for you, Mr. Hoggett. Not so good for me. Still, 'tis no use fussing. Mebbe summat'll turn up, but I don't like the look of it and that's flat."

CHAPTER XIV

I

THEY GOT BACK AT LAST, TRAILING WEARILY UP THE slope to Aikengill. An ambulance stood there, its headlights blazing importantly, and Giles snorted in derision.

"Looks smart, doesn't it, but it couldn't have helped us much for all the spit and polish. I wonder how they got coffins down from the Ramshead steading? On their shoulders I reckon. No other way."

"You can cadge a lift in that outfit," said Macdonald. "They'll drive you back to your own car on a stretcher if you'd like one."

"I shouldn't," said Giles Hoggett, and Macdonald said tersely:

"Then beat it on your own feet and get home. You've done more than enough for one night and your wife will be thinking you're dead. I shall probably be here till morning. Off you go—and thanks for the lift, if I may put it that way."

Giles trudged off thankfully, and Macdonald and Jock took their burden in at the front door of Aikengill, which Woolfall held open. The square hall was lighted by an oil lamp: Dr. McTay was waiting for them, and the two ambulance men took over the improvised stretcher and carried it into the sitting-room while Macdonald and Jock stretched their weary shoulders.

"I'll get some drinks," said Gilbert Woolfall. "I reckon we've earned them—" He broke off as Daniel Herdwick came out of the sitting-room.

"Before you go into your own dining-room you'd better know you've got a visitor, Mr. Woolfall," he said. "By heck, I said it was a daft set-out and daft it is. You hadn't been gone half an hour and I was making up t' fire in there when I heard t' front door open. 'Twas on t' latch, same as when you went out. I came to t' sitting-room door thinking you'd changed your mind and coom back. But 'twasn't you, 'twas the reverend. Believe it or believe it not, he was nosing around in t' hall here. Well, I was fair flummoxed, but since he was here I told him he could stay here till you coom back. He didn't like it, but there 'twas. I wasn't letting him go. And in the dining-room he is."

"What did he come here for?" asked Macdonald.

"You go and ask him," said Herdwick. "He's got a story to tell you and he'd better tell it his own way. If you believe him it's more than I do, but I'm past patience with him. Tried to do the high and mighty, but I soon showed him 'tweren't no manner of good. You've come here, I said, and here you can stay till t' police have a word with you."

"Well, I'm damned!" exclaimed Gilbert. "I always said he was at the bottom of it somehow—"

"'Not unconnected with' is better," said Macdonald. "That's Hoggett's way of putting it. Well, I'd better go and see what the reverend gentleman has got to say for himself. It's odd that he always seems to turn up on the edges of the case so to speak."

"May I come with you?" asked Gilbert. "I really do want a drink, and after all it's my house he entered unbidden. Surely I've a right to ask why."

"All right. Come and ask him," said Macdonald.

They went through the sitting-room, where Dr. McTay and the ambulance men were busy with splints and bandages. Macdonald cast a glance at the pallid face of the unconscious boy.

"Is he going to give us the slip?" he asked.

"Depends on the head injuries," said the doctor cautiously. "I think he'll do. His heart's ticking over nicely—but I can't tell you what damage is done till we've X-rayed him. I'll be moving him in a few minutes—can't do much here."

"Can you tell what hit him—blunt instrument or rock?"

"He hit his head on a rock all right, the scalp's lacerated and there's grit in the wound, but he's got plenty of superficial bruises as well. Maybe he'll be able to tell you himself some time."

Macdonald, followed by Woolfall, went through the sitting-room into the dining-room. Here only a couple of candles served for illumination. The Rev. Simon Tupper looked a sorry sight. He was sitting in a roomy spindle-back chair and he had fallen asleep. His head had slipped sideways, his mouth was wide open and he was snoring intermittently, his melancholy snores vibrating his slack body. His feet were resting on another chair, and it was his boots that Macdonald studied first: once well polished, the black boots showed signs of rough going. They were mired and scratched, the heel of one of them half-wrenched off. His clothes also showed evidence of contact with the earth, and brambles and burrs and dead prickly twigs of heather still stuck to the clerical black. His once dignified dog collar was twisted and crumpled, his grizzled sandy hair awry.

"Well, if he hasn't been in a rough-house, I'll eat my hat," exclaimed Woolfall.

The crumpled little parson woke up with a snore that ended in a snort. He sat up, gaping confusedly and blinked at the two tall fellows who stood over him. It was Gilbert who spoke first:

"I have been told that you walked into my house uninvited, sir. Considering recent events, I think I am justified in asking what you came for."

Mr. Tupper gulped unhappily and his troubled face puckered up as though he were going to cry, but he lifted his feet off the chair and sat up with an effort at dignity. "I deplore your tone," he began, but Macdonald put in:

"I advise you to answer the question, sir. I am a police officer, and events in this place demand explanations, not recriminations."

"Do you realise that I am the incumbent of this parish, officer?"

"Yes. I realise it fully. With all respect to your cloth, I still advise you to answer Mr. Woolfall's question."

"I asked you what you came here for," repeated Gilbert.

"I have been the victim of a hoax, a heartless and profane

hoax," replied Mr. Tupper, his voice rising in agitated falsetto. "I was aroused after I had retired by a ring at my bell, and on going to the front door I was told by a rough fellow that you, Mr. Woolfall, had met with a fatal accident and that you had asked for a minister of religion to come to you." He broke off, as though aware of the incredulity in the faces of his audience.

"Did you know the man who brought the message?" asked Macdonald.

"No. I did not. I was very troubled, very amazed. I asked him who he was, and he replied that he had been to see his folks in High Gimmerdale and had been asked to bring me this message. He ended up: 'You'd better go, mister. He's mortal bad. No time to waste.' With that he left me. I was in a quandary. I did not know what to do."

"Did you telephone to Mr. Woolfall's house to find out the facts?" asked Macdonald.

Mr. Tupper's face crumpled more than ever. "I went to the telephone," he said, "but I could not get an answer from exchange. And while I waited I thought that it was my duty to go to Mr. Woolfall without delay." He broke off, and then added unhappily: "I was very much troubled. Through no fault of my own I have been blamed for the tragedy of Mrs. Ramsden's death. Very hard things have been said. Very hard. Very uncharitable. I realised that I had forfeited the confidence of my parishioners." He broke off and rubbed his hair into even worse confusion and when he spoke again it was almost in a wail of appeal. "Can't you understand? I dared not let it be said that I had failed in my duty to the dying. It was my duty to go. And it was all so very inconvenient," he cried, in petulant anti-climax. "I had not got my car. I did not wish to ring up the garage. Daleham had been most disrespectful. To put it shortly, I got dressed and set out on foot. It was all I could do."

"Let's get the time fixed, sir," said Macdonald. "What time was it when the man called you up?"

"It was eleven fifteen. I noticed the time. I left the house by eleven forty-five."

Macdonald considered for a moment. At eleven fifteen he himself had been approaching the ridge of Hawkshead: Hoggett had been well on his way up the track beyond the church. Woolfall and Jock Shearling had been fast asleep—or said they had been fast asleep.

"Did you not tell anybody at your home that you were going out, sir?"

"There was no one to tell. My wife is away. It was all very difficult, very difficult indeed," moaned Mr. Tupper. "It is five miles by road from Ewedale to High Gimmerdale, but there is a footpath over the fells which is shorter, considerably shorter. I thought I could get there in an hour. It seemed the best thing to do at the time, but it took me longer than I anticipated. And then on the steepest bit of the path I slipped and had a bad fall, a very bad fall. I rolled down the slope. Indeed I think that I was nearly senseless for a while. When I recovered, I made what speed I could, but it was very painful. I had been badly shaken, and I am no longer very robust. When I reached Aikengill, I saw there was a glimmer of light in the windows and finding the front door unsecured I went in. Was it not a natural thing to do? I had been summoned to come, I had made a great effort and I was almost exhausted. I came into the hall, and immediately Herdwick found me he was not only suspicious, he was abusive. I am not accustomed to being spoken to in such a manner. It was all most unpleasant, most unpleasant. He did not believe me, *would* not believe me…"

"It sounds a bit of a tall story to me, I must admit," said Gilbert Woolfall unsympathetically, "so perhaps in the circumstances Mr. Herdwick isn't to be blamed."

"Are you having the effrontery to tell me that you do not believe what I have told you?" demanded Mr. Tupper.

Macdonald intervened here: "This is a police case, sir. Speaking as a policeman, I find a little corroboration worth a lot of belief. Is there any point at which your story can be corroborated?"

"I have given you my word, that should be sufficient," retorted Mr. Tupper. "As I told you, I was alone in the house. I had to make a decision and I did what I thought to be right. In doing my duty I have suffered much hardship: you have only to look at the deplorable state I am in to realise what I have been through. To be insulted on top of everything, to be regarded with suspicion and spoken to with contumely, is more than my forbearance can tolerate."

"I don't want to argue, sir, but I might point out that you are not the only person who has had a tough time to-night," said Macdonald. "With Mr. Woolfall, Jock Shearling, and Mr. Hoggett, I have just come in from carrying a casualty several miles up the valley. We found a badly injured man in the valley bottom. It is essential that we should know the actions of everybody who was out and about in High Gimmerdale to-night. You have told us a story of which there is no corroboration, and one which, by its lack of common-sense, carries no conviction."

"What else could I have done?" wailed Mr. Tupper.

"You say that you could get no answer from the telephone exchange, sir. I will have that investigated. But one thing you could have done: there is a police constabulary in Ewedale. Any serious accident should be reported to the police. Why did you not call in at the police constable's house and report to him this very odd story which had been told to you by a stranger, and a rough fellow at that, according to your own statement?"

"I did not envisage the matter as police business. I did what I thought to be right," said Mr. Tupper tremulously. "And now, officer, I must ask you to use your authority to obtain transport for me that I may return to my home. I am exhausted. I refuse to be interrogated further."

"I can get a police car to take you home," replied Macdonald. "If you had only used a minimum of common-sense you could have got one to bring you out. The police would have been only too anxious to investigate your story."

"Ee, but did he want t' police to investigate aught?" demanded Daniel Herdwick's sardonic voice from the kitchen door. The farmer came stolidly into the room and stood looking down at the tremulous parson. "'Tis this way, Rector. I've no call to quarrel with you: you're parson, and you've a position to keep up. 'Tis right you should ask for a bit of respect—but I reckon it works both ways. If so be you forget yourself and speak to me as you did speak when I found you poking around in Mr. Woolfall's hall, well, you'll get the rough side of my tongue, too. We're in a fair old mix-up here and no mistake. There's trouble around. Don't you go making it worse and not better."

"You accused me of lying," quavered Mr. Tupper.

"Maybe I did: I was up all last night and best part of to-night as well, what with a heifer calving, keeping Maggie and me on our feet when we was fair tired-out, and I'll admit I was none too sweet-tempered. I told you 'twas a fool story you told me. I still say so. But I shouldn't ha' gone so far if you hadn't tried to treat me like dirt. 'Twon't work. I tell you so straight." He turned to Macdonald. "Now I've got that bit said, is there anything against me going back to bed? I've got to work, come morning."

"Nothing at all," replied Macdonald, "except that morning's nearly here. I advise everybody to go to bed. I'll ring through for a police car for Mr. Tupper."

"And I'm going to have my drink," said Gilbert. "Where's Jock? He ought to have a drink, too."

"Jock's in your uncle's arm-chair, as fast asleep as a baby," said Herdwick. "I don't reckon he meant to go to sleep. It just came over him. Don't blame him, neither." With a tremendous yawn the farmer stumped off.

Gilbert Woolfall, with the whisky bottle in one hand and a tumbler in the other, glanced at Mr. Tupper. The Rector's head was nodding feebly from side to side as sleep claimed him too.

"Lord, what a night!" groaned Woolfall. He turned to Macdonald. "Say when."

"Not for me. I've got to keep awake till I've done some telephoning, got rid of this complication (pointing to the somnolent Rector), and told our chaps what to do next."

"How much did you believe of his story?"

"At this hour of the night and in these circumstances, I don't believe anything or anybody. I'm a hundred per cent sceptic," said Macdonald. "Take yourself off to bed. After I've packed off the reverend I'll go to sleep myself. We're all too tired to be reasonable. We'll sort it out in the morning."

"Amen to that," said Gilbert, as he lowered a good tot of whisky.

I I

Woolfall went into the sitting-room and shook the reluctant Jock into wakefulness and dragged him upstairs. "Sleeping in a chair's no good to you, Jock. You'll wake up cramped and aching. Come and lie flat for an hour or two, it's worth the effort of getting upstairs."

They trudged off and left Macdonald to the telephone. He phoned to Carnton and eventually got put through to the sergeant.

"It's Macdonald speaking, from High Gimmerdale. I want a police car sent up to Aikengill. The Reverend Tupper is here: he seems to have been the victim of a hoax, and he walked out here and isn't fit to walk back. I want a responsible officer to go back home with him and to stay at the Rectory until further orders. I'll explain that further when your man arrives."

"Very good, sir. I'll come out myself."

"Good. Now I don't want Chief Inspector Bord called up at this hour. I think he's going to have a busy day in front of him and there's nothing he can do until daylight, but phone this report through to him in a couple of hours time: ready? Here it is: Chief Inspector Macdonald walked back from Slaidburn as arranged and met Mr. Hoggett just below Ramshead. They found an unconscious man in the valley bottom. Mr. Hoggett went back to Aikengill for help and returned with Mr. Woolfall and Jock Shearling. The casualty was carried back to Aikengill where Dr. McTay examined him and took him to the infirmary by ambulance. Woolfall and Shearling are both here, at Aikengill. I shall stay here until Chief Inspector Bord arrives. Got all that? Read it back… That's all right. Come out as soon as you can and take Mr. Tupper home. Very good."

Replacing the receiver, Macdonald waited for a moment and then asked exchange to connect him with the Ewedale exchange.

"This is a Police Inquiry," he said. "Chief Inspector Macdonald, C.I.D., speaking. You will be having an inquiry from the Carnton police concerning any calls put through your exchange since ten o'clock last night. I thought I'd warn you, so that you can leave a report before you go off duty. What I particularly want to know is this: did any subscriber on the Ewedale exchange try to get a number between eleven o'clock and midnight?"

"No, sir. I can tell you that straight away. I came on duty at 10.0. There was no Ewedale call after 10.30, neither incoming nor outgoing. It's usually very quiet on this line at night."

"Did you leave the switchboard for any reason between eleven and twelve? If so, say so. There's been a complaint from a Ewedale number that no answer could be got from exchange about 11.20."

"No one called, sir. I'll swear to that."

"Well, think it over. If you did leave the switchboard for a moment, better say so. No one is going to blame you for a moment's inattention at that hour."

"Well, sir, the High Gimmerdale number you're calling from now has been put through to us for connection three times to-night, for Kirkholm, Lancaster, and Carnton. Have you had any delay over any of those calls?"

"No. I haven't. All right. But think it over. Good night."

"Good night, sir—but you can take it that it's the truth when I tell you no Ewedale subscriber tried to get me between eleven and midnight."

Macdonald put back the receiver and allowed himself to yawn. Then he went into the kitchen and had a long drink of cold water and a wash. He would have liked a cup of tea, but there was no electric power, and the fire which Herdwick had made was burning low. The police car from Carnton was to be expected within the next quarter of an hour, so Macdonald prowled round the house simply to keep himself awake. He could have taken the twelve-mile walk over the hills from Slaidburn in his stride, so to speak, but the trek up the valley taking his turn with the stretcher had used up all his reserves of energy, and he knew that if he sat down in the warm sitting-room he would simply fall asleep, as Jock Shearling had done—and as Mr. Tupper had done.

Macdonald looked in at the dining-room door: the Rector was snoring gently, his mouth wide open, his head tilted backwards somewhat askew, looking remarkably foolish. It was a silly face rather than an ill-disposed one, thought Macdonald. Now that sleep had eliminated the petulant effort at dignity characteristic of Mr. Tupper's waking hours, the sagging muscles and network of worried lines revealed an aspect of puerility. But sheer stupidity had led some men to do very unexpected things in Macdonald's experience. Was it possible that stupidity and fear had led this man to do a thing which no amount of self-deception could persuade him was justifiable? The setting alight of the cellar was a job which had needed no particular vigour or skill. Given some petrol to start the blaze, anyone could have done it, an old man as easily as a young one, a woman or a boy. The house was presumed to be empty: the fire could be calculated to do just what it had done—destroy the contents of the study. If no life had been lost, it was probable that a verdict of accident might have been accepted very easily. The fire insurance company would have paid for the damage. With a somewhat sardonic humour Macdonald realised that Mr. Tupper's activities this evening had proved one thing—that he was capable of walking over the fells from Ewedale and that he knew the path. But what had he come for? Macdonald was too sleepy to be constructive: he found his mind harking back to contemporary verse:

> "…either you had no purpose
>   Or the purpose was beyond the end you figured…"

He shook himself and continued his perambulations in the silent house. If he had got to the state of quoting T. S. Eliot sub-consciously he must be wool-gathering. Then he remembered the little gaunt church and realised that "Little Gidding" must have been playing hide-and-seek in his mind all the time.

He went upstairs and looked in on Woolfall and Jock Shearling. They didn't stir. It would have taken a shaking to wake either of them. "And they turned in at nine o'clock, both of them, confound them," thought Macdonald sleepily, "and neither knew anything more about the other until Hoggett came and woke them... That'll be the sergeant's car, God be praised."

Macdonald went down and had a talk with the sergeant before he roused the sleeping Rector.

"Mr. Tupper came out here because of a message from an unknown visitor stating that Mr. Woolfall was in a dying condition," said Macdonald, realising that the sergeant, also, was looking sceptical. "There are three possibilities: that Mr. Tupper was dreaming, that a malicious hoax was played on him, or that someone wanted to get him out of his own house for their own purposes. It's possible that the Rectory may have been burgled in his absence. That's why I want you to go back there with him and stay there, so that nothing is interfered with."

"Very good, sir. I understand," replied the sergeant, who was obviously quick in the uptake. He added: "In case of damage, or obvious breaking and entering, do I report to Chief Inspector Bord?"

"Yes. You'll have to. But tell him I'd like to look into it myself. He'll understand. If I have a couple of hours' sleep, that'll do me. At the moment I'm so sleepy I could sleep on my feet. I want to stay here for the moment, just in case any other practitioners get busy."

"Would you like me to send another man up, sir?"

"No. I'd rather leave things as they are. Now I'll go and wake your passenger. He's feeling the worse for wear."

Macdonald went and woke Mr. Tupper: the two candles on the mantelshelf were just burning out, and the whole tableau was bizarre in the extreme. Helping the tottery little man to his feet, Macdonald said: "I've given the sergeant orders to go into the house with you and to stay there until further orders."

"But that's quite unnecessary, quite unnecessary," quavered Mr. Tupper.

"Well, I don't think it's unnecessary," retorted Macdonald, "so you'll have to put up with it."

"But people may imagine things, may make malicious suggestions…a policeman in the house…it's open to misinterpretation," wailed Mr. Tupper.

"They can imagine what they like," snapped Macdonald. "No law-abiding person can object to police protection, and police protection is what you're going to have, sir. Now come along—I shall be telling you to come quietly in a minute. I'm tired of to-night."

At last the crumpled and still protesting cleric was packed in the back of the smart police car and Macdonald bolted the front door and went into the sitting-room and sat down thankfully on Thomas Woolfall's comfortable settle. The windows were paling as dawn drew near and the first curlew called his questing note. Before his mate had time to call back, the C.I.D. man was already asleep.

CHAPTER XV

I

FAST ASLEEP THOUGH HE WAS, MACDONALD WOKE UP immediately when there was a sound in the silent house. He stretched himself on the settle and listened to movement overhead, and then footsteps on the stairs. It was a brilliant morning now, and the sun was shining across the room. Macdonald sat up as Jock Shearling tiptoed clumsily into the room.

"Hallo. You're bright and early," said Macdonald. "I should have thought you could have treated yourself to another hour after the sort of night you had."

"T' cows ha' got to be milked," said Jock simply. "I'll get some kindling and make a cup o' tea. 'Twon't take a minute."

Macdonald stood up and stretched himself, wriggled his shoulders, flexed his arms and decided he felt none the worse for the night's activities. Before he'd got his shoes on he could already hear the crackle of sticks in the kitchen grate and the purposeful rhythm of the bellows. By the time he'd strolled into the kitchen the kettle was already singing above the blazing sticks.

"I reckon you can boil a kettle faster like that than on an electric plate," he said to Jock.

"Twice as fast," rejoined Jock, still busy with the bellows, and adding handfuls of dry kindling at intervals. "A right hot fire dry sticks do make."

The heat came out gratefully across the kitchen and Macdonald collected teapot and cups and saucers and they were soon enjoying a scalding brew. Jock glanced round the kitchen.

"'Tis a right good job Betty's coming along to clean up," he said. "If Mrs. Ramsden could see this house now she'd have a fit and no mistake: a proper muck it's in. She'll cook you some breakfast, Betty will. She'll be along soon now."

"I shan't say no. I'm hungry enough to eat a pretty mouthful. What about you?"

Jock was rummaging in earthenware bread pan and pantry cupboard. He found some bread and cheese and made himself a hefty sandwich. "This'll do me," he said, and then hesitated just as he was at the door. "Mr. Woolfall's still asleep, don't blame him. I should let him be. And I'd like to say him and me was in bed and asleep by half-past nine last night. Leastways I was. But there's nought to prove I didn't get up and go out up yonder and knock yon chap down t' fellside. Time to and spare I had, before Mr. Hoggett came a-calling of us. Reckon that'll be another story for Miss Wetherby to put around. Well, reckon I'd better go and get on with milking. Talking's not going to help, and

Hodges'll be right mad if them cows aren't milked before t' lorry comes."

He went off, and Macdonald filled the kettle again and had another cup of tea before he went upstairs to the bathroom and rummaged for Woolfall's shaving tackle. Before he shaved he went and looked in at Woolfall. The latter was still fast asleep: Macdonald walked across the room and stood beside the sleeping man, but he didn't stir. As he went out into the passage again, Macdonald remembered what Bord had told him about the way the house was built, and how little sound travelled through the solid walls. It seemed obvious that what Jock said was true: he could have got up and gone out last night without Woolfall being any the wiser.

Washed and shaved, Macdonald went downstairs again and a few minutes later Betty Fell came to the kitchen door, her cheeks flushed with the cool breeze, her eyes bright. She stared at Macdonald through the open kitchen door, and he called:

"Come in, Betty. Jock said you were coming to make breakfast and clean up. We had a busy night of it—maybe you've heard already?"

She shook her head. "No. I've just cycled up. I haven't seen anybody to talk to. 'Tweren't more trouble here, surely?"

"Not here. I found a fellow who'd got knocked out, or else had a tumble and knocked himself silly, up the valley below Ramshead. We had to carry him in. Jock came along to help, so he had another poor night." He caught the consternation in her face and added: "Jock's all right. He's in the shippon, milking. Now you get on and cook breakfast. Mr. Woolfall's still in bed. We can take him a tray up later on. He's not used to the amount of exercise he got last night. What've you got in that basket?"

"Eggs, bacon, butter, scones, and some honey. Do you like coffee? Mrs. Ramsden always made coffee for Mr. Woolfall—and please, who was't you found up Ramshead?"

"We don't know yet, except that it's the same young fellow whom Mr. Woolfall spoke to on the fell a few days ago. Who he is we've no idea. He's been taken to hospital. Now I've got some telephoning to do, so you get on with the breakfast."

Macdonald rang through to Carnton. Although it was only just half-past seven, Inspector Bord had just arrived at his head-quarters and was able to give Macdonald the sergeant's report from Ewedale Rectory.

"It was a burglary all right—that's to say it appears to be a burglary," said Bord. "A window was broken and the place is all upside down. The sergeant said you wanted to have a look round before anything's moved, so I've sent a man to relieve him. The reverend's in bed. He was pretty near collapsing last night so Sergeant Horner said. We're sending a doctor up to order the patient to stay in bed."

"Good idea. Keep him out of the way," said Macdonald.

Bord snorted. "It's a rum story, Chief. We'll have a crack together soon and exchange views. I'm not that keen about talking over the phone. Exchange must be feeling inquisitive by this time, what with one thing and another. Not that they'd listen in. No, but by gum, if I thought they did it'd be the riot act for somebody. Now I thought I'd go along to the infirmary and see if anything can be done about identifying the casualty."

"Good idea," said Macdonald. "Get every detail you can. The surgeons may be able to tell you quite a bit."

"I'll get all I can. I'm sorry you had such a night of it."

"You needn't be. I won't say I enjoyed it all the time, but it was a well-spent night. Now I'm going to have my breakfast. You might ring through to Slaidburn for me and ask one of their chaps to drive my car back here. It's the sort of job they won't mind being asked to do, and we're busier this end than they are."

"I'll see to it. D'you want any help? I can send you a man up if you want one."

"I'll let you know if I want anybody. Has your C.C. squared my old man?"

"By gum, yes, he has. It's all in order—red tape and official instructions and compliments galore all round. On the highest level. Sorry I forgot to tell you."

"Nice to know it's in order," chuckled Macdonald.

A moment later he walked to the dining-room, aware of a smell of sizzling bacon and fragrant coffee that was almost painfully delicious. Betty Fell had laid the breakfast and tidied the room, but upon the sideboard lay a most deplorable and ill-treated clerical hat, one of the flat felts which all curates had worn when Macdonald was young. It looked so ridiculous and out of place on the old oak sideboard, among Thomas Woolfall's pewter tankards, that Macdonald laughed aloud, and Betty looked in with an inquiring face.

"I found that under the table," she said. "Goodness knows how it got there—or how long it's been there."

"Not very long," said Macdonald. "Mr. Tupper was here last night. You're sure to hear about it from somebody, so you may as well know."

He saw a shadow pass over her face and went on: "Look

here: the smell of that bacon and coffee's so good I shall come and snatch it off the stove and wolf it down in a minute. Give me my breakfast—and come and talk to me while I'm eating it."

Betty ran back to the stove and in a few moments had set coffee and hot milk, bacon, and eggs, on the table, and Macdonald sat down to enjoy himself.

"I'll make you some toast: the fire's coming clear now," she said. "I'd have made porridge but there wasn't time."

"Porridge be translated," said Macdonald. "Bacon and eggs are what I want. I've never been so hungry in my life and never has coffee smelt better."

He had ten minutes to himself, during which he made short work of a surprising amount of bacon and three new-laid eggs, and when Betty reappeared with a laden toast rack and a half-pound pat of farm butter, Macdonald said:

"Sit down, and tell me what you're worrying about."

She looked at the deplorable hat. "What was he doing here?" she asked. "He's a parson, and nobody'll blame him—"

"Rubbish. Everybody's blaming him," retorted Macdonald. "Whether he deserves it or not, it's not for me to say, but I think Mr. Tupper was as frightened and miserable all day yesterday as a man could be. He walked out here in the middle of the night, tumbled head over heels in the dark, tried to bully Mr. Herdwick when he got here and was bullied by Mr. Herdwick instead. Let's forget about him. Betty, how long have your people lived in Low Gimmerdale?"

"I don't know how long, but 'tis over a hundred years. One of my folk married a Woolfall once—in 1850 that was."

"That's interesting," said Macdonald. "I expect your

parents have talked to you about this house. Can you tell me who lived here before Mr. Thomas Woolfall bought it back?"

"I'll try," she said. "I don't know about all of them, but I've heard tell of quite a lot. The old parson lived here till 1905. They say he bought the place cheap, and he let the land off to Mr. Lamb down in Kirkholm. Farming was in a bad way those days and sheep was hardly worth more'n a few shillings. When the parson died, a Mr. Hornby bought the house and land. He came from Kendal way. My mother says the house was like a pigsty when parson died, and 'twasn't much better when Hornbys had it. Nine children they had and Mrs. Hornby couldn't manage them. Hornbys farmed here till 1930, when Mr. Hornby died and the place was sold again. 'Twas said Mr. Herdwick bid for it, but he didn't bid enough. Anyway, 'twas bought by a Mr. Hogg. I remember Mr. Hogg, he was here when I was a little lass. He came from the Midlands and brought some of his own sheep with him— cross-bred border Leicesters. But he didn't understand fell farming, and he lost his flock and let off the fell rights to Mr. Herdwick. 'Twas expected Mr. Hogg would fail and have to give up, but he managed somehow with a few dairy cows in the bottom and some pigs. Mr. Hogg was here until 1946. When he died everyone thought Aikengill would be on the market again, and then 'twas found Mr. Thomas Woolfall had bought it during the war some time, and when Mr. Hogg died, Mr. Woolfall came and set the place to rights. You can't think what this house was like before Mr. Woolfall came—awful old place 'twas, all dark and miserable." She broke off. "I've just been going on. Was that what you wanted to know?"

"Yes. Exactly what I wanted to know," said Macdonald.

"You've got a good memory, Betty. Let's see if I've got it right. The parson was here till 1905—a 'perpetual curate' was what they called him, wasn't it? Then a farmer from Kendal bought the property—Mr. Hornby—and he was here until 1930, when Mr. Hogg bought it. He came from the Midlands and didn't make much of a do of it, and he sold it to Mr. Woolfall who let Hogg stay on as tenant until he died in 1946. I'm interested in this house, you know. You say it was dark and miserable. Did Mr. Woolfall make any structural alterations?"

"Goodness, yes. He altered it out of all knowing. There used to be a passage right along one side of t' house—matchboarding it was, and it cut off a big bit from all these rooms. And the study was just a sort of lumber room, never used. The windows were all grown over with ivy. Mrs. Ramsden said the room'd never been properly turned out since the old parson had it, and its floorboards were all rotten. It was Mr. Woolfall made the house like it is now—or like 'twas before this fire. Mr. Gilbert says he's going to put it to rights again and I hope he does."

"I think he will," said Macdonald, pouring himself out another cup of coffee. To all appearances, he was enjoying an aimless gossip: in actual fact he was learning a number of things which were very relevant to his case.

Lighting a cigarette, he went on: "When Hornbys were here with nine children, where did they go to school?"

"Why, in the little school here," said Betty. "My mother remembers that. 'Twas a church school, of course, but the Council paid teacher, same's in Low Gimmerdale. 'Twas comic like: at one time 'twas only Hornbys in school. There weren't no other children in High Gimmerdale. Then it came down to only two children and teacher got ill, so those two went down to Low Gimmerdale to our school. There was about twelve of us in school when I was there. Now all the children are taken down to Ewedale in the school bus. 'Tis better really, they get better teaching."

"Whom does this school building belong to, Betty, have you any idea?"

"I suppose it belongs to the church," she replied. "I know Mr. Tupper said it ought to be sold and the money given to the Ewedale Church School. We had a good laugh over that. Who ever'd buy it and what'd they buy it for? 'Tis only that tiny room and no water and no light—not fit to live in."

Macdonald laughed. "You should know that, Betty."

"Well—we thought about it," she admitted, "but 'tweren't no good. You couldn't sleep and eat and cook and wash clothes in there. Not even a fireplace—just an old iron stove, and fetch your water from the beck, and that's a right long way to carry buckets."

"Well, thanks for answering all my questions," said Macdonald. "You're a proper countrywoman, you remember all about who farmed in the different steadings, even years before you were born yourself."

"Well, I've heard Mother and Dad talking, and then Mrs. Ramsden, she used to ask about who lived here. Perhaps it's because I've always thought I should like to live here. I love this house, I like looking down on its long roof."

She got up, her face flushed, and said: "I'd better be getting busy cleaning up. 'Tis in a proper mess, the whole house is."

"Thank you for my good breakfast—and listen for Mr.

Woolfall. He'll be hungry, too, though I don't expect he'll wake for a couple of hours yet."

I I

Macdonald strolled outside into the keen sunny air and turned up the hill towards Lambsrigg. It was a solid, prosperous stone building, but it had none of the beauty of Aikengill: the proportion of wall to roof, the angle of the gable, the setting of the windows were all wrong from the point of view of design. But Lambsrigg had been built by people of some pretensions. The front door opened on to a wide flagged walk, and in front of this was a lawn which had been recently scythed, and parts of it clipped by a lawn mower. There were some wallflowers in the beds, and daffodils round the hedges. By the front door, a tall, stoutly built woman was raising her voice in vigorous protest to a wizened old man. Macdonald guessed (rightly) that the woman was Maggie Herdwick and the old man was Tegg, the shepherd. Miss Herdwick was obviously very indignant, Tegg not at all put about: in fact he was having a good laugh to himself.

"I never saw the like, never in me life," he wheezed. "'Tis right comic, that be. Dead men's shoes I've heard tell on, and that do put me in mind o' dead men's shoes."

"Don't you be talking so much nonsense, Tegg," she snapped. "Look at all the trouble I take to keep a decent bit of garden to make the house look nice, and then you go and do a thing like that. It makes me right mad!"

Macdonald walked serenely up the flagged path towards the house, very much interested in this altercation, and Tegg greeted him gleefully.

" 'Tis the London detective!" he said. "You come right up here and take a look at this. Never saw such a thing in me life, never. You take a look and tell us the rights of it."

Macdonald had a good look at the strip of grass which had been clipped short by the mower. Across the pale green of the mown area were brown marks where the grass was dead, and these marks had obviously been made by a man's footsteps. Wherever he had trodden, the grass had died, and the dead patches made a queer meandering line, showing that the walker had strolled casually across the lawn and wandered about a bit. It was certainly a very odd effect.

Tegg continued to chuckle. "What do 'e make o' that? 'Tis a job for a detective, I say. Dead men's shoes!"

"Oh, have done with your nonsense, Tegg. I've no patience with you!" snapped Maggie. "You ought to have more sense."

"Maybe I did ought, and I'm not t' only one," retorted Tegg with spirit. "If tha' can't speak civil I'll ha' done with tha'. I got me pension and 'tis all the same to me if I don't do no more shepherding. Then if tha's rid o' me and quit o' Jock Shearling too, tha'll be in a proper mulock." With which spirited retort he stumped off, with something very like a wink towards Macdonald.

The latter turned to Maggie Herdwick. "Good morning. It's bad luck to see your lawn looking all piebald. My guess is that Tegg got weed-killer on his clogs."

"And you wouldn't be far out," she replied crossly. "I did put weed-killer on the cobbles and flags yesterday. They looked such a sight with grass and nettles coming up in all the cracks. I was ill last summer and nothing got done and you could hardly see the flagstones for weeds and that. I haven't got time to pull them up, and none of the men will give a hand these days like they used, so I just doused the stones in weed-killer, and what must Tegg do but go tramping over it while it was still all wet and then walk it on to my lawn, because it's the quickest way for him to get to the ewes in that paddock. And 'twasn't as though he didn't know, either, because I told him."

"I expect it will soon grow out," said Macdonald consolingly. "When the rain washes the weed-killer away the grass will grow over the patches."

"Maybe it will, but I don't like the look of it," she said. "There's something uncanny looking about it. I could shake that old fool, with his dead men's shoes."

"I thought it was rather a good effort of imagination on Tegg's part," said Macdonald. "It does look a bit ghostly, I admit. He's a great age, isn't he?"

"He's about eighty," she replied. "He's been a very good shepherd in his time, and he's still very clever with the ewes: he hardly ever loses a lamb. But he's a dratted old nuisance all the same: he's that independent you can't say a word to him." She sniffed indignantly and then added: "Do you want to see my father? I hope not, because he's still asleep. Two nights he's had with hardly any sleep, and all this night watching they've been doing—he's getting old, you know. He's nearly seventy, though he doesn't look it, and he gets tired faster than he used."

"In that case I won't disturb him," said Macdonald. "I'm trying to get to know the folks hereabouts, and I'm interested in Tegg. He's a wonderful man for eighty, still being able to get about the fells."

"He's done it all his life," she replied. "We've a saying hereabouts—'You can do what you've always done'—and it's true. One day Tegg'll say he can't tramp the fells any more, and then he'll die, quite sudden like. His father went that way I'm told: came in from seeing to the ewes, sat down in his chair, and died."

"Not a bad way to die," said Macdonald, and she nodded.

"Might do worse. But I'm forgetting my manners—come in and sit down, do. I've got a lamb in the oven, and I must see to it. Come in."

She led the way round the house (not through the front door, that was evidently more for appearances than use) but by the foldyard to the kitchen. Here they found Tegg again. There was a very low fire in the grate, and a newborn lamb lay on a sack in the oven. Tegg lifted it out and stood it on its spindly legs, supporting it as it tottered uncertainly. "Her'll do champion," he said happily. "'S afternoon I'll put 'er to Darkie. Darkie's got plenty for two."

"Take your dirty clogs off my clean floor, do," exclaimed Maggie Herdwick indignantly. "Leave the lamb to me. I've never lost a lamb yet—not one that could live. What's the use o' scrubbing the flags if you muck 'em up as soon as they're done?"

"You're ower sharp, mistress," said Tegg. "If so be you minded your tongue as well as you mind them flagstones, 'twould be better belike."

He put the lamb back in the oven and walked off, and Macdonald said: "Was it this same Tegg who worked in Aikengill for the old parson? Mr. Hoggett happened to mention that to me."

"Oh no. That was Tegg's father—old Aaron. This one's young Aaron," she replied. "He's been a shepherd all his life. He started at Roeburndale, but he's worked at Lambsrigg for nigh on fifty years—nearly all my life that is. I remember old Aaron, but not when he was at Aikengill. A right dirty old man he was, too, and what that house was like when *he* cleaned it, the lord knows. 'Twas always a mess that house was till old Mr. Woolfall came there. He changed it so you'd hardly have known 'twas the same house inside."

"I expect you got to know Mrs. Ramsden quite well, Miss Herdwick."

"Well, I did and I didn't. She was always one to keep herself to herself like, and I hadn't much patience with her finicking ways: I'm used to a farmhouse. It's clean enough, this house is, but homely. Mrs. Ramsden, she likes to think Woolfalls was better-me-like, but she was a real hard worker. 'Twas a sad and shocking thing her dying like that. If Rector had done as he aught, that wouldn't never have happened."

"What do you think happened, Miss Herdwick?"

"Don't ask me. 'Twas those thieving villains I reckon. But I'll say this. I don't like to see Jock Shearling getting his foot in there so easy like. And that Betty—bold as brass, she is. She's up there now, isn't she?" Her mouth shut with a snap and her work-worn hands were trembling a little. She added hastily: "Not that I'm saying anything. I don't know nought about it. But I don't hold with their goings on."

She cocked her head as she heard a sound overhead. "That'll be Father. I must get his breakfast."

Macdonald turned to the door, recognising that she

wanted him out of the way. "I must be getting along," he said. He glanced out at the foldyard and the flagstones round the door where withered grass showed that weed-killer had been put down.

"What weed-killer do you use?" he asked. "You wouldn't use any of the arsenic mixtures in a farmyard."

"None o' that poisonous stuff," she said. "'Tis a white salt. You mix it with water. Don't harm nothing—except the weeds."

"That'd be sodium chlorate?" asked Macdonald.

"Maybe. I don't remember all them names. I asked the corn miller for some weed-killer that'd be safe to use here. Cost a pretty penny and there wasn't that much of it."

Macdonald left her and walked back to Aikengill deep in thought. Maggie Herdwick was an unusual woman. She hadn't asked a single question.

Before he went into Aikengill to find if Gilbert Woolfall had got up, Macdonald went down to the cellar where the fire had started. Most of the water had seeped away through the drain, but the flags were inches deep in malodorous black slime. There was a stone ledge along one side of the cellar: it rested on blocks of stone, and any kindling or logs which had been stacked on it would have been drier than those on the floor. Jock had said that the wood had been green "running with sap." Macdonald stood and stared at the slab, deep in thought, until he heard a sound behind him and turned to see Betty Fell.

"I heard you come in," she said. "Mr. Hoggett's just rung up and I told him you were all right. Mr. Woolfall's come down to breakfast and he hasn't got any cigarettes."

"I've got two, so he shall have one," said Macdonald. "How far are we from a cigarette shop, Betty?"

"Kirkholm's nearest. That's six miles."

"I'd better ring up Mr. Hoggett," said Macdonald.

CHAPTER XVI

I

MACDONALD WENT INTO THE HOUSE AND FOUND Gilbert Woolfall enjoying his breakfast.

"Any more news from the Front?" inquired Gilbert.

"Only that Miss Herdwick has been indulging in a bout of gardening to celebrate the spring, involving the application of weed-killer in bulk," replied Macdonald. "Young Aaron Tegg walked in the weed-killer and then perambulated over the lawn. The result is what young Aaron calls 'Dead men's shoes.' You ought to go and see it. It's an odd sight."

"What's that got to do with the matter in hand?" asked Woolfall.

"I don't know. I'll leave you to consider the application," said Macdonald. "It seems a bit hard to interrogate you at breakfast, but I hope you'll co-operate. I want an answer to a lot of questions, beginning with what Hoggett calls the 'hocus-pocus' over the transfer of stipends, continuing with the present location of parish registers and the sources from which your uncle obtained information for his historical researches, and some details of the residents in this house during the last half-century or so."

"I'll do my best, but I'm not really an authority on any of those points," said Gilbert. "It's true that I read most of Uncle Thomas's scripts, but my memory for historical facts has never been very reliable. However—lay on."

They talked for a solid hour, and Macdonald made notes of such facts as he considered essential, after basing his questions on the information he had acquired from the Hoggetts and from Betty Fell. At the conclusion of his questions, he read out his notes and said to Woolfall: "Does that summary suggest anything relevant to you?"

"Good God, yes!" burst out Woolfall. "I'd got all the facts for myself; I can't think why I didn't tumble to it."

"All we have got is a suggestion," said Macdonald. "If it's correct, then the motive for some recent activities is fairly plain. Fortunately, the idea is verifiable, and I can get the authorities to supply the necessary facts. But kindly remember that what I've postulated is a hypothesis and no more. Don't imagine it's all over bar the shouting. Meantime I've got a lot to do. I want to do a bit of research in the cellar to begin with. You can co-operate by talking business with Miss Betty Fell, thereby occupying her in this room for at least ten minutes." Seeing the reluctant expression on Woolfall's face, Macdonald added: "Betty is fairly quick in the uptake, and what Betty notices will be passed on to Jock. I don't want anything passed on to anybody."

"All right. I'll see to it," said Woolfall.

"Then I'm going up to Ramshead again," said Macdonald, "and after that to see the reverend, who is confined to his bed. There is one other job I should like to delegate to you."

"What is it this time?" asked Woolfall anxiously.

"Go and buy some cigarettes," said Macdonald.

I I

Macdonald walked up to Ramshead at a good swinging pace. He was a bit stiff to begin with, but the harder he walked the better he felt. It was a glorious morning, sunshine and birdsong combining to enhance the magnificence of the grey fells. Macdonald walked fast not only because he liked it but because he wanted to know what was the shortest time in which a man could reach the Ramshead cottage from High Gimmerdale. Hoggett had taken an hour to do the distance, walking at his leisure, but he had run back in less than half an hour. Macdonald believed he could knock at least ten minutes off the outgoing time but doubted if he could beat the return run. That had been a very good effort.

As he walked, Macdonald argued out afresh the main points of the case he was formulating: he had a theory, but its validity had yet to be proved, and he was fully aware that there were several alternative theories which could be propounded with equal ease. In most similar cases some suspects could be ruled out because they had not the physical strength for acts of violence, but in this case no great strength was involved. The firing of the cellar could have been done by anybody. Next came the assault Macdonald believed had been committed against the vagrant lad whom they had found last night. When Macdonald had flattened himself against the rock to let Hoggett pass, it had not only been to avoid startling Hoggett and provoking a sudden tackle from that once redoubtable rugger player: it had been to demonstrate to himself how easy it would be to trip up an unsuspecting man on that steep fellside. A stick between his legs would have done it, and once a man had started rolling down that gradient it was very improbable he would have been able to check himself; a knock on the head when he hit the rocks at the bottom might well be calculated to put paid to the casualty. As for the walking distance involved, since "young" Aaron Tegg at eighty-plus could take Ramshead (very literally) in his stride, age could not be said to debar the elderly from joining in suspected activities.

Turning by the outcrop of rock where he had waited for Hoggett to pass last night, Macdonald went on up to the cottage. The front door was jammed in place by its stone, but the shippon door stood open, as it had done last night. But, unlike last night, the sun was streaming into the little dark lean-to building—a very different matter from misty moonbeams and the light of a torch. Along one wall was a pile of bedding, dry heather, and bracken, deep and springy. It still showed where it had been weighted down by a recumbent body. There were a couple of big sacks on it, and a sack stuffed with bracken had done duty as a pillow. Macdonald had seen many a worse bed: he moved the bedding, pushing it aside, and found that at the foot of it, under the bracken, was a stone trough, doubtless fashioned long ago to hold drinking water for the beasts who had wintered there. In the trough, well concealed under the bracken, was a haversack, holding half of a loaf of bread, some red-skinned polony, two eggs, and a tin of herrings. In addition was a small tin holding a mixture of tea and sugar, and an enamel drinking mug and plate. Rummaging along the ledge of a beam, above his own eye level, Macdonald found a tin billy-can and a tin cooking plate which had been used for frying. "That seems clear enough. The chap could come here any night and find shelter, a fireplace, fuel for the gathering and a safe hideout," thought Macdonald. He went outside again and looked down towards the beck: then he made his way down, searching patiently in the hope of finding anything which might give an indication of where the lad had started his headlong flight. He found two things: one was an enamel can such as country folk use for fetching milk from a farm: this lay in the heather, not far above the place where the boy had lain. Higher up the slope was a more interesting find—a shepherd's crook. "Good Lord, of course that'd be it," said Macdonald. "What easier instrument for tripping a man up? The shepherds can catch a sheep by the leg while the beast's going full tilt. It'd be the easiest thing in the world for them to trip a man with it."

He tied his handkerchief round the crook and holding the can by its handle climbed up once more to the track.

When he came within sight of the shippon door again, he saw a wizened figure in the doorway: there was no mistaking "young Aaron." The old shepherd was staring through the door, which was now open again. (Macdonald had closed it.) Macdonald hoped to get up there quietly and take the old man unawares, but he had forgotten there would be a sheep dog. A sharp bark from the collie and Tegg turned round, staring about him with his long-sighted eyes, his leathery face creased into a multitude of wrinkles. Macdonald went on steadily and Tegg suddenly grinned a toothless grin. He waited until the younger man was only a few yards away and then he said:

"Ee, art goin' to take my job on? Tha'll ha' to learn to 'andle a crook more workmanlike than that there."

"The crooks I handle aren't shepherds' crooks," replied Macdonald, who was quite sure that Tegg was by no means slow in the uptake. "I found this thing down on the fellside yonder. Is it yours by any chance?"

"Nay. I got mine here," replied Tegg. "Had it d'un-a-many years. Younger than tha' I was, mister, when I first had 'un."

He turned and pointed into the shippon. "Someone been making 'emselves at 'ome, seemingly."

"Aye. That's about it," agreed Macdonald. "Did you know the place was being used, Tegg?"

"Nay. That I did not," retorted the old man vigorously. "I don't come nigh the place. Sixty year 'tis since that place was lived in. I was a lad o' twenty and I coom up Ramshead with Adam Theave. Moses Woolton lived here, and nobody'd set eyes on him for weeks, not since afore the great snow. That was a snow, that was. No getting oop here, 'twas too deep. Starved and dead he was, and t' old cow in t' shippon dead too. Starved. Frozen like, hard as boards. I never forgotten that. Many's t' time I reckoned I saw Moses oop here when I been up at nights, lambing times. His dog was alive tho'—curled up in a corner under t' old saddle. Eaten the leather she had, eaten t' rushes on t' chairs and t' rag mats on floor. But she 'adn't touched Moses. I carried her down home and nursed her like a babby. A good dog she was. This 'n's the same breed."

"That's a sad story," said Macdonald, and Tegg nodded.

"Aye. Tha' can't picture Ramshead in a winter like that'n. T' sheep was all buried in drifts. 'Twas March too. 'Tis worse come springtime. Hay's all finished, roots all finished, nothing to give t' beasts. Moses, reckon 'e lived on porridge and taties and a bit o' salt pork, and 'e'd got none left. Caught 'e was. Couldn't get down through t' snow and went to bed and waited for t' snow to let up, and it didn't let up. No one's never lived here since."

"I don't wonder. How did he ever keep a cow up here?"

"Ee, but 'e'd got some small intaks—pasture and a bit o' meadow. T' walls is all down now and t' land's gone back to fell. But folks had lived up here time out o' mind. But not since Moses died."

Macdonald jerked his mind back from the grim story to his present job. "Tegg, do you reckon it was the sheep thieves who fired Aikengill?"

"Who else?" asked the old man.

"Could they have driven the sheep over Hawkshead?"

"Could they?" The old man laughed. "You watch, mister. I'll show tha'."

Without moving he gave a short whistle. The dog lying so quiet beside him was away like smoke, almost too fast for Macdonald's unaccustomed eyes to follow it. Keeping perfectly still, whistling different notes and occasionally calling words which were unintelligible to Macdonald, Tegg's old eyes followed the dog's progress up the fell as it ran in a wide circle. From nowhere the sheep appeared, bleating and lamenting: at first scattered, running here and there, backward and forward, but gradually being driven into a compact flock as the indefatigable dog ran round them in decreasing circles. Then, after a longer whistle, the dog brought them down to within a few yards of the shepherd and Tegg changed his note again and raised his arms. Slowly, with uncanny skill, the dog edged the bunch forward, allowing none to break away, and drove them in at the shippon door until the small building was packed tight with the ewes and lambs, and the dog sat down panting, on guard beside the door, and Macdonald could have sworn there was a smirk of pride and pleasure on the collie's face.

"Aye," he said. "You've shown me. That's a grand dog, Tegg. Did you train her?"

"Aye. Took her out with her mother, and by gum, the mother taught 'er more'n I did. Didn't half snap at the young 'un when she made a mulock o't. That's the way to train a young dog. Take 'em out with old 'un."

"But the lad we found last night hadn't got a dog, Tegg," persisted Macdonald.

"I know naught about that. In me bed I was an' slep' t' night through, sundown to sunrise. Had enough I had, t' night before. 'Tis no manner o' use asking me aught, mister. All I know is there's a score o' good sheep gone from Ramshead. If 't hadn't been that dratted fire, we'd caught 'em at it, me and Daniel Herdwick. They diddled us." He paused and added: "You've got to use your own wits, mister, not mine."

"I'm trying to," replied Macdonald. "Have you lived in High Gimmerdale all your life, Tegg?"

"Aye, and me feyther before me. I was born in t' cottage where I live now, and I buried me wife and childern in our churchyard. I went to t' school down yonder—and a wun'nerful lot I learned. I can sign me name and that's the lot."

"And count the sheep?" asked Macdonald.

"No need. I know fra' the look of 'em, and I know which ones was took. Now you get on with your job, mister, and I'll get on with mine."

"Can you tell me whose this milk-can is?" demanded Macdonald.

"Nay, how should I know? Tisn't mine. That's all I do know."

I I I

Before Macdonald got back to High Gimmerdale, he met a small flock of lambs and ewes which were being driven back to pasture on the fellside after a week of more luxurious fare in the paddock of Lambsrigg. These were the last batch of ewes to lamb—the shearlings, who had had their first lambs, (being only a year old themselves). Jock was driving them, with his dog running around with anxious care, bullying the laggards and rounding up the stragglers.

Macdonald stopped Jock and asked: "Do you know whose this crook is?"

"Aye. 'Tis mine. Where did you get that from?"

"I found it on the fell below Ramshead, near where that lad fell down last night, and the can nearby."

Jock stared, and a vivid colour came over his square face.

"So that's the way of it," he said. "Thought that might be it when I missed it. Handy to trip yon chap up with."

He stood silent for a moment, fury in his face. "You must reckon I'm a gey gert fule to go chucking my own crook down, all handy like for you to find."

"Steady!" said Macdonald. "Getting mad about it

won't help. D'you know when you had it last, and where you left it?"

"I had it when I was up t' fell yesterday afternoon, and I left it where I always leave it, beside Tegg's, in t' foldyard down yonder." Again he broke off. "Leastways, I think I left it there. I allus does."

"Are you certain you brought it back with you? Didn't Betty come up to find you after she'd been talking to me yesterday?"

"Aye. She did that. We walked back together. She'd remember. Better ask her. Or mebbe Tegg noticed if mine were there, together with his, in t' foldyard." He looked towards the sheep, who were fussing around, trying to break back. "See here, I got to take this bunch back up to their own pasture, or they'll be all ower t' place. Can I go, or are you going to run me in? I know what's in your mind plain enough."

"Then you know more than I do. Of course you can get on with your job—but can you tell me whose the can is?"

"'Tis Mrs. Ramsden's milk-can. You ask Hodges. He ought to know. He must ha' seen it often enough when she came to fetch her milk."

Jock hurried after his sheep and Macdonald went on to the foldyard gate of Lambsrigg. Here he found Hodges, who had just finished brushing the yard out, after taking the cows out to pasture. Hodges was a man of about thirty, heavily built and powerful, fair-skinned and blue-eyed, but with a sullen expression on his face which wasn't promising from the point of view of an interrogator. Macdonald knew that Hodges was a bachelor (unusual for a man of his age in the country) and that he lived with his mother. It was Mrs. Hodges whom the

Rector had been to visit when he refused to let his taxi wait to take Mrs. Ramsden back to Kirkholm.

Macdonald leant on the foldyard gate, aware that Hodges had seen him but was deliberately ignoring him. In the circumstances, this was unusual, and Macdonald watched the man for a while, his mind playing with the policeman's theme: "What's all this about?"

He waited until Hodges had emptied his barrow on the muck heap and then went into the yard.

"Good morning. Mr. Hodges, isn't it? I'm a detective officer—I expect you know that."

"Aye." Hodges faced him sullenly, standing leaning on the heavy broom he had wielded so easily over the cobbles.

"I've just found this crook on the fellside. It's Jock Shearling's. Do you know where he generally keeps it?"

"Nay. 'Tis no business of mine what the shepherds do with their gear. I'm cowman."

"But you clean out the foldyard: are you telling me you don't know where the gear is generally kept?"

"I'm telling you that one crook's same as another to me. Tegg's got one, the boss has got a couple, Shearling's got one and there's some owd ones about. You can see for yourself, they're standing inside t' barn door there, but they're nought to do with me and I don't know t'other from which."

Macdonald was mainly interested because the man was so obstinately sullen and unhelpful. He tried another tack and held out the milk-can. "Do you know whose this is?"

Hodges rubbed his head. "How should I know? 'Tis like any other milk-can. Tegg has one, Alice, the maidservant, has one, Mrs. Ramsden had one, I've got one, Jock's got one."

"Who puts the milk out—the milk supplied to Aikengill?"

"Miss Herdwick does. Better go and ask her."

"Right. I'll go and find her."

Macdonald walked across the yard to the kitchen door and came face to face with Daniel Herdwick. The big farmer called "good morning" cheerfully enough.

"I had my sleep out," he said. "I was fair tired out, what with one thing and another. 'Twas a rum go last night. Mebbe I spoke too sharp to Rector, but when I saw him poking around I reckoned it looked fishy-like. Mr. Hoggett, he'd just come and told us of an injured man up the valley, and then t' reverend turned up, looking for all the world as though he'd been a-scrapping, and as for his story, 'twas as silly a taradiddle as ever I did hear. If some chap came and told him Mr. Woolfall was in a bad way, wouldn't he ha' done what you suggested—gone to police station? 'Tis not that far away from Rectory. And who was the chap left him the message? That's what beats me."

"I'm hoping to find out more about that when I've seen Mr. Tupper," said Macdonald. "I've just been up the valley again, to Ramshead. I found this crook, and the milk-can, not far from where we found the injured man. Jock Shearling says the crook is his, and that he left it in the yard here yesterday. Do you remember seeing it about?"

"Well, now you're asking," said Mr. Herdwick. "Most days I'd a been able to give you a straight answer, but yesterday was all of a worry like. Morning I went up t' fell with Tegg and Shearling to check t' flock between Ramshead and Parsons Lot, and we found the count was short. Afternoon I went up t' other side, across t' beck, to make sure none had strayed that way. Doesn't often happen. Sheep stick to their own pasture, where they've been since they was lambs: they only stray if aught worries them. Tegg went down t' valley, and Jock went up to Ramshead, hunting in them gills and clefts. We had a day o't, sure enough: miles we tramped. By the time I got home I was that tired I just come straight into t' kitchen and fell asleep in me chair—so I wasn't noticing much. As for the gear in the yard, I shouldn't ha' noticed if it'd a been all over yard—provided I didn't fall over it." He stretched his big limbs and yawned. "And that wasn't t' lot. I went to bed early—reckoned I'd earned it—and blessed if I didn't wake up and hear one o' them heifers bawling. Due to calve she was, any time next week, and chose to do't on t' one night when I was dead beat. Maggie had to come and help me out. 'Tis Hodges' job, but he's got his own bit o' trouble, his mother can't last long, poor old soul, and I wasn't bringing him out, heifer or no heifer."

"That was bad luck," said Macdonald. "D'you know what time it was you woke up?"

"Ten o'clock, 'twas. I'd gone to bed before nine, and Maggie, too. And two mortal hours we was with that heifer: a right difficult calving, 'twas—but she's all right now. On her feet again. They generally do all right once they stand oop. T' calf's dead, but 'twas a bull, so it's no great loss."

"Were you still up when you heard someone running past the house and you came out to Aikengill again?"

"I'd gone back to my bedroom—took my boots off and lay down, but I was listening in my sleep as 'twere, lest that heifer was in trouble again. We made a pot o' tea when we came in, Maggie and me, and had a wash like. And then I heard someone running, and when I went to t' window I could see a light shining across t' garden in Aikengill. I went over to see what 'twas. Couldn't do no other, things being as they is." He sighed, and turned to Macdonald, banging one fist on the other. "I tell tha' I shan't stir to-night—no matter what. A chap can do so much and no more, and I've had enough these past two nights."

"Well, I'm sorry to come bothering you when you're tired," said Macdonald. "Can I speak to your daughter? I won't keep her a minute."

"Aye, she's here, in t' kitchen. Step in, and welcome."

When Macdonald asked Maggie Herdwick about the milk-can, she looked at him as though she thought he was weak in the head. Then she called:

"Alice! Come here."

Alice was the maidservant, a sixteen-year-old who came up daily from Low Gimmerdale.

"Alice puts the milk in t' cans," explained Maggie. "Alice, is this your can?"

"No. 'Tis not ours. Ours is like it—but it's chipped on t' side. Hodges's is like that—we both bought 'em at Mrs. Barrow's in Ewedale. No. 'Tis not Hodges—he marked his so's I should know't. Why, 'tis the can Mrs. Ramsden lost not so long ago. Her swore her had put it in t' cooling house, but 'twasn't nowhere. I lent her a jug and she said she'd get another can—but she was real put out."

"What happens about the cans, Alice?" asked Macdonald. "Did Mrs. Ramsden leave her can in the cooling house for you to fill?"

"That's right," said Alice. "She had two cans. When she

came across for t' milk in the morning she took t' full one and left the empty one. And the day one went missing, 'twas the day Mr. Woolfall met that strange fellow up on Hawkshead, and Mrs. Ramsden reckoned he'd looked in t' cooling house—'tis just by foldyard gate—and stolen t' can. 'Tis this one, sure enough."

And with a few added elaborations on this theme, Macdonald had to be content.

CHAPTER XVII

I

By the time Macdonald crossed the road to Aikengill, he saw with considerable satisfaction that his car had been returned from Slaidburn. He felt that he had done quite enough walking for the time being. He went into the house and found that Woolfall had returned (with the cigarettes) and was sitting by the fire in a room which already looked much improved by Betty Fell's efforts.

"She's a grand lass," said Woolfall. "What I'd have done without her I don't know. I'm a hopeless chap at domestic chores, and if I'd asked my own housekeeper in Leeds to come and clean this place up, she'd have walked out on me."

"Oh, you're the sort of chap who'll always get some good woman to look after you," said Macdonald. "It's that helpless look with which you face domestic crisis. I wish you'd tell me this: what do you know about Hodges, the cowman?"

"Not much. He's a dour sort of chap. He's the only son

of a widowed mother and she's dominated him and seen to it that he didn't go after the lasses. At least, that's what Mrs. Ramsden said; she told me that Jack Hodges was sweet on Betty Fell, and Betty wouldn't look at him and took up with Jock Shearling. That's why Hodges looks so sour—according to Mrs. Ramsden."

"So Hodges has got a down on Jock?"

"Something of the kind, but don't take it too seriously. Hodges is all right: he's always been a bit dumb, but he's a decent, honest, hard-working chap. Incidentally, I'm trying to set down some facts for you in writing, to reinforce what I told you this morning—but it's the Diocesan records you want."

"I'm going to put through some calls from Kirkholm, to get the record searchers on the go. Our chaps at C.O. can have a smack at the Ecclesiastical Commissioners and the Charity Commissioners simultaneously. And in the interim I'm going to see the reverend. I shall try to come back here before dark. If I'm known to be here, there's a better hope of a quiet night."

When Macdonald arrived at the Rectory, he was greeted by Mrs. Tupper. She was a gaunt, grey-haired woman, in clothes and hair-style reminiscent of the Edwardian gentlewoman. She had a big iron-grey bun, and her dark woollen frock was ankle length, severely belted, and collared to the chin, where it was held firmly in place by a good solid gold brooch. Macdonald, whose eye was nothing if not observant, wondered where on earth she had obtained such an out-moded garment and concluded that she must have made it herself, and promptly put her down (rightly, as he found later) as an industrious and thrifty soul. Her face, he thought, was distinctly more intelligent than her husband's, and Macdonald felt very sorry for her.

When he introduced himself, she asked him to come in, speaking with the self-possession of a woman who was well accustomed to controlling both voice and expression, though anxiety showed plainly enough in her eyes. She led him into a room which was evidently the dining-room: it was immaculately clean and tidy, but as cold and dreary a room as Macdonald had ever seen. Mrs. Tupper opened the conversation firmly:

"As you will realise, officer, we are in great trouble. The house was burgled in my husband's absence last night. The sergeant is satisfied that this room has not been interfered with, and I am therefore allowed to use it. I have been away for a few nights—*most* unfortunately. I went to stay with my sister at Morecambe, and Dr. McTay telephoned to me and I returned home immediately. First, I want you to realise that my husband is really ill. He is not fit to answer questions, and any further worry may lead to the most serious consequences. I beg, therefore, that you will allow me to tell you all that I can. If you insist on seeing him, well, what must be, must, but at least hear me first."

"Of course I will. I shall be most grateful to you for any help that you can give me in this perplexing and trouble-some business," said Macdonald. "I hope you will allow me to express my sympathy with you, personally. You must be suffering great distress of mind."

She looked at him in obvious astonishment, as though amazed at the kindly voice. Then she said resolutely:

"That is most charitable, officer. I realise that many things are being said which are the reverse of charitable. I would rather look things in the face and not attempt to minimise them. I know that my husband is suspected of connivance in the unhappy events at High Gimmerdale, and I realise that in certain respects he is to blame. But if what he did may have been foolish and ill-judged, it was certainly nothing worse. It all began with that dispute over the taxi—not waiting for Mrs. Ramsden and bringing her back in the taxi." Her pallid face suddenly flushed, and she demanded with some asperity: "Why should he have waited for her? Mrs. Ramsden had not only been lacking in courtesy and respect, she had said things about my husband which were most opprobrious. Of course, I know that she was only quoting old Mr. Woolfall. I believe that he went so far as to say that the Rector had appropriated funds not rightly his—or that the Church had appropriated them."

"Let us get things into proportion," said Macdonald quietly. "You said just now, with considerable courage, that you would rather look facts in the face. The matter of the taxi is irrelevant from my point of view. The results of the incident were unfortunate, out of all proportion to the original action, but that is no concern of mine. What I cannot understand is this: why, if Mr. Thomas Woolfall made aspersions about the use of funds, did not the Rector go to see him, with a lawyer if need be, and clear the matter up? Such matters pertain to documentary evidence. The evidence is set out in writing in various records and can be found and published if need be. Why did not the Rector challenge these aspersions?"

Mrs. Tupper gave a profound sigh. "Of course you are quite right, officer. I urged my husband to do exactly what you have suggested. But he refused to do so. He said it would be undignified."

"And the result of his refusal, to put it quite plainly, is this," said Macdonald, "that people believed the Rector was afraid to go into the matter, lest Mr. Woolfall proved to be right in his contention."

"He wasn't afraid of that: he was afraid of old Mr. Woolfall. My husband is really a very timid man," she said.

"Well, now let us consider the upshot," said Macdonald. "Popular beliefs or suspicions are nothing to do with the police. The only thing which concerns us is evidence—ascertainable fact. It is a fact that all Mr. Thomas Woolfall's papers dealing with the history of his family and parish were in his study, and that these papers were destroyed by the fire. We are satisfied that the fire was not caused by accident. Therefore we have to consider, among other things, whether any person or persons had a motive to destroy these papers."

"That's perfectly clear," said Mrs. Tupper, "but you spoke of evidence—ascertainable fact. Have you any evidence that my husband was connected with the fire?"

She certainly had courage, thought Macdonald, and lived up to her wish to "look things in the face." He replied promptly: "I have no such evidence. While I might have called on your husband to consult him on various matters, I had no reason to connect him with the fire at Aikengill until he arrived there last night. His state on arrival and the reasons he gave for coming were so strange that it is essential I should question him further. I would like to be quite frank with you. During his absence, this house was broken into, as far as can be ascertained, and Mr. Tupper's study was rifled.

Papers may have been stolen or destroyed. We have got to find out who stole or destroyed those papers."

Mrs. Tupper was very white now, but she answered quite steadily: "I don't pretend to misunderstand you, officer. You are suggesting that my husband's mind became deranged by worry: that he deliberately destroyed the evidence he feared existed in Mr. Woolfall's study: that he faked a burglary here when he was alone in the house, destroyed such records as he wished to destroy and undertook that walk to High Gimmerdale so that this house could be left empty and the 'burglary' discovered on his return. I am willing to be perfectly straight with you. I see that there is reason in what you say, but I know this. My husband could never have thought out such a scheme of action. Quite apart from the moral problem involved, he is too impractical. I know perfectly well he could never have done it. And in any case, what had he to be afraid of? The plain fact is that he not only had had no hand in any financial dealings with High Gimmerdale, he knew nothing whatever about the matter."

"While he was ignorant of the matter to start with, wasn't he sufficiently interested in what Mr. Gilbert Woolfall told him to look up the facts and get the whole thing clear?" asked Macdonald quietly. "I myself have only the most cursory acquaintance with the facts, but I have to admit that I think there is room for suspicion on one count. Now I have not told you all this to add to your distress. I want you to realise that it is essential, in order to clear your husband of any suspicion, that he should pull himself together and answer the questions I wish to put to him. It's no use for him to try to hide behind illness or exhaustion. He's got to answer questions."

Quite suddenly she smiled: it was a white-faced, tight-lipped smile but there was amusement in it.

"I really respect your methods, officer. You build up this formidable chain of suggestions in order to convince me that I can't get my husband out of his difficulties by saying that he's too ill to be questioned."

"It was you yourself who said you wished to face the facts," said Macdonald equably. "I ask you to realise afresh what has occurred in the last two days and nights: arson, manslaughter, and attempted murder. Suspicion has fallen on the majority of those living in High Gimmerdale. When you think that it is a shocking and outrageous thing that suspicion should fall on your husband, it should give you a measure of other people's feelings. I admit that your husband is under suspicion and that uncharitable things are being said about him: they are being said about other people, too. Now madam, I must ask to see Mr. Tupper."

She got up, indicating that Macdonald should follow her and they went upstairs. When Mrs. Tupper opened the bed-room door, the room beyond was in darkness: she spoke very firmly:

"My dear, the Scotland Yard officer is here, and he says that he must talk to you and ask you some essential questions. So sit up and do your best to help him. I will draw the curtains back—you really can't talk in the dark."

I I

When he thought over that bizarre interview later, Macdonald realised the truth of what the psychologists say about illness being used as a defence mechanism by people who find the problems of their lives too difficult to face. The illness thus developed is real enough: fear and misery can develop symptoms as bacteria or exposure can develop them. Mr. Tupper was certainly frightened and he was certainly ill, and Macdonald realised that he himself had to be cautious in his approach lest he precipitated the bugbear of the detective—a confession based on hysteria. The line he took, therefore, was essentially practical: he asked for a detailed description of last night's visitor to the Rectory.

"The first assumption made in this case was that the fire at Aikengill was caused by the sheep-stealers," he explained. "It is still the most probable assumption. The lad whom Mr. Hoggett and I found last night may have been one of this gang, or may have been attacked by them because they feared he could give evidence which would lead to their own arrest. All this aspect of the case is explicable enough. Where confusion arises is in the matter of the man who came here last night and who later, it is to be supposed, robbed the house. What connection is there between the original crimes of arson and sheep-stealing and the robbery here?"

Mr. Tupper, groaning heavily, had said that the whole hoax was calculated to incriminate himself.

"That may be," agreed Macdonald, "but why the robbery, particularly the theft and upheaval in your own study, sir? It's that which has got to be explained. Now, first I want a description of the man who came here last night."

Mr. Tupper was a very poor hand at descriptions, but of one thing he was quite certain—he had never seen the man before. He gave his age as "elderly"—between sixty and seventy, his clothing as an old raincoat, a scarf round his neck, and an old cap, very dirty. Macdonald next asked:

"Would you have taken him for a country man? You live in the country, sir, among farmers and farm workers, you are used to their speech. Did this man resemble the folks hereabouts, in speech and manner and appearance?"

Eventually Mr. Tupper agreed that the man had not spoken with the accent and idiom of Lunesdale: his speech was more like that of the industrial towns of Lancashire.

"Then we are faced with this situation, sir. A townsman, a stranger to this place so far as can be ascertained, comes to your house at night, showing himself to be familiar with the name of Mr. Gilbert Woolfall and the troubles at Gimmerdale—though there has not been time for the fire to be reported in the press—and induces you, sir, to walk out to High Gimmerdale at midnight, leaving this house conveniently empty for a thief to rifle."

Mr. Tupper's only reply was that he could do no more than tell the truth: everything he had said, he protested miserably, was true. It was not for him to provide explanations.

Macdonald then continued: "We will leave it at that for the moment, sir. Next, I want a description, so far as you can give it, of the documents which were in a deed-box in your study. This deed-box has been broken open and the contents thrown out or removed."

Mr. Tupper replied quite simply: "I do not know the details of these papers. They are none of them mine. They are old papers, registers, and deeds, I believe, which I found in the vestry. There is no safe in the church, and

I thought these documents would be more secure in my own study, especially as we had some things stolen from the church."

Mrs. Tupper, who had been sitting in silence thus far, put in: "The Rector, intended of course, to lodge these documents at the bank, when he had had leisure to examine them. They are very old and many of them illegible, and he realised that it would be a lengthy task to decipher them."

"I see," said Macdonald. "Since you, sir, were in charge of these papers, can you make any suggestion as to why they should be stolen by a man such as you have described?"

Mr. Tupper had no suggestion to offer. He closed his eyes in obstinate silence.

It was when they were downstairs again that Mrs. Tupper finally said her say. "You asked my husband if he had any suggestion as to why those papers were stolen, officer. I am not in the habit of ascribing evil motives to my neighbours, but the situation is so dangerous to my husband that I feel justified in speaking my mind. There is one explanation which would cover all these abnormal events and it is this: that Mr. Gilbert Woolfall discovered something among his uncle's papers which was disadvantageous to himself. He set light to the cellar in order that all those records should be burnt, apparently by accident. Further, he employed some fellow from the town he lives in to come here and steal the papers from my husband's study. You may say this is a far-fetched explanation, but it is not nearly so preposterous as suspecting my husband of these crimes."

"Well—it's an idea, but so far I haven't come across any evidence to support it," said Macdonald.

I I I

The next hour or so was spent in "routine operations." With the assistance of the sergeant, who came joyfully to lend a hand to the C.I.D., Macdonald was busy with the familiar job of testing for fingerprints, footprints, and other traces in Mr. Tupper's sadly disorganised study. Macdonald wished that he had Reeves there to assist him, and to discuss the chain of events in his own particularly pungent way. Of one thing Macdonald was pretty certain: the general upheaval, including the tossing of books from bookcases, the turning out of drawers (including a great confusion of Mr. Tupper's sermons in manuscript) and the overturning of furniture was but a blind to the essential theft of the papers from the deed-box. Fingerprints (with the exception of Mr. and Mrs. Tupper's) there were none: the job had been done by somebody wearing gloves, as various smudges testified—which fact proved nothing at all, as the sergeant observed. In common with Mr. Herdwick and, indeed, the majority of those who had had occasion to reason with Mr. Tupper, the sergeant felt little sympathy with the Rector: accustomed to exerting authority and demanding respect "ex officio" so to speak, Mr. Tupper seemed to have the unhappy faculty of rousing resentment when it was least expedient to do so.

"He could have put on a pair of gloves and done the whole thing himself, sir," said the sergeant.

"As far as possibilities go, he could have done most of the offences himself," agreed Macdonald, "but he couldn't have stolen the sheep."

"Aye, there's that," agreed the sergeant.

"And it's no use suggesting that Mr. Herdwick obliged the Rector by reporting a theft of sheep as a blind," went on Macdonald, "because Tegg says the sheep are missing. I wouldn't believe all that Tegg says automatically, but I believe him when he says there's a score of sheep missing, and Tegg's very mad about those sheep."

"Aye, there's that," reiterated the sergeant, who was a man of few words. Then he went on: "And from what I hear, Mr. Herdwick's not likely to oblige Mr. Tupper—cat and dog they were, I'm told."

"Very regrettable," said Macdonald solemnly. He was squatting on the floor, examining the linoleum from an unorthodox angle. "I think we shall have to admit that the evidence goes to prove that Mr. Tupper's story is well-founded, sergeant. Look at these."

"These" were marks which had been brought up on the well-polished lino by powder from an insufflator: it adhered to certain footprints sufficiently to show roughly the size of the shoes or boots which had been worn by the person standing on the lino. "Mr. Tupper hasn't got feet this size," went on Macdonald. "You say you didn't let him enter this room when you came in last night?"

"That I didn't, sir. You said nothing was to be interfered with. I had a job to keep him out, but I said orders was orders."

"How right you were," chuckled Macdonald. "Very fortunate for him, too, though he may not have realised it at the time. There's enough evidence here to show that the outsize feet walked over this floor after Mr. Tupper had last been in here."

"Funny the way them marks show up, sir," said the sergeant. "I've never used that powder outfit for footmarks."

"The reason it's so successful on this occasion is that the lino's so well polished," said Macdonald. "Still, it is rather impressive, as you say. Go and find me a cup of water, sergeant."

With an expression of "mine not to reason why" the sergeant obeyed. When he came back, with a fine disregard of Mrs. Tupper's polished linoleum, Macdonald tilted the cup of water over the floor and the sergeant watched, fascinated.

"What do you make of that?" asked Macdonald, pointing to one of the prints which still showed up noticeably, despite the fact that the powder was washed away.

"By gum, that's oil, that is," said the sergeant.

"Oil it is: tractor oil at a guess. Mr. Tupper wouldn't have got oil on his shoes so far as I can see."

"Tractor oil," muttered the sergeant hopefully. Then his face fell. "But the Rector said he didn't recognise the chap who brought the message," he declared.

"I'm pretty sure he didn't recognise him," said Macdonald. "Well, we've got all we can from here for the moment. We'll lock and seal the door until I can get some of the backroom boys on the job. It's wonderful what they smell out."

Before they left the study, the sergeant said: "What beats me is why Mr. Tupper didn't go over to the constabulary and report this message. He'd have got the whole thing in order and above board if he'd done that, and maybe we should have caught the chap who worked the hoax."

"I think I know why he behaved as he did, but it'd take too long to explain now," said Macdonald. "Now then, I want to get at your telephone and get our chaps busy at their end."

CHAPTER XVIII

I

TOWARDS THE END OF A LONG DAY, MACDONALD WENT to Carnton to exchange notes with Bord. The C.I.D. man sat down gratefully in the not very comfortable chair and repeated a phrase which Kate Hoggett had quoted to him from a book written by a farmer's wife.

"'Either it's a luxury to sit down or else it's a bore.' I must say that at the moment it's a luxury. As I walked up from Slaidburn last night, I was quite sure that I wasn't too old to start farming. At the moment I'm not so sure."

"Don't say that," said Bord. "You'll do champion. By heck, you can beat me at getting about—and I reckon I can give you a year or two, though no one'd think it."

"Thanks for the kind words," said Macdonald. "Now what about our casualty? How's he doing?"

"Nicely, they tell me. 'Quite comfortable,' Sister said, and since he's still unconscious I suppose it's true. We've placed him, Chief. Fingerprints. He's been had up a couple o' times for thieving. Put on probation first time—in Manchester that was—and then a sentence of three months. When he was discharged, the Prisoners' Aid people got him a job on a farm. He came from a bad home and he said he'd like farming. He stuck it six months—a hill farm 'twas, Kinder Scout way. The farmer said he didn't shape so bad, but then he ran away. That was a year ago. What's he been doing since is anybody's guess."

"Picking up what he can where he can," said Macdonald. "Sheep-stealing doesn't seem so far out of the picture after all. How old is he?"

"Twenty, according to records, but it's a bit of a mix-up. The folks he lived with weren't his own parents. His name's Len Williams and his parents were killed in the Merseyside blitz and he was evacuated to Cheshire. The folks he was billeted on hadn't any children and they adopted him: the family moved into Manchester after the war and young Len got into bad company—and so did the pair who'd adopted him. It's a common story enough."

"Bad luck on the kid. I've met plenty of similar stories," said Macdonald. "You might find out where his parents lived before they were blitzed."

"All right. That's easy enough. The records have been kept—very careful they are. You believe in going right back, Chief."

"Aye. Records, records all the way. I've got some of our chaps busy digging out records. It's marvellous what you can find out if you give your mind to it. Now here's another thing you can tell me—about Thomas Woolfall's death."

"Yes, by heck. I've been thinking about that, on and off, all day," said Bord soberly. "It wasn't my case. The Kirkholm chaps dealt with it. I was on the sick list at the time, but I know it was considered a perfectly straightforward case—accidental death. It was last December, in the first heavy snow we had. There'd been a lot of snow on the Pennines, and we hoped we were going to escape it, but two days after Christmas there was a big fall on the hills, and we got it in the valley, too. Bitterly cold, it was—I got pneumonia and I'm not likely to forget it. Old Mr. Woolfall often went out about sundown. He was a sturdy old chap, and he'd go up the fell above his house and watch the sunset. You often get very fine sunsets late in December. It was about six o'clock in the evening that Mrs. Ramsden telephoned to Herdwick's place, saying Mr. Woolfall wasn't in the house and she was worried about him. She'd been poorly herself—got lumbago—and she'd been lying down for awhile. She came down and got the old man's meal—he liked a good solid tea about six o'clock and didn't bother about supper. When she went to the study to tell him his tea was ready, he wasn't there. Well, to cut a long story short, they all turned out to look for him—Herdwick and Hodges, Shearling and even old Tegg. Shearling had been working late, lending Hodges a hand with the oat crusher and cutting up the mangolds. They were behind hand because snow is always a nuisance to farmers—slows them up."

"Was it snowing at the time?"

"By heck it was, a real heavy fall. That's what made it so difficult to find the old man. They knew more or less the way he'd have gone—it hadn't been snowing at the time he set out—but it'd been snowing heavily for best part of two hours before they started looking for him. It was nigh on a foot deep as it lay, and drifting in all the hollows. Tegg it was that found him, with his shepherd's crook, plumbing the drifts. The old man had fallen into the gill, right among the rocks, and hit the back of his head."

"Was he dead?"

"I think he was dead, but they couldn't be sure. Hodges and Shearling carried him in. Then there was all the trouble of getting a doctor up. Mrs. Ramsden swore he wasn't dead, only unconscious. By that time no car could get up there, not with that amount of snow on those hills. Young Dr. Murray got up there at last. Daleham took him up on a tractor—and he'd got some pluck to do it, considering the drifts. That must have been a ride, by gum it must. It was ten o'clock they got up there and they might have spared the trouble. Mr. Woolfall had died hours ago. They couldn't fix the time of death, what with his lying under the snow all that while, but Dr. Murray said he must have died soon after he fell. The verdict was accidental death and the coroner thanked all the chaps who'd gone out searching—quite a story the papers made of it."

"Who was the last person to see Mr. Woolfall?"

"Tegg. He'd gone up the fells himself, before the snow really started, bringing some of the sheep down to the walled intacks. Tegg knew it was going to snow and to snow hard— these old shepherds always know. He'd caught sight of Mr. Woolfall climbing up by the gill, as he often did. He must have fallen on his way back, for he was lying only a couple of hundred yards away from the house."

Both men fell silent for awhile. Then Macdonald said: "It's no use hoping to get any further evidence along those lines—but one can't help thinking. I take it that once the snow started, visibility was almost nil?"

"Aye. You couldn't see a yard in front of you. The snow started as the sun went down—that was about 3.50, though of course you lose the sun much earlier behind the fells. Probably the old man went out about half-past three and got to the top about four o'clock. Tegg hadn't got a watch of course. He said it was just about sundown, and the sky was flaming—angry like—where there was a break in the clouds towards the west."

"Well, perhaps it was accident, but if it was murder the elements helped to make it foolproof," said Macdonald.

I I

It was dusk when Macdonald set out to drive back to High Gimmerdale. He had thought of going to supper with the Hoggetts: he had talked to Kate over the telephone and learned that Giles was none the worse for what Kate called "his night out." "He's absolutely uppish about it," she said. "That run must have gone to his head. I believe he's as stiff as a poker, but he won't admit it. At the moment he's fast asleep in front of the fire with the wireless on. If I turn the wireless off he'll wake up at once and say he was listening."

"Don't be too hard on him," said Macdonald. "He really did a very fine run. I hope you'll both have a good night."

"Thank you. I hope you will, too," said Kate. "Do you expect to?"

"Blessed is he that expecteth nothing in my job," said Macdonald. "Tell Giles our casualty is doing nicely."

Macdonald drove direct to Aikengill, but when he'd got his car out of the way, he turned up the hill behind the house and took the track which led to Summerfold, the cottage where Tegg lived. At intervals during the day, Macdonald's mind had returned to Tegg and to some of the abrupt sentences the old shepherd had spoken that morning. Macdonald believed that Tegg knew a number of things which it would be very useful to know if only "young Aaron" could be persuaded to put his knowledge into words. Men who live solitary lives—and most shepherds spend the greater part of their time alone—often have an awareness that is implicit rather than explicit. "Words aren't their medium," meditated Macdonald. "The things they do so skilfully aren't the result of thought, but of long practice: the skill becomes ingrain, like a conditioned reflex, and words have nothing to do with it."

The track leading to Summerfold was not only rough, it was steep. Most men of eighty would have had a heart attack if they had attempted to climb it, but Tegg had climbed it all his life. "You can do what you've always done," said Maggie Herdwick.

Summerfold was a very small stone cottage—two rooms upstairs and a kitchen and dairy below—but even in the fading light the comeliness of its proportions was evident, that grace which distinguishes all the stone houses from Lunesdale to Penrith, and which vanishes (as Macdonald knew) as soon as you cross the border to the land of "but and ben."

There was no light showing in the kitchen window, but Macdonald knocked with his fist on the door and waited. He got no answer, and after a while he tried the handle and found that the door was on the latch. He opened it and called, aware of the mixed smells of habitation. The fire in the open chimney was quite dead, and the tang of turves and woodsmoke wafted across in the down-draught from the chimney, mingled with other less easily identifiable smells—that of sheep, for the shepherds' clothes got saturated with the oiliness of the fleeces when they handled the sheep: a smell of home-cured bacon, not too well cured at that and the smell of unwashed humanity. The place was neat enough in its sparseness. Tegg "did for" himself and he evidently didn't believe in being cluttered up with a lot of domestic gear. A solid old kitchen table, two heavy ladder-back chairs, one cushioned with a variety of ancient paddings, a built-in wall cupboard and several shelves—these were the essentials. A huge iron kettle hung on the crane in the open chimney, and a correspondingly outsize frying pan stood on the hearth stone: an enamel teapot, plates, and mugs, with some ancient horn-handled knives and forks completed the domestic arrangements.

Macdonald stood there with a vague sense of discomfort: it was after sundown, and he had expected confidently to find the old shepherd at home. Feeling more of an intruder than he usually did when he ventured uninvited into other folk's dwellings, Macdonald crossed the stone-flagged floor and went up the steep wooden ladder which was the only approach to the rooms above. The primitive sparseness of the cottage seemed to rebuke his curiosity.

There were two bedrooms, small and ill-lit, with a loft of sorts above. Both bedrooms and bedding would have been condemned as unfit for human use by any sanitary inspector, but Macdonald sensed that Tegg was comfortable enough in his primitive way. He lived as his forebears had lived, with few added amenities save a paraffin lamp in place of the home-made candles of earlier generations. Having satisfied himself that the cottage was empty, Macdonald went to the door again and stood for a moment, while a huge tom cat rubbed hopefully round his legs and miaowed in a voice frightful enough to induce shudders: the creature evidently hoped to get into the house, but Macdonald firmly shut the door and left it disconsolate on the doorstep.

I I I

Walking down the track again, Macdonald went on to Lambsrigg and met Hodges, who was just going home.

"Have you any idea where Tegg would be?" asked Macdonald.

"Reckon he's gone home," replied Hodges. "He keeps his own times, Tegg does."

"I've just been up to his cottage. He's not there," said Macdonald.

"No? Then he's somewhere else," grunted Hodges.

"When did you last see him?" asked Macdonald.

"Scarce seen him all day. He's nought to do with me," said Hodges and continued on his way.

Macdonald walked across the foldyard and knocked on the kitchen door, whence the light streamed out cheerfully. Maggie Herdwick opened the door and looked at him in an exasperated way: she and her father were at tea, and the table was a cheerful sight, laden with food, the fragrance of hot scones and pastry reminding Macdonald that he was hungry enough himself.

"I'm sorry to bother you," he said. "I've been trying to find Tegg. He's not in his cottage and I wondered if he was about the place anywhere."

"He's not here," said Maggie, and her father chuckled behind her.

"If he's not by his own fireside, you'll have a job to find him," said Herdwick. "Out ferreting, maybe, or setting nooses in the rabbit runs. Or likely he's gone to the pub down Ewedale or Low Gimmerdale."

"Does he often do that?" asked Macdonald, conscious that they thought he was being tiresome and a bit foolish.

"He likes his pint, same's the rest of us, and a crack with his cronies," said Herdwick. "Sometimes he has a real blind. Not often, just once in a way. They say no liquor ever brewed makes Tegg drunk. It's this way: he's paid good money these days, and lambing time brings him more brass than he knows what to do with. Tegg don't spend aught—he's nothing to spend it on, but sometimes he goes out to t' locals and pours his brass down's throat—don't blame him. So mayhap he's having a night out. He'll be home morning—always gets home on his own legs, Tegg does."

Herdwick yawned: a huge jaw-splitting yawn. "Rather him than me," he said. "I tell you what, I'm going to sleep t' night through to-night, and so's Maggie here. We've had enough o' being out of our beds all hours and that's a fact."

"'Tis true," she said, "but if we're not knocked up again to-night I shall be surprised. District Nurse came in and said Mrs. Hodges is real bad. I said I'd go round if need be. There's no one else, and Hodges's that obstinate, won't have her moved to t' infirmary. Makes me mad, he does."

"Well, that's a woman's job, that is," said Herdwick. "I tell you this straight, thunder and lightning's not going to wake me this night once I'm in me bed."

Macdonald went back to Aikengill, where Woolfall was drowsing over a good fire, and a promising fragrance came from the kitchen quarters.

"I'm glad you've got back," said Gilbert. "Help yourself to a drink. Betty's gone home now, but she's left us a bird roasting in the oven and everything else put ready. Has anything definite turned up?"

"No. It's a matter of marking time until I get some reports in," said Macdonald. "The chap we brought in is doing well enough, so our tramp wasn't wasted effort. I'm just going to telephone to the Kirkholm chaps. Tegg's off the map. Herdwick says he may be at one of the locals, so I'm going to get them to find out."

When he came back, Woolfall asked: "Why worry about Tegg? Where does he come in?"

"Everywhere," said Macdonald. "The more I think about it, the more I'm certain Tegg could tell us quite a lot if he chose. He's lived here all his long life and I believe he's capable of noticing more than anyone else here, but he's so used to keeping his own counsel that he'll only talk if he chooses to talk."

"Tegg," said Woolfall slowly. "I hadn't thought of him. He's as dumb as they make them."

"Not always," said Macdonald. "You ask him what happened in the great snow when Moses Woolton starved up on Ramshead. Tegg can tell a story in his own way if he chooses."

"Well, you're a chap for getting stories out of folks," said Gilbert. "Tegg's never honoured me with a word beyond 'good day.' Come and inspect that bird in the oven. It smells good to me."

After a good meal, the two men sat over the fire, too sleepy to talk much. Woolfall nodded himself to sleep and Macdonald drowsed at intervals. It was shortly after ten that the telephone rang, and Macdonald went to answer it while Woolfall nodded on undisturbed.

It was Sergeant Berry calling, to tell Macdonald that Tegg had not been seen in any of the locals, neither had he returned home. Two of the Kirkholm police had been up at Summerfold and round about, and had found no sign of the old shepherd.

"Well, it's Operation Sheepfold then," said Macdonald. "It's a slim chance, but we can't leave it."

"Are you coming out again, sir?" demanded Berry, sounding astonished enough.

"Yes. I'm coming. I can sleep for a week afterwards. You've notified Slaidburn?"

"Yes. They've started already, and the chap who guided you up is with them. He knows Bowland better than any of them."

"Good. I'll set out by myself within five minutes," said Macdonald. "Get your chaps moving straight away and keep to instructions."

Going back into the sitting-room, Macdonald found Gilbert Woolfall fast asleep. He saw that the fire was safe in the wide hearth and Gilbert not in danger of falling into it. Then he pulled on his Burberry and went out into the chill night air. He wasn't sleepy any longer, and he knew his legs would keep going somehow, but he admitted that there were moments when the delights of hill country palled.

I V

As he plodded up the rough track, Macdonald wondered whether he had brought out men from two county police forces on a fool's errand. It was true that Tegg had been neither seen nor heard of since Macdonald himself had left the old shepherd on Ramshead that morning, but what kept recurring to Macdonald's mind was Tegg's final phrase: "You get on with your job, mister, and I'll get on with mine." The more he thought about it, the more convinced Macdonald became that Tegg was working his way up to Hawkshead again to see if he could find any traces of the missing sheep. Left to himself, the shepherd might know by a hundred traces whether sheep had been driven up to the head of the valley and over the top, and by what route they had been driven down on the Slaidburn side. Macdonald was pretty certain that if the idea had occurred to him earlier and he had offered to accompany Tegg, the latter would have had none of it. Alone, with his dog, Tegg might find out something that no one else could observe. "You get on with your job, mister, and I'll get on with mine." It might have been Tegg's way of saying that he had a particular job to do. One thought cheered Macdonald—the thought of the dog. It was a fine dog. It would go ill with anyone who attacked the shepherd while the dog was at liberty.

Up the track to the steep below Ramshead: on again to the crest of Bowland and the stone-walled fold, or shepherd's shelter, on the summit. Were there other similar walled shelters, wondered Macdonald, where the sheep could be folded while the drovers had a rest?

He trudged on, feeling that his legs were going automatically, having no reference to himself. At the summit he sat down, not so much for a rest, as to listen. The world was incredibly still: if anything was in movement on the fellside around him, surely he ought to be able to hear it in the stillness. The men would be coming up from Slaidburn in an hour or so, searching the fells as they came: others would be coming up from Kirkholm. Then, suddenly, Macdonald forgot all about the others. He had heard a dog bark: the short warning bark that Tegg's dog had given when Macdonald climbed up from the beck below Ramshead that morning: the same bark which Betty Fell's dog had given when he came towards her the first time he had walked up to the head of the valley. It was the sheepdog's way of giving warning of an interloper, and it was a long way away. "It wasn't because of me the dog barked," thought Macdonald. "They don't give warning until you're close enough at hand to be a nuisance." Somewhere, away down the fell slopes to the east, was a shepherd and his dog—and somebody else: somebody unexpected, because no well-trained sheepdog will bark at his master's friends. The communication between master and dog is too comprehensive for that.

Weariness forgotten, Macdonald got up and began to bear downhill eastwards: he had only memory of the sound to guide him, but presently he knew that he was moving in the right direction. The sheep were on the move: eerily their backs caught the light, the fleeces dewed over and shining in the moonlight. Then they scented Macdonald, and broke away from him, going uphill, while a curlew called its warning note far away. "Right so far," he thought. "The dog's farther down, because the sheep are going up fell." Then he came to a wall: one of those unexpected long lines of dry-stone walling by which industrious men of long ago marked out the fell rights. He stopped and listened again.

If there was a wall, there might well be a sheepfold. He stood still for some time and then heard a commotion higher up—the sheep bleating. Someone, he argued, was coming down from the summit, on the far side of the wall. Not risking a move, Macdonald crouched down, so that he should not be silhouetted against the sky, his ears straining to catch the rustle of heather and dry grass which would indicate the other's coming. Oddly enough, the dog didn't bark again: so the shepherd was keeping his dog silent. Into Macdonald's mind flashed the memory of Betty's dog, as it crouched ready to spring. Not very far away another dog was crouching like that, tense and quivering, panting a little, jaws slobbering, all its pent-up energy waiting for the order "go." Then came the rustle of heather and swish of dry grasses: no sound of a footstep, only the movement of brushwood: it passed Macdonald and went farther down the slope, and then he began to follow.

When Tegg's voice spoke, just across the wall, it came as such a startling shock that Macdonald's heart pounded, his skin prickled and a wave of heat seemed to well over him: the shepherd's voice wasn't a yard away.

"Eh, maister, tha' made a praper fule of me, tha' did, but tha's made a bigger fule o' tha' self. If tha'd trusted me, belike I'd held me jaw. Thee and me's known t'other a tidy time. But tha' shouldn't ha' tried to fule me. Here I be, and here I bide, till them chaps coom oop fra' doon yonder. Tha's gone too far this time."

"What the hell are you jawing about, you old fool?" came the answer. "D'you know the police are out after you, from Kirkholm to Lancaster?"

"Happen they be. I'll bide here till they coom," said Tegg. "I know what tha' was oop to, selling ewe mutton to black market chaps. It paid tha' better that way, a sight better. Maybe I'd've said nought but for firing that house. Tha' shouldn't ha' done that, maister, tho' I know why 'twas——"

Macdonald waited no longer. He knew what was coming. He had no time to climb the wall: he set his hands on the top of it and put all his strength into a gate-vault: he'd done that vault dozens of times as a young man, but he wasn't a young man any longer. It was determination and past training that got him over, but as his weight pivoted on the stones which his hands gripped, the dry walling gave and he landed in an avalanche of stones just as a heavy stick was crashed down on the old shepherd's head. With a snarl like a wild beast, the dog leapt at the aggressor, right at his throat, and the man went down, hit simultaneously by the collapsing wall and the impetus of Macdonald's spring.

Staggering clear of the stones, Macdonald shouted:

"You'd better lie still, Mr. Herdwick. The dog'll tear your throat out if you fight him. You've asked for it and you've got it."

Across the waste of Bowland Forest another note shrilled, terrifying the sheep, rousing the curlews, and the owls who called back in mournful cacophony. The police whistle was heard by Sergeant Berry and his men toiling up from Gimmerdale: it was heard by old Blackburn and the police coming up from the Yorkshire border. It was heard by the man who lay half stunned by an avalanche of stones, and it was heard by the dog, who growled hideously over his victim. Only old Tegg didn't hear it: his wizened face untroubled, his unseeing eyes wide open to the moonlight, the shepherd lay on his back, his crook beside him, in the oldest sheepfold on Bowland Forest.

CHAPTER XIX

I

"I ALWAYS SAID THERE WAS SOME HOCUS-POCUS," insisted Giles Hoggett. Before Kate had time to deal with her husband's beliefs, Macdonald weighed in:

"It's no use saying there's hocus-pocus in general terms. You've got to produce chapter and verse to substantiate a charge, and if you thought there was any chance that the Diocesan lawyers and the Charity Commissioners connived at anything illegal, you're a disgrace to the university which taught you Logic."

"I didn't mention those particular functionaries," protested Giles, but Kate said:

"Stop arguing and listen. I want to get it properly sorted out. Now, Macdonald, please tell us exactly what happened."

"In the year 1690," began Macdonald, "one Martin Woolfall left a benefaction to his native place, namely four hundred acres and the house known as Lambsrigg Hall, together with outbuildings and extensive rights of fell grazing together with the sheep on said fells for the following purposes: to ensure that a minister of religion should reside in the Chapelry of High Gimmerdale and that a school should be maintained for the education and enlightenment of the youth of that Chapelry. Is that clear?"

"Perfectly clear," said Gilbert Woolfall. "I know it by heart—but I didn't see the point."

"The point is this," said Macdonald. "The rents from the property were to pay the parson *and* maintain the school, and the income from the property was to be administered by Trustees, the said Trustees having power to appoint new Trustees on the death or resignation of any one of them. All this was faithfully carried out until 1904, when the little grammar school became an elementary school, conforming to the education act of that year, and the part of the income set aside for the payment of the schoolmaster (who had also been the parson) was no longer needed when an elementary school teacher was paid for by the county authorities."

Gilbert Woolfall put a word in here. "It's important to remember that the Woolfalls left High Gimmerdale in 1870— the same year the first education act was passed. If I had used my wits, I should have realised that at least some portion of the school endowment was no longer spent on the school for some years before 1904, because the costs of the elementary school were increasingly borne by the rates."

Macdonald took up the story. "After the Woolfalls left High Gimmerdale, the chief trustees of the Woolfall Benefaction were the Herdwicks, and the Herdwicks were the Treasurers of the Benefaction. In 1904, Lambsrigg Hall and its land were sold to the Herdwicks and the stipend was transferred to the living of Ewedale with every legal nicety, the proportion of money calculated to pertain to the school being scrupulously transferred to the Trustees of the Woolfall Benefaction—the Trustees in question being dominated by the Herdwicks."

"I begin to see what happened," said Kate, with a sigh of relief.

"That was all I did," said Macdonald. "I began to see. The only facts I had were those that Woolfall quoted to me—that the Will of 1690 endowed both a parson and a school. Unlike Hoggett, I had a profound conviction that the Diocesan lawyers and the Charity Commissioners of 1904 would have administered the funds with absolute probity and correctness: in short, they would not have annexed that portion of the funds earmarked for the school and added it to the stipend: they would have left the income for the school in the hands of the Trustees of the Benefaction. But I also wondered if, in 1904, the Charity Commissioners were as prompt to demand accounts from such Trustees as they are to-day."

"In point of fact, the school funds were just lost sight of," said Gilbert Woolfall. "No questions were ever asked."

"Well, it wasn't till we disinterred all the records that we were able to understand what really happened," said Macdonald. "I had made a guess—a wild guess if you like. I knew that money had been left to endow the school—Woolfall told me so—and the schoolroom was there, complete with the initials of the founder—M.W. But the school had been closed a long time. Problem, what had happened to the income? We know now that in 1904 the Charity Commissioners advised that the income be allowed to accumulate in order to build a new church school, but, as Woolfall says, no further inquiries were ever made. The money was left in the hands of the Treasurer to the Trustees—Daniel Herdwick—and there was nobody in High Gimmerdale who bothered to inquire about it. Until Mr. Thomas Woolfall bought back the home of his forefathers."

I I

"It's important to bear in mind that Mr. Thomas Woolfall was not born in High Gimmerdale," went on Macdonald. "He was born in Bradford in 1879, nine years after the Woolfalls sold Aikengill. All that Thomas Woolfall knew about the place was hearsay, what his father had told him, and it's likely that a town-bred boy wasn't much interested in a place he'd never seen. It wasn't until he was an old man that Thomas's thoughts recurred to the home of his fathers. He bought it and set it in order, and in the long disused study he found old papers and set to work deciphering them, and began to write the history of the Woolfalls. To put it shortly, Thomas disinterred long-forgotten facts, and his researches happened to constitute a menace to somebody. That seemed a fairly reasonable assumption on my part, but it was only an assumption. Nevertheless, I asked myself this: if any funds from the Benefaction had been embezzled, who was most likely to have profited by this hypothetical fraud? The persons involved were as follows: the Rector—who should have known all the facts; Jock Shearling and Betty Fell, the latter being descended on the distaff side from the Woolfalls themselves; Mrs. Ramsden, who had heard old Thomas talking of his researches; Aaron Tegg, who had lived in High Gimmerdale all his eighty years; and Hodges, the cowman. The answer seemed obvious to me: if embezzlement were at the bottom of it, Daniel Herdwick was the likeliest suspect."

"I was very dense," said Gilbert slowly. "On the same evening that Mr. Tupper called on me, Herdwick came in and got talking. He told me, with justifiable pride, how hard his father and grandfather had worked to enable them to buy Aikengill. It seemed a remarkable achievement to me that three generations of sheep-farmers had been able to save £5000 to buy their steading. It didn't occur to me that as Trustees of the Benefaction the Herdwicks had been taking money out of it for years. The last 'perpetual curate,' the Rev. Curtis who lived in Aikengill, was far too ancient and easygoing to bother himself about school funds."

"Well, that constitutes the 'motive' part of the argument," said Macdonald. "Herdwick was an avaricious man: he wasn't going to part with good money, let alone be proceeded against for embezzlement, because old Thomas Woolfall was meddling with old papers. Thomas Woolfall had realised there had been some 'hocus-pocus' somewhere, but being anti-clerical by conviction, he was only too willing to believe that the Rev. Tupper and his predecessors had been wolves in sheep's clothing. And Thomas died before he realised his mistake."

"I suppose we've got to accept that we shall never know if poor old Uncle Thomas was knocked out by Herdwick," said Gilbert sadly. "I'm certain that's what happened. And how mad Herdwick must have been when I turned up and began to read all Uncle Thomas's papers."

Giles put in a word here. "Aye," he said. "It must have seemed outrageous to Herdwick that a townsman, a prosperous business man, should have behaved as you did. Herdwick expected—with reason—that you would have no interest in Aikengill and would sell it as promptly as possible. How he must have sweated with impotent fury at the thought of you nosing out all the things he'd hoped would now be quietly forgotten."

"Yes. I see all that," said Kate, in her clear decisive way, "but that's only part of the story. There's the sheep-stealing—how does that come in?"

"It's interlocked with the other," said Macdonald. "The sheep-stealing was confusing, but old Tegg blew the gaff about that before he died. From the point of view of satisfying Mrs. Hoggett's demand for clarity, it'll be easier if I state now exactly what happened. Herdwick was approached by one of his own kith and kin in Liverpool—a black market dealer in meat. Herdwick was offered a much higher price for his sheep than he could get on the legal market, and he began to sell them, driving them up over Hawkshead in twos and threes to be collected by the black market drovers on the Slaidburn side. When Tegg missed the sheep, the answer was 'sheep thieves.'"

I I I

"Now we've cleared the decks a bit, let's get down to the plan Herdwick made to burn Uncle Thomas's study and the documents in it," said Macdonald. "It was a most astute and cunning operation, combining cover for arson with profits from sale of the sheep on the black market. Herdwick must have thought long and hard before he got his scheme into order, carefully timed. He drove a score of his own sheep over Hawkshead when Tegg was busy with the late lambers in the low paddocks. The sheep Herdwick drove were folded in the ancient sheepfold on the slopes of Croasdale, and there they were collected by the black marketeers well before midnight. On the night of the fire, Herdwick set light to the cellar, probably when Maggie Herdwick went out to help with Mrs. Hodges, and then set out up the fell with Tegg, ostensibly on the track of the sheep thieves. When they got to Ramshead they could see the fire at Aikengill, and down they came. It was a clever plan, but it wasn't beyond the scope of detective work to see how it could have been worked."

"Do you think he knew that Mrs. Ramsden was in the house at the time?" asked Kate.

"I'm quite sure that he didn't," said Macdonald. "Herdwick supposed, in common with everyone else, that Mrs. Ramsden had gone back to Dent. The last thing he wanted was anybody in the house when he fired it; they might have woken up and given the alarm before the study was well alight. The fact that Mrs. Ramsden was killed was a disaster for Herdwick; it meant the sort of police investigation he wanted to avoid. If it hadn't been for Mrs. Ramsden's death there wouldn't have been nearly such an intensive inquiry. When Mrs. Ramsden's body was found, Herdwick saw the red light; it might mean a murder charge, and he knew the danger involved. People in the district who would never otherwise have admitted knowing anything would have begun talking if it came to a charge of murder—against Jock Shearling for instance. Herdwick wanted a scapegoat, and he thought about the fellow whom Mr. Woolfall had seen on the fellside."

"But did Herdwick know that this lad had been sheltering in Ramshead?" asked Kate.

"No. He'd have put a stop to it pretty soon if he had," replied Macdonald. "Herdwick wouldn't have risked someone staying up there when he himself had planned to drive his own sheep over Hawkshead to meet his black-market friends. I'm afraid that Herdwick got guessing when I went up to the Ramshead steading that afternoon. The difficulty of detecting in remote country like Gimmerdale is that the detective is always noticed. In a city street a C.I.D. man is just one of a multitude and he passes unnoticed. On the fellside he's marked at once. Herdwick knew that Hoggett had taken me up towards Ramshead." He turned to Giles. "You asked me if I'd searched the old steading. I said no. I didn't want people to realise I was taking too much interest in it—but several people knew I'd been up there: Betty Fell knew, Jock knew, Tegg knew. And somehow Herdwick got suspicious. He went up there himself, that night. He'd gone to bed very early and his daughter as well. They'd been awake all the previous night, remember. Maggie went to sleep at once. Herdwick came downstairs, altered the clock, went up to the steading carrying Jock's crook and a milk-can and routed Len Williams out of the shippon and flung him down the fellside. Len has told us that part of it. The crook was thrown after him, and the can: the one to throw suspicion on Jock, the other to suggest the lad had been tripped up when he went down to the beck for water. Then Herdwick went home."

"How long did all this take?" asked Giles.

"He could have done it in seventy minutes or less," said Macdonald. "I got up to Ramshead in fifty minutes, you ran down in twenty, but Herdwick knew the ground. He probably did it faster than we could by taking advantage of his knowledge of the ground. I reckon that if he left home soon after half-past nine, he could have been back home well before eleven. And then he had a bit of luck: the heifer started bawling. He fetched Maggie down to help. She hadn't a clock in her bedroom and she was much too sleepy to notice the time anyway. If her father said it was half-past ten when it was really half-past eleven she didn't notice the difference—why should she? And by the time she saw the clock again Herdwick had changed it back. She realised later the trick he'd played on her to get his seventy minutes accounted for. She admitted it under interrogation."

"How much did she know—or guess—about what had been going on?" asked Kate.

"She didn't *know* anything," said Macdonald. "She couldn't be charged as accessory—but I think she guessed a lot. It's always the same with country people: you can say they don't know, so far as factual evidence is concerned, but they guess. Maggie had brooded over the whole story, and I think there wasn't much of it she didn't guess at."

"It's pretty dreadful for her," said Kate.

"It would be pretty dreadful for most women," mused Macdonald, "but Maggie's tough. She's not a Herdwick for nothing. We have traced old Nathaniel Herdwick in Liverpool. Records again. It wasn't for nothing he left the city and went to a remote hamlet in the fells. He'd every reason to clear out. My guess is that Maggie will realise what she can from the debacle—and go back to Liverpool with the proceeds."

"So we've got Daniel Herdwick providing himself with an alibi to prove he couldn't have been up to Ramshead that night," said Giles, "but what we haven't heard is the full details about the unhappy reverend. Let's hear about him next. I've always been interested in the reverend."

"Perhaps Mr. Tupper deserved a severe shaking up," said Macdonald. "Certainly he got one. I rather fancy there'll be a change of incumbency very shortly, and I think Mr. Tupper will be both chastened and a thought more industrious in his next cure. He was generally disliked—that was common knowledge. He was disliked in the first case because he tried to be superior, in the second because he was lazy. Folks said he wasn't neighbourly and didn't do his duty by visiting. In those two indictments are the reason for all his tribulations, added to the fact he's fundamentally stupid. Because he was superior and unneighbourly he refused to let the taxi wait for Mrs. Ramsden. Because he was lazy, and also stupid, he did not investigate the documents which he found in the vestry when he first came to Ewedale. Had he examined them all, as it was his duty to do, he could have found out all about the Woolfall Benefaction, and the income paid to the Treasurer of the Trustees for the benefit of the school."

"Incidentally, how was that income invested?" asked Kate.

"The sum due to the school was invested in Consols by the Trustees lawyers," said Macdonald. "The interest was paid to the Treasurer of the Woolfall Benefaction: it was as simple as that. And it's never been anybody's business to ask what has happened to that £75 yearly for over fifty years. But to get back to the Rector. When Mrs. Ramsden's death became known, the Rector was blamed by the whole of Ewedale. As

Mr. Tupper said, 'Very uncharitable things were said.' Mr. Tupper, between fear of his parishioners and the guilt of his own conscience, worked himself up into a panic. After all, in a sense it was true to say that Mr. Tupper's behaviour led to Mrs. Ramsden's death, and he knew that he would have to appear at the inquest and bear the brunt of the publicity which would follow. In addition to this, he was terrified of Mr. Woolfall."

"Why on earth was he frightened of me?" demanded Gilbert.

"Conscience, again. He knew that he ought to have examined all the documents pertaining to High Gimmerdale as well as to Ewedale, and he hadn't done it. I believe myself that Mr. Tupper had a suspicion that Mr. Herdwick, as chief trustee, had not reported all the transactions of the Trust— but Daniel Herdwick was a very tough customer for the reverend to tackle. 'Timid' is the word Mrs. Tupper uses of her husband. It's a euphemism to cover lack of moral courage and the feeling that it's wiser to let sleeping dogs lie."

"That's all understandable enough; he's a wretched little worm anyway," said Gilbert unsympathetically, "but did he burgle his own study?"

"No. He did not. The story he told us was substantially true," said Macdonald. "You see, Herdwick was the best psychologist of the lot of us, and Herdwick had a sense of detail. He had destroyed the papers in Thomas Woolfall's study, but he knew that certain records existed in Mr. Tupper's possession. I think it's time that Giles tried his hand at a reconstruction here—he's been doing nothing but listen."

Giles sat up: "Macdonald's practically indicated what happened. Herdwick decided to get a right-and-left: to nab the parish records and inculpate the incumbent. The reverend was so terrified of public opinion that he would not dare refuse a summons to the dying: he was in such a panic about publicity at the inquest that the thought of being seen going to the police station was abhorrent to him, and anyway, he was sure the police wouldn't believe anything he said. So after dithering over the telephone for a bit he decided to do the heroic thing and walk up to High Gimmerdale. And his study was burgled in his absence by..."

Giles hesitated and Kate cut in promptly: "This is my one assumption: the study was burgled by Herdwick's black market relative, the one who bought the 'stolen' sheep. It was to his interest to keep Daniel out of prison in case Daniel split on him. It couldn't have been anybody else."

"Perfectly correct," said Macdonald. "He has been arrested by the Liverpool police while marketing illicit mutton, and Mr. Tupper had his moment of victory when he identified his visitor."

I V

"We're nearly through, but not quite," said Gilbert. "Len Williams, please."

"More or less as I postulated," said Macdonald. "A shirker from military service, but records showed he came from Merseyside originally. The odd thing is that Len Williams got a lift in the Slaidburn direction in the black-marketeer's cattle van. Then, having decided that the driver was too much of a tough to work for, Len dropped off the lorry and decided to foot it up on to Bowland and cadge a job at the waterworks camp, well out in the wilds. He missed his way, came over Bowland Forest and found the Ramshead shack by chance. He's been using it on and off for a month, and he saw, actually *saw*, Herdwick, when the latter drove his own sheep over Hawkshead."

"Then that's everything explained," said Kate comfortably, but Gilbert Woolfall put in:

"No, it's not. I've got a private question. Why was Macdonald interested in Maggie Herdwick's weed-killer?"

"Because she used sodium chlorate. It's a very potent weed-killer. Ask Giles," replied Macdonald.

Giles gave a long, long whistle. "Well, I'm damned!" he exclaimed. "I'd never have thought of that. Sodium chlorate is highly inflammable. If you soaked kindling and billets in sodium chlorate dissolved in water and dried the water out, the result would be the arson specialist's dream. The billets would burn with a blazing heat that would ignite anything."

"That's it," said Macdonald. "When I went down to the cellar and told Woolfall to keep Betty Fell out of the way, I scraped up some of the ash and deposit left on the stone ledge where the water hadn't got to. The analysts did the rest: they found common salt, the residue left after sodium chlorate has burnt—or been deoxidised. Quite a point, wasn't it? The Herdwicks were the only people in High Gimmerdale who had any sodium chlorate."

It was at the end of the evening that Giles asked: "Will Herdwick be found guilty of murder?"

Macdonald nodded. "He certainly will. He murdered Tegg. I saw him do it. I was sorry, I liked Tegg, but perhaps it wasn't a bad ending. He loved his sheep and his fells, and he couldn't have gone on with his job much longer. I think Tegg would rather have died out of doors, in the old sheepfold, than in his little truckle-bed."

"I'm sure that's true," said Gilbert. "Tell me, do you still think of buying a farm, Macdonald?"

"Yes. I do. But not a sheep farm."

"I believe Jock's quite handy with cows," said Gilbert, "and Betty's a champion cook. I shall hate to part with them, but I have a feeling you can set their feet on the farming ladder, Macdonald."

"If that's an offer, it's an uncommonly handsome one," said Macdonald. "Now I've only got to find a farm."

"If you're going to have Jock and Betty to work it for you, I withdraw all my objections and warnings," said Giles.

"Now, isn't that a good idea," said Kate. "I was frightfully worried that Macdonald was working at an idea that Betty and Jock were involved in burning the study. After all, one of Betty's forebears married a Woolfall, and I was afraid it was going to turn out one of those tiresome stories about a forged will, with Betty claiming the Woolfall property, or something idiotic like that. Did you ever consider that possibility, Macdonald?"

"Well, I tried to consider all possibilities, including Jock and Tegg and Hodges and the reverend—and even Mr. Gilbert Woolfall. But none of them fitted all the circumstances—the sheep-stealing, arson, and assault. I was very glad when I realised that Jock and Betty had nothing to do with it."

"It makes rather a nice ending to the story," mused Kate. "Now we've only got to find you a farm."

THE END

If you've enjoyed *Crook O' Lune*,
you won't want to miss

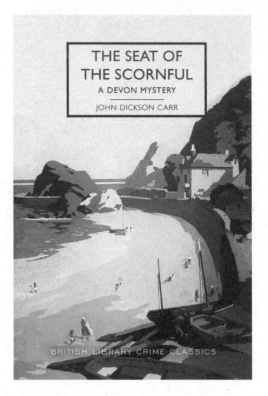

the most recent BRITISH LIBRARY CRIME CLASSIC
published by Poisoned Pen Press,
an imprint of Sourcebooks.

Praise for the
British Library Crime Classics

"Carr is at the top of his game in this taut whodunit... The British Library Crime Classics series has unearthed another worthy golden age puzzle."

—*Publishers Weekly*, STARRED Review, for *The Lost Gallows*

"A wonderful rediscovery."

—*Booklist*, STARRED Review, for *The Sussex Downs Murder*

"First-rate mystery and an engrossing view into a vanished world."

—*Booklist*, STARRED Review, for *Death of an Airman*

"A cunningly concocted locked-room mystery, a staple of Golden Age detective fiction."

—*Booklist*, STARRED Review, for *Murder of a Lady*

"The book is both utterly of its time and utterly ahead of it."

—*New York Times Book Review* for *The Notting Hill Mystery*

"As with the best of such compilations, readers of classic mysteries will relish discovering unfamiliar authors, along with old favorites such as Arthur Conan Doyle and G.K. Chesterton."

—*Publishers Weekly*, STARRED Review, for *Continental Crimes*

"In this imaginative anthology, Edwards—president of Britain's Detection Club—has gathered together overlooked criminous gems."

—*Washington Post* for *Crimson Snow*

"The degree of suspense Crofts achieves by showing the growing obsession and planning is worthy of Hitchcock. Another first-rate reissue from the British Library Crime Classics series."

—*Booklist*, STARRED Review, for *The 12.30 from Croydon*

"Not only is this a first-rate puzzler, but Crofts's outrage over the financial firm's betrayal of the public trust should resonate with today's readers."

—*Booklist*, STARRED Review, for *Mystery in the Channel*

"This reissue exemplifies the mission of the British Library Crime Classics series in making an outstanding and original mystery accessible to a modern audience."

—*Publishers Weekly*, STARRED Review, for *Excellent Intentions*

"A book to delight every puzzle-suspense enthusiast."

—*New York Times* for *The Colour of Murder*

"Edwards's outstanding third winter-themed anthology showcases 11 uniformly clever and entertaining stories, mostly from lesser known authors, providing further evidence of the editor's expertise…This entry in the British Library Crime Classics series will be a welcome holiday gift for fans of the golden age of detection."

—*Publishers Weekly*, STARRED Review, for
The Christmas Card Crime and Other Stories

poisonedpenpress.com